WOES
OF THE TRUE
POLICEMAN

ROBERTO
BOLAÑO

Translated by Natasha Wimmer

PICADOR

First published 2012 by Farrar, Straus and Giroux, New York

First published in the United Kingdom 2012 in paperback by Picador

This edition published 2014 by Picador
an imprint of Pan Macmillan, a division of Macmillan Publishers Limited
Pan Macmillan, 20 New Wharf Road, London N1 9RR
Basingstoke and Oxford
Associated companies throughout the world
www.panmacmillan.com

ISBN 978-1-4472-3330-5

London Borough of Southwark		
N		
SK 2383051 4		
Askews & Holts		17-Jan-2014
AF FIC		£8.99

Printed and bound by CPI Group (UK) Ltd, Croydon CR0 4YY

Visit **www.picador.com** to read more about all our books
and to buy them. You will also find features, author interviews and
news of any author events, and you can sign up for e-newsletters
so that you're always first to hear about our new releases.

WOES
OF THE TRUE
POLICEMAN

ROBERTO BOLAÑO was born in Santiago, Chile, in 1953. He grew up in Chile and Mexico City. He is the author of *The Savage Detectives*, which received the Herralde Prize and the Rómulo Gallegos Prize, and *2666*, which won the National Book Critics Circle Award. He died in Blanes, Spain, at the age of fifty.

Also by Roberto Bolaño in English translation

The Skating Rink

Nazi Literature in the Americas

Distant Star

The Savage Detectives

Amulet

Monsieur Pain

By Night in Chile

Tres

The Romantic Dogs

Antwerp

The Insufferable Gaucho

Between Parentheses

2666

The Secret of Evil

The Unknown University

The Third Reich

Last Evenings on Earth

The Return

To the memory of Manuel Puig and Philip K. Dick

PROLOGUE: Between the Abyss and Misfortune

Woes of the True Policeman is a project that was begun at the end of the 1980s and continued until the writer's death. What the reader has in his hands is the faithful and definitive version, collated from typescripts and computer documents, and bearing evidence of Roberto Bolaño's clear intention to include the novel in a body of work in a perpetual state of gestation. There are also a number of epistolary references to the project. In a 1995 letter, Bolaño writes: *"Novel: for years I've been working on one that's titled* Woes of the True Policeman *and which is MY NOVEL. The protagonist is a widower, 50, a university professor, 17-year-old daughter, who goes to live in Santa Teresa, a city near the U.S. border. Eight hundred thousand pages, a crazy tangle beyond anyone's comprehension."* The unusual thing about this novel, written over the course of fifteen years, is that it incorporates material from other works by the author, from *Llamadas telefónicas* (Phone Calls) to *The Savage Detectives* and *2666*, with the peculiarity that even though we meet some familiar characters—particularly Amalfitano, Amalfitano's daughter, Rosa, and Arcimboldi—the differences are notable. These characters belong to Bolaño's larger fictional world, and at the same time they are the exclusive property of this novel.

This brings us to one of the book's most striking and unsettling qualities: the fragile, provisional nature of the narrative (*desarrollo narrativo*). If in the contemporary novel the barrier between fiction and reality, between invention and essay, has been toppled, Bolaño's contribution takes a different path that perhaps finds its model in Julio Cortázar's *Hopscotch*. *Woes of the True Policeman*, like *2666*, is an unfinished novel, but not an incomplete one, because what mattered to its author was working on it, not completing it. And this brings us to a series of reconsiderations. By now we've accepted the rupture of linearity (digression, counterpoint, the blending of genres). Reality as it was understood until the nineteenth century has been replaced as reference point by a visionary, oneiric, fevered, fragmentary, and even provisional form of writing. In this provisionality lies the key to Bolaño's contribution. We may ask ourselves when a novel begins to be unfinished, or when it hasn't yet begun to be unfinished. When the author is in the middle of writing it, the end can't be the most important thing, and many times it hasn't even been determined. What matters is the active participation of the reader, concurrent with the act of writing. Bolaño makes this very clear in his explanation of the title: "*The policeman is the reader, who tries in vain to decipher this wretched novel.*" And in the body of the book itself there is an insistence on this conception of the novel as a life: we exist—we write, we read—so long as we're alive, and the only conclusion is death. This consciousness of death, of writing as an act of life, is part of Bolaño's biography, since the Chilean writer was condemned to write his limitless fiction against the clock. In *Woes of the True Policeman* there are a number of concrete references to this fractioning and provisionality: "a crucial feature of the French writer's work: even if all his stories, no matter their style (and in this regard Arcimboldi was eclectic and seemed to subscribe to the maxim of De Kooning: *style is a fraud*), were mysteries, they were only solved through flight, or sometimes through bloodshed (real or imaginary) followed by endless flight, as if Arcimboldi's characters, once the book had come to an end, literally leapt from the last page and kept fleeing." This is faithful to the itinerancy, to the frequently fruitless searching and the fleeing, that mark Bolaño's writing. This is why Amalfitano's students understood "that a book was a labyrinth and a desert. That there was nothing more important than ceaseless reading and traveling, perhaps one and the same thing." This provisionality gives the writer great freedom, since he permits himself the same risks as his most daring contemporaries with whom he explicitly identifies himself; but at the same time his texts maintain traditional suspense, full as they are of nonstop adventure. That is, his novels never stop being novels as we've always understood them. And the fracturing is what obliges the editor of his unpublished works to respect the legacy of a writer for whom all novels are part of one great novel always in progress and always in utopian search of an ending.

So far as the title is concerned, it also lends itself to a series of reflections. *Woes of the True Policeman* is certainly the least characteristic of Bolaño's titles, and nevertheless it is clear, from typescripts and computer texts, that it is the definitive title. We are presented with a descriptive phrase, long, lacking the rhythm to which Bolaño has accustomed us, and not provocative or surprising at all (what can savage detectives or killer whores mean?). And yet it hides a clue in a text full of clues, a metaphor that transports us not only to *The Savage Detectives* but most particularly to another scarcely characteristic title, that of Padilla's unfinished novel, *The God of Homosexuals*. Each contains a clue: as previously stated, the true policeman is none other than the reader, relegated from the start to the woe of constantly uncovering false clues, in the same way that the king of homosexuals is none other than AIDS, a metaphor for the fatal disease that prevents Padilla from finishing his novel.

Thus we have here a "detective," who is Amalfitano, the critic, around whom the whole meta-literary dimension of the novel turns. There's a policeman, who is the reader. And there's a true protagonist, who is Padilla. Detective, reader/author, herald of death: these are the protagonists of a search that never ends (that has no ending). This obliges us to focus even more intently on the development of the narrative, which suggests that the suspense lies not in the denouement but in the unfolding of events. This is the same way we read *Don Quixote*, a novel that remains alive despite its ending, since it isn't the knight errant who dies but the mediocre squire.

And as in *Don Quixote*—that is, as in the best contemporary fiction—the fragment is as important as the potential unity demanded of the novel, with this addendum: the fragments, the situations, the scenes, are discrete units that nevertheless make up a greater whole that isn't necessarily visible. It could almost be said that we are returning to the origins of literature, to the story, or rather to a succession of stories that build upon one another. Naturally there is a thread that links Amalfitano, his daughter, Rosa, his lover Padilla, Padilla's lover Elisa, Arcimboldi, the Carreras, the singular poet Pere Girau; and—elsewhere—Pancho Monje, Pedro and Pablo Negrete, and Gumaro the chauffeur. The same is true of the different geographic spaces we traverse, be they Chile, Mexico—Santa Teresa and Sonora—or Barcelona, all familiar to readers of Bolaño. There is even a very strong link between the beginning and the end of the book, between Padilla's passion for literature and the final discovery that Elisa *is* death. But what makes the novel memorable isn't its unity (facilitated by the growing protagonism of Padilla, a victim, like Don Quixote, of literature and love—in this case the morbid love of our times), but the different situations and what each of them suggests.

We find ourselves, as so frequently in contemporary fiction, in the realm of violence, alienation, estrangement, outrageousness, illness, sublime degradation. The stories follow one after another: about the stewardess and the mango juice, the recruit and the confusion caused by the word *kunst*, the informal dinner with the Italian patriots, the visit to the numerologist, the communicative striptease, the five generations of María Expósito, the dead man in the servants' quarters, or the Texan and the Larry Rivers exhibition. There are send-ups of the Potosí school of Maestro Garabito, of Rosa's teachers, and, prophetically, of frustrated writers like Jean Marchand, who decides to give up his literary ambitions to devote himself to the careers of other writers: "He sees himself as a doctor at a leper colony in India, a monk pledged to a higher cause." And purported saviors aside, literature has—as it always has had in Bolaño, beginning with *Nazi Literature in the Americas*—an ambiguous and crucial presence, in which homage mingles with criticism, veiled and therefore doubly harsh as well as hilarious. This is the ambiguous light in which Pablo Neruda appears in *By Night in Chile* or Octavio Paz in *The Savage Detectives*, in Mexico City's Parque Hundido. But certain writers, represented here by the *poetas bárbaros*—today's poètes maudits, already present in *Distant Star*—interest him particularly to the extent that they are poets of impurity, an impurity that closely resembles the kind that interests Ricardo Piglia. In fact, all of Bolaño's characters are impure, victims and privileged witnesses of violence in all its forms, which here reaches its height in the section "Killers of Sonora," and also in the god of homosexuals, that is "the god of those who have always lost," "the god of the Comte de Lautréamont and Rimbaud." And there are Arcimboldi's brilliantly summarized novels, of course, as well as Padilla's unfinished novel, and the letters that Amalfitano and Padilla write to each other. More than metaliterary, we might call these texts intraliterary, since everything is part of the plot.

Woes of the True Policeman is of special interest because of its close links to the best of Bolaño—its wealth of invention, its identification with losers—because of an ethic unhampered by ethical principles, because of its lucid reading of authors close to Bolaño, because of its radical independence, because it offers us a modern novel that doesn't relinquish the satisfactions of plot, because of its fierce loyalty to the places where Bolaño spent his formative years, its loyalty to a cosmopolitanism that is the expression of a way of life, and its loyalty to a joyful and desperate surrender to creation, far from social imperatives. His writing is always extremely clear, and yet it springs from the darkest places (sex, violence, love, exile, loneliness, breakups): "It's all so simple and so terrible," because "true poetry resides between the abyss and misfortune." And it's no coincidence that he's especially attracted to poets: it's they who give his prose the capacity to express tenderness, unhappiness, and rootlessness. How can so much humor exist amid such desolation, so much decency amid such violence? Because in each of Bolaño's books we ultimately find, as we clearly find here, the best Bolaño. An author horrified by our century's violence, from the Nazis to the crimes of the north of Mexico; an author who identifies with the losers, and who makes of his work an autobiography, which in large part explains the mythification of his persona—because the great absence represented by his death is made into presence over the course of a series of works that culminate in *2666*, where he seems to elaborate upon and condense all his experiences as a human being and as a writer. In *Woes of the True Policeman* we once again encounter a Bolaño who has become as familiar to us as he is indispensable. It remains bone-chilling to discover in this book an extraordinary vitality constantly threatened not only by the consciousness of physical illness but also by the moral sickness of an era. Vitality and desolation are inseparable.

Juan Antonio Masoliver Ródenas

WOES OF THE TRUE POLICEMAN

I. *THE FALL of the BERLIN WALL*

1

According to Padilla, remembered Amalfitano, all literature could be classified as heterosexual, homosexual, or bisexual. Novels, in general, were heterosexual. Poetry, on the other hand, was completely homosexual. Within the vast ocean of poetry he identified various currents: faggots, queers, sissies, freaks, butches, fairies, nymphs, and philenes. But the two major currents were faggots and queers. Walt Whitman, for example, was a faggot poet. Pablo Neruda, a queer. William Blake was definitely a faggot. Octavio Paz was a queer. Borges was a philene, or in other words he might be a faggot one minute and simply asexual the next. Rubén Darío was a freak, in fact, the queen freak, the prototypical freak (in Spanish, of course; in the wider world the reigning freak is still Verlaine the Generous). Freaks, according to Padilla, were closer to madhouse flamboyance and naked hallucination, while faggots and queers wandered in stagger-step from ethics to aesthetics and back again. Cernuda, dear Cernuda, was a nymph, and at moments of great bitterness a faggot, whereas Guillén, Aleixandre, and Alberti could be considered a sissy, a butch, and a queer, respectively. As a general rule, poets like Blas de Otero were butches, while poets like Gil de Biedma were—except for Gil de Biedma himself—part nymph and part queer. Recent Spanish poetry, with the tentative exception of the aforementioned Gil de Biedma and probably Carlos Edmundo de Ory, had been lacking in faggot poets until the arrival of the Great Faggot of All Sorrows, Padilla's favorite poet, Leopoldo María Panero. And yet Panero, it had to be admitted, had fits of bipolar freakishness that made him unstable, inconsistent, and hard to classify. Of Panero's peers, a curious case was Gimferrer, who was queer by nature but had the imagination of a faggot and the tastes of a nymph. Anyway, the poetry scene was essentially an (underground) battle, the result of the struggle between faggot poets and queer poets to seize control of the *word*. Sissies, according to Padilla, were faggot poets by birth who, out of weakness or for comfort's sake, lived within and accepted—most of the time—the aesthetic and personal parameters of the queers. In Spain, France, and Italy, queer poets have always been legion, he said, although a superficial reader might never guess. What happens is that a faggot poet like Leopardi, for example, somehow reconstrues queers like Ungaretti, Montale, and Quasimodo, the trio of death. In the same way, Pasolini redraws contemporary Italian queerdom. Take the case of poor Sanguinetti (I won't pick on Pavese, who was a sad freak, the only one of his kind). Not to mention France, great country of devouring mouths, where one hundred faggot poets, from Villon to Sophie Podolski, have nurtured, still nurture, and will nurture with the blood of their tits ten thousand queer poets with their entourage of philenes, nymphs, butches, and sissies, lofty editors of literary magazines, great translators, petty bureaucrats, and grand diplomats of the Kingdom of Letters (see, if you must, the shameful and malicious reflections of the *Tel Quel* poets). And the less said the better about the faggotry of the Russian Revolution, which, if we're to be honest, gave us just one faggot poet, a single one. Who? you may ask. Mayakovsky? No. Esenin? No. Pasternak? Blok? Mandelstam? Akhmatova? Hardly. There was just one, and I won't keep you in suspense. He was the real thing, a steppes-and-snow faggot, a faggot through and through: Khlebnikov. And in Latin America, how many true faggots do we find? Vallejo and Martín Adán. Period. New paragraph. Macedonio Fernández, maybe? The rest are queers like Huidobro, fairies like Alfonso Cortés (although some of his poems are authentically fagotty), butches like León de Greiff, butch nymphs like Pablo de Rokha (with bursts of freakishness that would've driven Lacan himself crazy), sissies like Lezama Lima, a misguided reader of Góngora, and along with Lezama all the queers and sissies of the Cuban Revolution except for Rogelio Nogueras, who is a nymph with the spirit of a faggot, not to mention, if only in passing, the poets of the Sandinista Revolution: fairies like Coronel Urtecho or queers who wish they were philenes, like Ernesto Cardenal. The Mexican Contemporaries are also queers (no, shouted Amalfitano, not Gilberto Owen!); in fact *Death Without End* is, along with the poetry of Paz, the "Marseillaise" of the highly nervous Mexican poets. More names: Gelman, nymph; Benedetti, queer; Nicanor Parra, fairy with a hint of faggot; Westphalen, freak; Pellicer, fairy; Enrique Lihn, sissy; Girondo, fairy. And back to Spain, back to the beginning: Góngora and Quevedo, queers; San Juan de la Cruz and Fray Luis de León, faggots. End of story. And now, to satisfy your curiosity, some differences between queers and faggots. Even in their sleep, the former beg for a twelve-inch cock to plow and fertilize them, but at the moment of truth, mountains must be moved to get them into bed with the pretty boys they love. Faggots, on the other hand, seem to live as if a dick were permanently churning their insides, and when they look at themselves in the mirror (something they love and hate with all their heart), they see the Pimp of Death in their own sunken eyes. For faggots and fairies, *pimp* is the one word that can cross unscathed through the realms of nothingness. But then, too, nothing prevents queers and faggots from being good friends, from neatly ripping one another off, criticizing or praising one another, publishing or burying one another in the frantic and moribund world of letters.

"You missed the category of talking apes," said Amalfitano when Padilla at last fell silent.

"Ah, those talking apes," said Padilla, "the faggot apes of Madagascar who refuse to talk so they don't have to work."

2

When Padilla was five his mother died, and when he was twelve his older brother died. When he was thirteen he decided that he would be an artist. First he thought he liked theater and film. Then he read Rimbaud and Leopoldo María Panero and he wanted to be a poet as well as an actor. By the time he was sixteen he'd devoured literally all the poetry that fell into his hands and he'd had two (rather unfortunate) experiences at the local community theater, but that wasn't enough. He learned English and French, took a trip to San Sebastián, to the Mondragón insane asylum, and tried to visit Leopoldo María Panero, but once the doctors had seen him and listened to him talk for five minutes, they turned him away.

At seventeen he was a tough, well-read, sarcastic kid, prone to bursts of anger that could lead to violence. Twice he resorted to physical aggression. The first time, he was walking through Parque de la Ciudadela with a friend, another poet, when two young skinheads insulted them. They might have called them faggots, something like that. Padilla, who was usually the one to taunt others, stopped, went up to the bigger kid, and punched him in the neck, making him gasp and choke; while the kid was trying to keep his balance and get his breath, he was felled by a swift kick to the groin; his friend tried to help but what he saw in Padilla's eyes was more powerful than the bonds of friendship and he chose to flee the scene. It was all over very quickly. Before Padilla moved on, he had time to aim a few kicks at the bald head of his fallen opponent. Padilla's young poet friend was horrified. Days later, when he took Padilla to task for his behavior (especially his final outburst, the gratuitous kicking of his enemy when he was down), Padilla answered that when fighting Nazis, everything was permitted. On Padilla's adolescent lips, the word *everything* sounded luscious. But how do you know they were Nazis? asked his friend. They had shaved heads, said Padilla tenderly, what kind of world do you live in? Also, he added, it's your fault, because that afternoon, remember, we were talking about love, Love with a capital *L*, and the entire time you just kept arguing with me, calling my ideas naïve, telling me to get my head out of the clouds; every word you said, sabotaging my dreams, was like a punch in the gut. Then the skinheads turned up, and added to all my pain and suffering, of which you were well aware, was the pain of ignorance.

Padilla's friend never knew whether he was serious or not, but from then on, in certain circles, going out late at night with him became a guarantee of safety.

The second time, he hit his lover, a kid of eighteen, good-looking but not too bright, who one night transferred his affections to a rich architect, thirty and not too bright, either, with whom he was indiscreet enough to make the rounds of the places he used to hang out with Padilla, flaunting his happiness plus a weekend jaunt to Thailand and summer in Italy and a duplex complete with Jacuzzi, which was more than Padilla—who was only seventeen at the time and lived with his father in a dark three-bedroom apartment in the Eixample—could take. This time, however, Padilla acted with premeditation: he waited until five in the morning, hiding in a doorway, for his ex-lover to come home. Once the taxi had gone he was on him, and the attack was swift and brutal. He didn't touch his face. He hit him in the belly and the genitals and, once his ex-lover was on the ground, aimed kicks at his legs and rear. If you turn me in I'll kill you, baby, he warned before he vanished down the dark streets, gnawing his lip.

His relationship with his father was good, though somewhat distant and perhaps a little sad. The abrupt and enigmatic messages they flung at each other with seeming carelessness tended to be misinterpreted on both sides. Padilla's father believed that his son was very intelligent, of higher-than-average intelligence, but

7

at the same time deeply unhappy. And he blamed himself and fate. Padilla believed that his father might long ago have been an interesting person or might have had the chance to become one, but the deaths in the family had turned him into a spiritless, resigned man, sometimes mysteriously happy (when a soccer match was on TV), but usually quiet and hardworking, a man who demanded nothing of Padilla beyond perhaps the occasional bit of trivial conversation. Nothing more. They weren't rich, but since his father owned the apartment and hardly spent a thing, Padilla always had a decent amount of money at his disposal. With it he bought movie and theater tickets; went out to dinner; bought books, jeans, a leather jacket with metal studs, boots, sunglasses, a small weekly supply of hash, very occasionally some cocaine, albums by Satie; paid for his college tuition, his metro passes, his black and purple blazers, the rooms in Distrito V where he brought his lovers. He never went on vacation.

Padilla's father never went on vacation, either. When summer came, Padilla and his father slept until late, with the blinds down and the apartment plunged into a gentle dusk, redolent of the previous night's dinner. Then Padilla would go out to roam the streets of Barcelona, and his father, after washing the dishes and giving the kitchen a once-over, would spend the rest of the day watching television.

At eighteen Padilla completed his first book of poetry. He sent a copy to Leopoldo María Panero at the Mondragón asylum, put the original in a drawer in his desk—the only one with a lock and key—and forgot all about it. Three years later, when he met Amalfitano, he retrieved the poems from the drawer and begged him to read them. Amalfitano thought they were interesting, maybe too faithful to certain conventions, but elegant and polished. Their subjects were the city of Barcelona, sex, illness, crime. In one of them, for example, the poet described in perfect alexandrines some fifty ways of masturbating, each more painful and terrible than the last, as a nuclear twilight settled slowly over the city's suburbs. In another he minutely chronicled the death of his father, alone in his room, as the poet cleans the house, cooks, rations out the provisions (ever dwindling) in the pantry, searches for good music on the radio, reads curled up on the sofa in the living room, and tries in vain to reorder his memories. His father takes his time dying, of course, and stretching between his sleep and the poet's wakefulness, lost in the mist, is a ruined bridge. Vladimir Holan is my model in the art of survival, he told Amalfitano. Wonderful, thought Amalfitano, one of my favorite poets.

Up until this point, Amalfitano had hardly seen Padilla, who only very rarely showed up in class. After the reading and the favorable comments, he was never absent again. Soon they became friends. By then Padilla wasn't living with his father anymore; he had rented a studio near the university, where he hosted parties and gatherings that Amalfitano soon began to attend. Poems were read and later on in the evening the guests put on little plays in Catalan. Amalfitano found it charming, like the *tertulias* of South American literary circles in the old days, but with more style and taste, more flair, something like what the *tertulias* of Mexico's Contemporáneos might have been if the Contemporáneos had written plays, which Amalfitano doubted. Also: there was a lot of drinking and sometimes one of the guests had a breakdown that usually ended—after much screaming and sobbing—with the sufferer shut in the bathroom and two volunteers trying to calm him down. Every so often a woman made an appearance, but usually it was just men, most of them young, students of literature and art history. A painter also came, a strange man, maybe forty-five, who wore only leather and who sat silently in a corner during the *tertulias*, not drinking, chain-smoking little hash cigarettes that he selected, pre-rolled, from a gold cigarette case. And the owner of a pastry shop in Gracia, a cheerful, animated fat man who talked to everyone and who was, as Amalfitano soon realized, the one bankrolling Padilla and the other boys.

One night, as they were performing one of the *Dialogues with Leucò* translated into Catalan by a very tall, fair-skinned boy, Padilla surreptitiously took one of Amalfitano's hands. Amalfitano didn't let go.

The first time they made love was one Sunday morning, with

the dawn light filtering through the lowered blinds, when everyone else had gone and all that was left in the studio were cigarette butts and a jumble of glasses and scattered cushions. Amalfitano was fifty and it was the first time he had slept with a man. I'm not a man, said Padilla, I'm your angel.

3

At some point, as they were coming out of a movie theater, remembered Amalfitano, Padilla confessed that in the not-too-
distant future he planned to make a movie. The movie would be
called *Leopardi*, and according to Padilla it would be a Hollywood-
style biopic about the famous and multidisciplinary Italian poet.
Like John Huston's Toulouse-Lautrec movie. But since Padilla's
movie wouldn't have a big budget (in fact it had no budget), the
main roles would be played not by great actors but by fellow writers, who would work for the love of art in general, love of the
gobbo in particular, or simply to be included. The role of Leopardi
was reserved for a young poet and heroin addict from La Coruña
whose name Amalfitano had forgotten. The role of Antonio
Ranieri was reserved for Padilla himself. It's the most interesting
of all, he declared. Count Monaldo Leopardi would be played by
Vargas Llosa, who, with a brooding look and some talcum powder,
would be perfect for the role. Paolina Leopardi would go to Blanca
Andreu, and Carlo Leopardi to Enrique Vila-Matas. The role of
Countess Adelaida Antici, mother of the poet, was to be offered
to Josefina Aldecoa. Adelaida García Morales and Carmen Martín
Gaite would play peasants from Recanati. Giordani, faithful friend
and epistolary confidant—a bit of a drip, really—would go to
Muñoz Molina. Manzoni: Javier Marías. Two Vatican cardinals,
tremulous Latinists, loathsome Hellenists: Cela and Juan Goytisolo.
Uncle Carlo Antici was reserved for Juan Marsé. Stella, the publisher, would be offered to Herralde. Fanny Targioni, the fickle
and too-human Fanny, to Soledad Puértolas. And then there were

some of the poems, which—to make them more comprehensible to the audience—would be played by actors. That is, the poems would be given physical presence instead of being ladders of words. Example: Leopardi is writing "The Infinite" and from beneath the table springs Martín de Riquer, in a small but effective role, though Padilla doubted that the eminent academic would accept the ephemeral glory of the cinema. The "Night Song of a Wandering Shepherd in Asia," Padilla's favorite poem, would be played by Leopoldo María Panero, naked or in a tiny bathing suit. Eduardo Mendicutti would play "To Silvia." Enrique Vila-Matas: "The Calm After the Storm." "To Italy," the poet Pere Girau, Padilla's best friend. He planned to shoot the interiors in his own Eixample apartment and at the gym of an ex-lover in Gracia. The exteriors: Sitges, Manresa, the Barrio Gótico of Barcelona, Girona, Olot, Palamós. He even had a completely original and revolutionary idea for re-creating Naples in 1839 and the cholera epidemic that ravaged the city, an idea that he could have sold to the big Hollywood studios, but Amalfitano couldn't remember what it was.

4

On the Ruin of Amalfitano at the University of Barcelona

The rector and the head of the literature department entrusted Professor Carrera with the mission of informing Amalfitano of his situation at the university. Antoni Carrera was forty-eight, a former anti-Franco militant, someone who at first glance led an enviable life. He seemed reasonably content, a happy man. His salary and that of his wife, a high school French teacher, covered the mortgage on an old house that he had renovated to suit himself and the occasional whims of an architect friend. The house was magnificent, with six bedrooms, a huge, bright living room, a garden, and a little sauna that was Professor Carrera's greatest domestic pride.

His son, seventeen, was a good student, or so his parents thought. He was six foot two, and every Saturday aftenoon the Carreras went to watch him play basketball at a club in Sant Andreu. All three were in good health. Antoni Carrera and Anna Carrera had gone through some hard times and once, long ago, had even come close to divorcing, but that was in the past and their marriage had gradually stabilized; now they were good friends, they shared some things, but in general each led his or her own life. One of the things they shared was their friendship with Amalfitano. When he arrived at the university he didn't know anyone, and Carrera, taking pity on him and following the unwritten rules of scholarly hospitality, held a dinner at his house—his welcoming, wonderful house—and invited Amalfitano and three other department colleagues. It was a peculiar affair. The professors didn't know each other, nor did they have any particular interest in getting to know Amalfitano (Latin American literature no longer roused passions); the professors' wives looked terminally bored; Carrera's own wife wasn't in the best of moods. And Amalfitano didn't appear at the agreed-upon time. In fact, he was very late, and the hungry professors got impatient. One suggested that they begin without him. Most would have seconded the motion, but Anna Carrera had no interest in starting the same dinner twice. So they ate cheese and Serrano ham and reflected on the impunctuality of South Americans. When Amalfitano arrived at last he was accompanied by a strikingly beautiful adolescent. At first the Carreras assumed, stunned, that it was his wife. Humbert Humbert, thought Antoni in terror, seconds before Amalfitano introduced her as his only daughter. I'm a widower, he remarked later, unprompted.

The dinner, as Anna had feared, proceeded in the usual fashion. The Amalfitanos, father and daughter, weren't very chatty. The professors discussed seminars, books, university politics, and gossip, though no one could say exactly what the topic was at any given moment: gossip turned into seminars, university politics into books, seminars into university politics, books into gossip, until every permutation was exhausted. In fact they were really only talking about one thing: their work. When they tried to get Amalfitano to tell the same kind of stories about his previous university (it was very small and I taught only one course, on Rodolfo Wilcock, he said, politely and abashedly), the result was disappointing. No one had read Rodolfo Wilcock, no one cared about him. His daughter talked even less. Despite all their efforts, the professors' wives got monosyllabic replies to their questions: did she like Barcelona, yes, could she speak some Catalan yet, no, had she lived in many countries, yes, did she find it difficult to keep house for her widowed father, the classic absentminded literature professor, no. Though at the coffee hour (*after* eating, thought Carrera, as if father and daughter were used to eating in silence) the Amalfitanos began to take part in the conversation. Someone, taking pity on them, brought up a subject having to do with Latin American literature, which led to the first lengthy remarks by Amalfitano. They talked about poetry. To everyone's surprise, and to the disgust of some (feigned surprise and disgust, of course), Amalfitano held Nicanor Parra in higher esteem than Octavio Paz. After that, as far as the Carreras—who hadn't read Parra and didn't care much about Octavio Paz—were concerned, everything began to go well. By the time the whiskey was brought out, Amalfitano was frankly winning, witty, brilliant, and Rosa Amalfitano, as her father's happiness drew everyone into its embrace, grew more talkative, more forthcoming, though she never shed a certain reserve, a watchfulness, that made her even more charming in a way that struck Anna Carrera as most unusual. An intelligent girl, an attractive and responsible girl, she thought, realizing that imperceptibly she had begun to love her.

A week later the Carreras invited the Amalfitanos for dinner again, but this time, instead of the professors and their wives, the fifth person at the table was Jordi Carrera, the pride of his mother, a slender adolescent with a shyness that was in some ways like Rosa's.

As Anna hoped, they became friends on the spot. And the children's friendship ran parallel to their parents' friendship, at least during the time the Amalfitanos lived in Barcelona. Rosa and Jordi began to see each other at least twice a week. Once a week or once every two weeks Amalfitano and the Carreras talked on the phone, dined together, went to the movies, attended exhibitions and concerts, spent hours—the three of them—in the Carreras' living room, by the fireplace in winter or in the garden in summer, talking and telling stories about when they were twenty, thirty, and possessed of an invincible courage. Concerning the past—their personal pasts—the opinions of the three diverged. Anna looked back on those days with sadness, a fond and rather serene sadness, but sadness nonetheless. Antoni viewed his heroic years with indifference, as something necessary but almost nonexistent; he despised nostalgia and melancholy as pointless, sterile emotions. Amalfitano, on the other hand, was dizzied, thrilled, depressed by remembering, capable of weeping in front of his friends or bursting into laughter.

They usually talked late into the night, when Carrera would give Amalfitano a ride back to his apartment on the other side of Barcelona, wondering how he had come to confide in him so easily, how he had learned to trust him in a way that he hardly ever trusted anyone. Amalfitano, meanwhile, usually made the trip half-asleep, watching through half-closed eyes the empty streets, the yellow signs, the dark and bright windows, at peace with himself in Carrera's car, sure of arriving home safe and sound, of coming in the door quietly, jacket on the coatrack, glass of water, and before getting into bed, a last glance into Rosa's room, out of pure habit.

And now the rector and the department head, always so prudent, so circumspect, had assigned Carrera—because you see him socially, one might call him your friend, he'll listen to you (was there a threat there? a joke that only the rector and the department head understood?)—this delicate mission which had to be carried out tactfully, with decorum, persuasively, and at the same time firmly. With unshakable firmness. And who better than you, Antoni. Who better than you to find a solution to this problem.

So Amalfitano wasn't surprised when Carrera told him that he had to leave the university. Jordi, under instructions from his parents, had taken Rosa to his room, and from the end of the hallway came the faint sound of the stereo. For a while Amalfitano was quiet, looking down at the rug and at the feet of the Carreras sitting one next to the other on the sofa. So they want to get rid of me, he said at last.

"They want you to go voluntarily, as quietly as possible," said Antoni Carrera.

"If you don't they'll take you to court," said Anna Carrera.

"I've been talking to some people in the department and it's the best you can hope for," said Antoni Carrera. "Otherwise, you risk everything."

"What's everything?" Amalfitano wanted to know.

The Carreras gave him looks of pity. Then Anna got up, went

to the kitchen, and came back with three glasses. When her husband, the night before, had told her that Amalfitano's days at the university were numbered, and why they were numbered, she had begun to cry. Where's the cognac? she asked. After a few seconds in which Amalfitano couldn't understand what the hell this woman wanted, he answered that he didn't drink cognac anymore. I gave it up, he said, closing his eyes, his lungs filling with air like someone about to scale a hill. Not a hill, thought Amalfitano as he imagined the whole faculty hearing about his indiscretions, a mountain. The mountain of my guilt. On the sideboard there was a bottle of apple brandy.

"Don't complain now," said Antoni Carrera, as if reading his thoughts. "After all, it's your own fault. You should have been more careful choosing your friends."

"I didn't choose them," said Amalfitano, smiling. "They chose me, or life did."

"Don't wax poetic, for God's sake," said Anna Carrera, secretly angry that a man who was still handsome—and she really did find him handsome, tall and lean as he was, like a matinee idol, with that shock of white hair—would rather sleep with boys (probably pimply ones) than women. "You fucked up and now you have to suffer the consequences, do what's best for you, and for your daughter, especially. If you fight it, the literature department will bury you in shit," she said as she filled three glasses to overflowing with Viuda Canseco.

What a nice, blunt way to put it, thought Antoni Carrera, admiringly and gloomily.

Anna handed them the glasses: "Drink up, we'll need it. What we should really do is send the kids to the movies and get drunk."

"That's not a bad idea," said Amalfitano.

"The university is rotten," said Antoni Carrera without conviction.

"But what does that mean?" asked Amalfitano.

"It means that in the best of cases, you'll be left with a near-indelible stain on your record. Worst case, you could end up in jail as a corruptor of minors."

Who was the minor, my God? thought Amalfitano, and he remembered the faces of the poet Pere Girau and a friend who sometimes turned up at Padilla's studio, an economics student he had never slept with but whom he had seen in Padilla's arms, the memory excited him, the boy surrendering to Padilla in a way that Amalfitano would never be able to, begging him between sobs and entreaties not to pull out, to keep going, as if the poor bastard were a woman, thought Amalfitano, and could have multiple orgasms. I disgust myself, he thought, though the truth is he didn't disgust himself at all. He remembered other boys, too, whom he'd never seen before and yet who claimed to be students of his, Padilla's gang, Padilla's hangers-on, whom he favored upon grading exams (but not overly so) and whom he later saw at parties and on late-night pilgrimages to the James Dean, the Roxy, the Simplicissimus, the Gardel, Chance Encounters, the Doña Rosita, and the Atalante.

"How could you risk so much?" asked Antoni Carrera.

"I always used condoms," said Amalfitano, remembering Padilla's body.

The Carreras looked at him in confusion. Anna bit her lower lit. Amalfitano closed his eyes. He thought. About Padilla and his condoms. And suddenly the act appeared to him in a terrifying light. Padilla *always* used condoms when they slept together! And I never noticed. What horrific thing, what gallantry, lay hidden in that gesture? wondered Amalfitano with a lump in his throat. For a moment he was afraid he would pass out. The music coming from the room where Rosa was persuaded him not to.

"The rector has really behaved in a civilized fashion," said Antoni Carrera.

"Put yourself in his place," said Anna Carrera, still thinking about the condoms.

"I have," answered Amalfitano despondently.

"Then will you do what we suggest? Will you be reasonable?"

"I will. What's the plan?"

The plan was for him to make an official request for a leave of absence, claiming some physical ailment. A nervous breakdown, for example, said Antoni Carrera, anything. For two months he would continue to receive his full salary, after which he would resign. The university, of course, would furnish all the requisite positive recommendations and draw a veil over the affair. Naturally, he should by no means show his face at the department offices. Not even to get my things? asked Amalfitano. Your things are in the trunk of our car, said the Carreras in unison, downing their drinks together too.

5

I, thought Amalfitano, who was a creative, loving, happy child,
the brightest at my elementary school lost on the muddy plain and
the bravest at my high school lost in the mountains and the fog, I
who was the most cowardly of adolescents and who spent afternoons of slingshot fights reading and dreaming over the maps in
my geography book, I who learned to dance rock and roll and the
twist, boleros and the tango, but not the *cueca*, though more than
once I bounded under the leafy bower, handkerchief at the ready
and driven by something deep inside me because I had no friends
in my burst of patriotism, only enemies, purist hicks scandalized
by my heel-tapping *cueca*, my needless and suicidal heterodoxy, I
who slept off drinking binges under a tree and who met the imploring eyes of Carmencita Martínez, I who swam one stormy
afternoon at Las Ventanas, I who made the best coffee in the apartment I shared with other students in the center of Santiago, and
my roommates, southerners like me, would say wonderful coffee,
Óscar, you make the most wonderful coffee, though actually it's a
little strong, actually it's too Italian, I who heard the call of the
Absolute Lazy Motherfuckers, time and time again, on buses and
in restaurants, as if I had gone mad, as if Nature, sharpening my
senses, wanted to warn me of something terrible and invisible, I
who joined the Communist Party and the Association of Progressive Students, I who wrote pamphlets and read *Das Kapital*, I who
worshipped and married Edith Lieberman, the most beautiful and
loving woman in the Southern Hemisphere, I who didn't realize
that Edith Lieberman deserved it all, the sun and the moon and a

thousand kisses and then another thousand and another, I who drank with Jorge Teillier and talked psychoanalysis with Enrique Lihn, I who was expelled from the Party and who kept believing in the class struggle and the fight for the revolution of the Americas, I who taught literature at the University of Chile, I who translated John Donne and bits of Ben Jonson and Spenser and Henry Howard, I who signed proclamations and letters from leftist groups, I who believed in change, in doing my bit to wipe away some of the world's misery and abjection (without knowing yet—innocent that I was—the real nature of misery and abjection), I who was a romantic and who in my heart of hearts just wanted to stroll bright boulevards with Edith Lieberman, up and down, feeling her warm hand in mine, at peace, in love, while storms and hurricanes and great earthquakes of fate built up behind us, I who predicted the fall of Allende and yet did nothing to prepare for it, I who was arrested and brought in blindfolded to be interrogated, and who withstood torture when stronger men were broken, I who heard the cries of three Conservatory students as they were tortured and raped and killed, I who spent months at the Tejas Verdes concentration camp, I who came out alive and was reunited with my wife in Buenos Aires, I who kept up my ties with leftist groups, that gallery of romantics (or modernists), gunmen, psychopaths, dogmatists, and fools, all brave notwithstanding, but what good is bravery? how long do we have to keep being brave? I who taught at the University of Buenos Aires, I who translated J.M.G. Arcimboldi's *The Endless Rose* for a Buenos Aires publishing house, listening as my beloved Edith speculated that our daughter's name was an homage to the title of Arcimboldi's novel and not, as I claimed, a tribute to Rosa Luxemburg, I who watched my daughter smile in Argentina and crawl in Colombia and take her first steps in Costa Rica and then in Canada, moving from university to university, leaving countries for political reasons and entering them for academic ones, carting along the remains of my library, as well as the few dresses belonging to my wife, who was in increasingly poor health, and the very few toys belonging to my daughter, and my only pair of shoes, which I called the Invincibles, miraculous leather tooled in the shop of an old Italian shoemaker in the Buenos Aires neighborhood of La Boca, I who spent sweltering evenings talking to the new radicals of Latin America, I who watched smoke drift from a volcano and aquatic mammals that looked like women frolicking in a coffee-colored river, I who joined the Sandinista Revolution, I who left my wife and daughter and entered Nicaragua with a guerrilla column, I who brought my wife and daughter to Managua and when they asked me what battles I had fought in, I answered none, I said that I was always behind the lines, but that I had seen the wounded and the dying and many dead, I had seen the eyes of those on their way back from the fighting, and such beauty mixed with such shit made me retch every day of the campaign, I who was a professor of literature in Managua and who knew no greater privilege than to give seminars on Elizabethan literature and teach the poetry of Huidobro, Neruda, de Rokha, Borges, Girondo, Martín Adán, Macedonio Fernández, Vallejo, Rosamel del Valle, Owen, Pellicer, in exchange for a miserable salary and the indifference of my poor students, who lived desperate, precarious lives, I who ended up leaving for Brazil, where I would make more money and could pay for the medical care that my wife needed, I who swam with my daughter on my shoulders on the most beautiful beaches in the world while Edith Lieberman, who was more beautiful than the beaches, watched us from the shore, barefoot on the sand, as if she knew things that I would never know and that she would never tell me, I who was left a widower one night, one plastic night of shattered windows, one night at a quarter to four as I sat at the bedside of Edith Lieberman, Chilean, Jew, French teacher, and in the next bed a Brazilian woman dreamed of a crocodile, a windup crocodile that chased a girl through mountains of ashes, I who had to carry on, father and mother now to my daughter, but who didn't know how to do it and who heaped suffering upon suffering, I who hired a servant for the first time in my life, Rosinha, northeasterner, twenty-one, mother of two little girls left behind in the village, my daughter's good fairy, I who one night after listening to Rosinha's tales of woe slept with her and probably brought her only misfortune, I who translated Osman Lins and was Osman Lins's friend though my translations never sold, I who in Rio met the nicest leftists on the planet, I who—for their sake, for my own sake, for the love of art, out of a sense of defiance, out of a fucked-up sense of obligation, out of a sense of conviction, for no reason, for fun—got mixed up in the old trouble and had to leave Brazil with time enough only to pack the little we could take with us, I who in the Rio airport watched my daughter cry and Rosinha cry and Moreira say what's wrong with these women and Luiz Lima say write us as soon as you arrive and the people coming and going through the airport lounges and the ghost of Edith Lieberman up higher than the Christ of Corcovado, I who at the same time could see nothing, not the people coming and going, not my friends, not Rosinha, not my daughter, not the silent and smiling ghost of Edith Lieberman that we were leaving behind, I who arrived in Paris with no job and scarcely any money, I who worked hanging posters and sweeping offices while my daughter slept in our *chambre de bonne* on the rue des Eaux, I who strove and strove until I got a job at a high school, I who found work at a German university, I who took my daughter on trips to Greece and Turkey, I who took my daughter on a trip down the Nile, always the two of us, with friends who came close but couldn't reach the secret heart of our affection, I who found work at a Dutch university and taught a seminar on Felisberto Hernández that got me noticed and even made me a little bit famous, I who wrote for the weekly *So Much the Worse*, published by French anarchists and Latin American leftists and I who discovered how nice it was to be a dissident in a civilized country, I who discovered the first signs of age (or exhaustion), long present in my body but previously ignored, I who went to live in Italy and work in Italy and travel in Italy, land of my grandparents, I who wrote about Rodolfo Wilcock, beloved son of Marcel Schwob, I who took part in conferences and colloquia all over Europe, flying from place to place like a corporate honcho, sleeping in five-star hotels and dining in Michelin-starred restaurants, all in order to talk about literature, about the people who made literature, I who finally washed up at the University of Barcelona, where I threw myself into my work with earnestness and zeal, I who discovered my homosexuality at the same time that the Russians discovered their passion for capitalism, I who was discovered by Joan Padilla the way a continent is discovered, I who was swept away and re-discovered pleasure and paid the price, I who am the source of mockery, disgrace of the halls of academe, labeled a filthy South American, faggot *sudaca*, corruptor of minors, queen of the Southern Cone, I who now sit in my flat writing letters, beseeching friends, seeking a job at some university, and time goes by, days, weeks, and no one gets back to me, as if everyone had suddenly stopped existing, as if in these times of crisis literature professors weren't needed anywhere, I who've done so many things and believed in so many things and who is now meant to believe that he's nothing but a dirty old man and that no one will give me a job, no one cares . . .

6

Horacio Guerra, professor of literature and official historian of Santa Teresa, distinguished polymath according to some friends from Mexico City, where he went every four months to *soak up ideas*, was, like Amalfitano, fifty years old, though unlike the latter he was beginning to enjoy a certain reputation—earned, God only knew, by the sweat of his own brow.

Born of humble stock, he had worked stubbornly his whole life to get ahead. He was awarded a scholarship by the government of Sonora, and finished his university studies at twenty-eight; he wasn't a great student, but he was curious and, in his own way, diligent. At twenty-one he published a book of sonnets and cataphoras (*Spell of the Dawn*, Tijuana, 1964) that won him the respect of some influential reviewers at northern Mexico newspapers and inclusion, six years later, in an anthology of young Mexican poets edited by a young lady from Monterrey which managed to briefly engage Octavio Paz and Efraín Huerta in a dialectical battle (both despised the anthology, though for reasons that were contradictory and mutually opposed).

In 1971 he moved to Santa Teresa and began to work at the university there. At first the contract was for only one year, during which time Horacio Guerra finished a study and anthology of the work of Orestes Gullón (*The Temple and the Wood: The Poetry of O. Gullón*, with prologue and notes by J. Guerra, University of Santa Teresa, 1973), an underappreciated Oaxacan poet and old friend of the university rector. His contract was extended for another year and then for five and then indefinitely. Now his interests multiplied. It was as if he had suddenly become a Renaissance man. From the sculpture and architecture of the school of Maestro Garabito to the poetry of Sor Juana Inés de la Cruz and Ramón López Velarde, pillars of Mexicanness, he dabbled in everything, sought to learn about everything, studied everything. He wrote a treatise on the flora and fauna of the Mexican northeast, and it wasn't long before he was named honorary president of the Santa Teresa Botanic Garden. He wrote a brief history of the city's old town, kept up a regular column called "Memories of Our City Streets," and finally was named official historian, a distinction that filled him with satisfaction and pride. All his life he would remember the ceremony, which was only an informal gathering but was attended by the bishop of Sonora and the state governor.

In academic circles his presence was inevitable: he might have been slow on the uptake and not particularly charming, but he made sure he was seen where he needed to be seen. The other professors were divided between those who admired him and those who feared him; it was easy to take issue with his ideas, his projects, or his teaching methods, but not advisable if one didn't want to be excluded from university activities and social life. Though a serious man, he was up on all the gossip and secrets.

In 1977 he published a book on the Potosí school of Maestro Garabito, who left his mark on the public buildings and plazas of the north of Mexico (*Statues and Houses of the Border*, University of Santa Teresa, thirty photographs and illustrations). Shortly after he was named professor, the book he considered his masterwork appeared: *Ramonian Studies*, on the life and work of Ramón López Velarde (University of Santa Teresa, 1979). The following year saw his book on Sor Juana Inés de la Cruz (*The Birth of Mexico*, University of Santa Teresa, 1980), a work that was dedicated to the rector and that sparked a kind of polemic: accusations of plagiarism appeared in two Mexico City newspapers but the slander didn't stick. By this point something had developed between Guerra and the rector, Pablo Negrete, that could superficially have been called friendship. They saw each other, yes, and sometimes they had a drink together, but they weren't friends. Guerra knew he was a glorified courtier—*courtier*, the term wounded and pleased him, filled him with pride and gloom, but it was the only one that fit the facts—and yet he believed that he, too, when the moment came, would be university president and that he would take under his wing another professor in circumstances similar to his own. For years now, too, he suspected that Pablo Negrete had been delegating to him only *practical* matters, resolving *worldly* matters without his counsel.

He lived in a permanent state of agitation.

At the time when Amalfitano met him, Horacio Guerra was a well-dressed man (this was a quality—like so many others—that he shared with the president, who over the years had become a dandy) among poorly or sloppily dressed professors and students. His manner was cordial, though he sometimes raised his voice excessively. His gestures for years now had tended to be peremptory. It was said that he was ill, but no one knew what was wrong with him. It was probably something do to with his nerves. He never missed a class. He lived in a fifteen-hundred-square-foot apartment in the center of Santa Teresa. He was still a bachelor. For a while now his students had been calling him by the nicer-sounding and more peaceable name of Horacio Tregua, *Truce* replacing *War*.

7

After Amalfitano had sent out fifty job applications and pestered the few friends he had left, the only school to show an interest in his services was the University of Santa Teresa. For a full week Amalfitano debated whether to accept the job or to wait by the mailbox for a better offer. In terms of quality, the only worse options were a Guatemalan university and a Honduran one, though neither had even bothered to send him a written rejection. In fact, the only universities that had gotten back to him to say no were the European ones with which Amalfitano had had previous dealings. All that was left was the University of Santa Teresa, and after a week of thinking it over, sunk in a deepening depression, Amalfitano sent word that he would accept the position. He soon received a copy of the contract, all the papers and forms he would need to fill out for his work permit, and the date when he was expected in Santa Teresa.

He lied to Rosa. He told her that his job was ending and that they had to leave. Rosa thought they would return to Italy, but she wasn't unhappy to hear that they were going to Mexico.

At night Amalfitano and his daughter talked about the trip. They made plans, studied maps of northern Mexico and the southern United States, decided which places they would visit on their first vacations, what kind of car they would buy (a used one, like in the movies, at one of those lots with a salesman in a blue suit, red tie, and snakeskin boots), the house they would rent, no more apartments, a little house with two or three bedrooms, a front yard, and a backyard where they could barbecue, though neither Amalfitano nor his daughter was entirely sure what barbe-cuing was: Rosa claimed it involved a grill set up in the backyard (next to the pool, if possible) where meat and even fish were grilled; Amalfitano thought that in Mexico it actually involved a pit—a pit out in the country, ideally—into which one shoveled hot coals, then a layer of earth, then slabs of goat, then another layer of earth, and finally more hot coals; the pieces of meat, according to Amalfitano, were wrapped in the leaves of some ancient tree, the name of which escaped him. Or in aluminum foil.

Those last days in Barcelona, Amalfitano sat at his desk for hours, supposedly working but really doing nothing. He thought about Padilla, his daughter, his dead wife, random scenes from his youth and childhood. Rosa, meanwhile, was never at home, as if the moment she had to leave Barcelona she was seized by an irre-sistible urge to walk its streets, to see and commit to memory every inch of it. Usually she went out alone, although occasionally she was accompanied by Jordi Carrera, silent and distant. Amalfitano would hear him arrive, and after a brief interval in which nothing seemed to happen, he would hear them go and it was then that he most regretted having to leave Barcelona. Then he would stay up, though with the lights off, until one or two or three in the morn-ing, which was when Rosa generally came home.

To Amalfitano, Jordi seemed a shy and formal boy. Rosa liked his silence, which she mistook for thoughtfulness when it was re-ally just a symptom of the confusion raging in his head. For both young people, each day that went by was like a sign, the an-nouncement of an impending future full of significant events; Rosa suspected that the trip to Mexico would mark the end of her adolescence; Jordi sensed that their time together would torment him someday and he didn't know what to do about it.

One night they went to a concert. Another night they went to a club where they danced for a long time like two strangers.

8

Who came to the airport? The Carreras—and, thirty minutes before boarding, Padilla and the poet Pere Girau. Jordi and Rosa's farewell was silent. The Carreras and Amalfitano's was traditional, a hug and good luck, write to us. Antoni Carrera knew the poet Pere Girau by reputation, but he greeted him politely. Anna Carrera, however, asked him whether his work had been published and if so where she could buy it. Jordi gave his mother an incredulous look. But you don't read poetry, he said. Rosa—who, standing next to Jordi, looked much smaller than she was—said: it's never too late to start, though I would choose something more classic, more solid. Like what, for example? asked the poet Pere Girau, who next to Jordi looked smaller, too (even smaller than Rosa), and who was hurt by the word *solid*. Padilla cast his gaze skyward. Amalfitano seemed to develop an interest in the fine print on his boarding passes. Catullus, said Rosa, he's quick and fun. Oh, Catullus, said Anna, I read him ages ago, in college, I think, wasn't it? Yes, said Antoni Carrera, we read him, of course. Jordi shrugged, but that was a long time ago, I'm sure you don't remember any of it now. I haven't been published yet, said the poet Pere Girau with a smile, though this year a collection of mine is coming out with Cavall amb Barretina, the new Catalan publishing house. And do you write poetry too? Anna asked Padilla. Yes, ma'am, but in Spanish, which means there's no chance I'll be published by Cavall amb Barretina. But there are other places where you could be published, aren't there? Or so I imagine. What do you think, Toni? Of course there are other places, said Antoni

Carrera, trying to give her a look that explained who Padilla was. Are all of your students poets? asked Rosa. Amalfitano smiled without looking at her. Not all of them, he said. Jordi thought: I should ask Rosa to come with me to the café for a drink, I should get her alone, I should bring her with me to the newsstand and say something, anything. Oh, these are students of yours, said Anna Carrera, at last understanding who they were. Yes, said Amalfitano, and then he smiled: former students. Shall we go get something to drink? Jordi asked. Rosa, after hesitating for a few seconds, said no, there wasn't time. No, there isn't time, said the Carreras and Amalfitano. Amalfitano was the only one to notice the boy's dejected slump and he smiled, youth is the pits. Well, well, well, said Anna Carrera. Yes, the hour approaches, said Amalfitano. I'm so envious, said the poet Pere Girau, I'd love to be on my way to Mexico tonight, wouldn't you all? I'm starting to feel that way, admitted Antoni Carrera. Padilla gave them a smile that was intended to be ironic but was only tender. It must be the moon, said Anna Carrera. The moon? asked Amalfitano. The moon, the moon, said Anna Carrera, the moon is huge, the kind that makes people go wild or take long trips to exotic countries. There are no exotic countries left in Latin America, said Rosa. Oh, no? asked Anna, who had always liked Rosa's wit. No, Anna, there are no exotic countries left anywhere in the world, said Jordi. Don't you believe it, said Amalfitano, there are still exotic countries and there must be one or two of them left in Latin America. Catalonia is an exotic country, said Padilla. Catalonia? asked the poet Pere Girau. The moon is certainly exotic, said Antoni Carrera sadly. Not even the moon, said Jordi, the moon is just a satellite. I love the full moon when I'm at the beach, I love to listen to the tide—is it coming in or going out? I'm never sure—while I'm moon gazing, said the poet Pere Girau. It's coming in, said Antoni Carrera, and it's called high tide. I thought high tide was when the water stopped rising, said Padilla. Actually, it's the time it takes it to rise, said Antoni Carrera. I adore the ebb and flow, said the poet Pere Girau, rolling his eyes back in his head, though low tide is more practical because you can find treasures. He rolled his eyes back in his head, thought Rosa, disgusting! Do you remember our honeymoon in Peniche, Toni? asked Anna Carrera. Yes, said Antoni Carrera. The tide was very low, hundreds of yards out, and in the early morning light the beach looked like some extraterrestrial landscape, said Anna. In Brittany you see things like that every day, said the poet Pere Girau. But what you're talking about has nothing to do with the moon, said Antoni Carrera. Of course it does, said Amalfitano. I don't think so, said Antoni Carrera. It certainly does, said Amalfitano. Peniche is an exotic place, too, said Padilla, in its own way and with its government workers. Have you ever been to Peniche? asked Anna Carrera. No, but a third of Barcelona has camped there, said Padilla. Funny, it's true, now everyone has been to Portugal, but when we went it was unusual to see another Catalonian, said Anna Carrera. It was political tourism, admitted Antoni Carrera quietly. My father took me to the Alentejo on vacation, said Rosa. Amalfitano smiled, in fact they had made only a brief stop in Lisbon, but he loved his daughter's finely honed malice, she might be Brazilian, he thought happily. What is an exotic country, essentially? asked Jordi. A poor but happy place, said Amalfitano. Somalia isn't exotic, of course, said Anna Carrera. And neither is Morocco, said Jordi. It can also be a country that's poor in spirit but deeply joyful, said Padilla. Like Germany, which at least to me seems very exotic, said Rosa. What's exotic about Germany? asked Jordi. The beer halls, the street food, and the ruins of the concentration camps, said Padilla. No, no, said Rosa, not that, the wealth. Mexico is a truly exotic country, said the poet Pere Girau, Breton's favorite country, the promised land of Artaud and the Mayas, home of Alfonso Reyes and Atahualpa. Atahualpa was an Inca, a Peruvian Inca, said Rosa. True, true, said the poet Pere Girau. Then he was quiet until the moment came for hugs and farewells. Take care of your father, Anna Carrera said to Rosa. Take care of yourself and think of us every now and then, Padilla said to Amalfitano. The plural, like a flower flung in his face, dealt Amalfitano a soft blow. So low, he thought sadly. Good luck and bon voyage, said the poet Pere Girau. Jordi looked at Rosa, made a gesture of resignation, and couldn't think what to say. Rosa turned to him and said let me give you a kiss, silly. Of course, said Jordi, and he bent down clumsily and they kissed on both cheeks. Jordi's cheeks burned as if he had a fever, Rosa's were warm and smelled like lavender. Anna kissed Rosa, too, and Amalfitano. Finally, they all hugged and kissed, even the poet Pere Girau and Anna Carrera, who weren't going anywhere. When they were in line to board, Amalfitano raised his hand and waved a last time. Rosa didn't turn around. Then the Carreras, the poet Pere Girau, and Padilla hurried up to the viewing area but they couldn't see the Amalfitanos' plane, though they did see a huge moon, and after a while, not knowing what to say to each other, each group went its own way.

9

How Were the Carreras Affected by Amalfitano's Departure?

At first both of them were busy at their respective jobs, and in a way, especially for Antoni, Amalfitano's departure was simply a relief, but after a few months, in the middle of an especially boring after-dinner hour, the two of them began to miss him. Gradually they realized that Amalfitano and his crazy stories were like the image of their own lost youth. They saw him as they saw themselves: young, poor, determined, brave, generous, invested in a perhaps ridiculous and feeble way with pride and nobility. By so often associating Amalfitano with defunct images of themselves, they ultimately stopped thinking about him. Only every so often, when a letter came from Rosa, were they reminded of the wandering queer, and then they would laugh, happy all of a sudden, remembering him with fleeting but sincere affection.

How Was Jordi Carrera Affected by the Departure of Rosa Amalfitano?

It was much harder for him than for his parents. Until Rosa left, it was as if Jordi lived at the North Pole. He and his friends and a few people who weren't his friends and others he didn't even know but saw in teen magazines, all lived in harmony—if not happily, since happiness was a sham—at the North Pole. They played basketball there, learned English, developed computer skills, bought lumberjack clothes, and assiduously attended movies and concerts. His parents often remarked to each other how inexpressive Jordi was, but this lack of expressiveness was his true self. Rosa's absence changed everything. From one day to the next, Jordi found himself sailing at full speed over a vast sheet of ice to warmer seas. The North Pole receded in the distance and faded in significance and his ice sheet kept shrinking. He soon began to suffer from insomnia and nightmares.

How Was Padilla Affected by Amalfitano's Departure?

Hardly at all. Padilla lived in a constant state of amorous self-expression and his feelings were extravagant but didn't last for more than a day. In his own way, Padilla was a scientist who left no room for God in his laboratory. He agreed with Burroughs that love is nothing but a mixture of sentimentalism and sex and he found it everywhere, which meant that he was unable to mourn a lost love for more than twenty-four hours. Inside, he was strong and he accepted the shifts and fluctuations of the romantic object with a stoicism that, unlikely as it seemed, he shared with his father. Once, the poet Pere Girau asked how in the world, after a person had loved and fucked a Greek god, he could love and fuck people of inferior looks—ugly queers, if you can believe it, and the usual horrible rent boys. Padilla's answer was that we loved beautiful people for the sake of convenience, that it was like a preference for known quantities, that the inner self was all that mattered, and that he could find beauty even in the shuffle of a donkey. And he wasn't the only one. For example, he said, take the Apollonian poets of nineteenth-century France who sated themselves with stub-dicked boys from the Maghreb, youths who in no way fit the strict definition of classical beauty. Stub-dicked boys? said the poet Pere Girau incredulously, but I'm Apollonian, too, aren't I, and I'd like to find someone to love who's at least as good-looking as the son of a bitch who left me. Girau, said Padilla, I love people and my insides are bursting, and all you love is poetry.

And Finally, How Was the Poet Pere Girau Affected by the Departure of Amalfitano?

Not at all, though occasionally he remembered how much Amalfitano knew about Elizabethan verse, how well acquainted he was with the work of Marcel Schwob, how pleasant and agreeable he was when they talked about contemporary Italian poetry (Girau had translated twenty-five poems by Dino Campana into Catalan), what a good listener he was, and how sharp his opinions usually were. In bed it was a different story, he was a late-blooming queer and he neglected the practical, neglected it badly. Though in the end, thought the poet Pere Girau bitterly, he's more practical than we are, because he'll always be a literature professor, which means he'll be protected financially at least, while we're plunged into the vulgar and savage fin de siècle.

10

During the flight each of them realized that the other was afraid, though not very, and each of them understood with a sense of fatalism that all they had was each other: Planet Amalfitano began with Óscar and ended with Rosa and there was nothing in between. Or maybe there was: a succession of countries, a whirl of cities and streets that brightened and darkened arbitrarily in memory, the ghost of Edith Lieberman in Brazil, an imaginary country called Chile that drove Amalfitano mad—although every so often he tried to find out what was going on there—and that Rosa, born in Argentina, couldn't care less about. If their plane went down in flames over the Atlantic, if their plane exploded, if their plane disappeared in the boundless space of the Amalfitanos, no memory of them would be left in the world, thought Amalfitano sadly. And he thought: we are two gypsies without a tribe, reviled, used, exploited, with no real friends, a clown and his poor defenseless daughter. Which led him to think: if instead of both of us dying in a plane accident only I die, of a heart attack or stomach cancer or in some gay brawl (the possibilities made Amalfitano sweat), what will happen to my angel, my darling, my wonderful, clever girl? and the carpet of clouds he could see if he craned his neck a little (he was in an aisle seat) opened up like the door to a nightmare, like an immaculate wound, Israel, he thought, Israel, let her head to the first Israeli embassy she can find and request citizenship, her mother was Jewish, so it's her right, let her live in Tel Aviv and study at Tel Aviv University, where she'll probably run into Skinny Bolzman (how many years has it been since I saw him? twenty?), let her marry an Israeli and live happily ever after, ah, he thought, if only it could be Sweden I would breathe easier, but Israel isn't bad, Israel is acceptable. And he thought: if neither of us dies but things go badly in Santa Teresa, if I lose my job and can't find another one, if I can only give private French lessons and we have to live in a seedy boardinghouse, if we start to shrivel up and succumb to our basest instincts in the middle of nowhere with no money to leave and no place to go, if we're smothered and numbed in a time that moves with endless slowness, without hope or prospects, if I end up like that Spanish widow I met in a café in Colón, the perfect victim, that mental Justine who worried every day that the Panamanians (the black ones, those big, athletic black men) would rape her delectable fifteen-year-old daughter, and she would be helpless, a woman with no husband and no money running a tiny café that made no profit, with no hope of returning to Spain, trapped in a Buñuel film from the '50s, what will I do then? thought Amalfitano, bewildered, trying to block stray images of Padilla and desolate, schematic New World landscapes in which he was the only cat among packs of hounds, a hoopoe among eagles and peacocks.

11

A month after they were settled in Santa Teresa one of the secretaries from the rector's office gave Amalfitano a letter from Padilla that was addressed to the university. In the letter Padilla talked about the weather in Barcelona, about how much he was drinking, about his new lover—another one—a twenty-eight-year-old SEAT auto worker, married with three children. He said that he had left the university (it wasn't the same without you) and that at last he had work, he was a proofreader at a publishing house, a friend got him the job, it was a little boring but secure and the pay wasn't bad, though a few lines later he said that in fact the pay was bad but he could get by. He also said that he had left the studio and that the painter who was sometimes there, the one with the gold cigarette case full of little hash cigarettes, had recently killed himself in New York. Life, according to Padilla, despite the crushing boredom of proofreading novels faker than a three-thousand-peseta note, continued to be strange and full of mysterious offerings. Finally, he reported that he had begun to write his first novel. About the plot, however, he divulged nothing.

Amalfitano answered the letter that same night, in his room, lying on his unmade bed, as his daughter devoured another video in the living room. In broad strokes he described his life in Santa Teresa, his work, how receptive his students were, *I don't know whether I've ever seen kids so interested in literature,* interested, in fact, in everything that was happening in the world, all continents and all races. He didn't say anything about his new lover, whose name was Castillo, or about how badly he was getting along with his daughter lately. He ended the letter by telling Padilla that he missed him. Though it may seem strange to you (or maybe not), I miss you. In a postcript he said that of course he remembered the man with the gold cigarette case, the one who always wore leather, and he asked why he had killed himself. In a second postcript he said that it was wonderful that Padilla was writing a novel, keep it up, keep it up.

Padilla's response was quick to arrive. It was concise and mono-thematic. My novel, he said, will be like an emission of strobo-scopic light, with lots of characters (though rudimentary or sketched arbitrarily and at random) and lots of violence and lots of wolf moons and dog moons and lots of erect and well-greased cocks, lots of hard cocks and lots of howling.

Amalfitano's response, on university letterhead and written between classes on the electric typewriter in his cubicle, tried to be judicious. Too many characters could turn any novel into a collec-tion of stories. Hard cocks, with glorious exceptions, were hardly ever literary. Howls were literary, but the place for them, their natural medium, was generally poetry, not prose. That way lies danger, he warned, and a few lines later he insisted on hearing the circumstances surrounding the painter's suicide. Otherwise, he assured Padilla once again that he missed him and wished him the best. About his new life in Santa Teresa he said practically nothing.

The next news he had from Padilla was a postcard of the port of Barcelona. This is where we saw each other for the last time, he said. The last time ever, I think sometimes. And he disclosed the title of his novel: *The God of Homosexuals.*

Amalfitano returned the ball. On a postcard of Santa Teresa depicting the statue of General Sepúlveda, hero of the Revolu-tion, he allowed that the title struck him as the right choice. It was a sad title, certainly, but the right choice. And who was this god of homosexuals? Not the goddess of love or the god of beauty, but some other god—which one? As to whether they would see each other again, he left that in the hands of the god of travelers.

Padilla's response was swift and lengthy: the leather-wearing painter had had seemingly no reason to kill himself. He was in

New York for a solo show of his work at the prestigious Gina Randall Gallery, you've probably never heard of her, but she's known to the cognoscenti as one of the most powerful art dealers in Babylon. So, ruling out any financial or artistic motives (in that order, insisted Padilla), what remained were sentimental or carnal ones, but the painter was famous for his indifference to a nice pair of hips and to spoken or unspoken romantic sentiments, which meant that this possibility also had to be discarded. And if the explanation wasn't money, art, or romance, what else could drive a man to suicide? Clearly: boredom or illness, the culprit must have been one or the other, you choose. Regarding the identity of the god of homosexuals, Padilla was categorical: he's the god of beggars, the god who sleeps on the ground, in subway entrances, the god of insomniacs, the god of those who have always lost. Here he talked (confusedly) about Belisarius and Narses, two Byzantine generals, the former young and beautiful, the latter old and a eunuch, but both of them perfectly suited to the Emperor's military needs, and he talked about the wages of Byzantium. He's a helpless god, ugly and resplendent, a god who loves but whose love is terrible and always, but *always*, turns against him.

The wages of Chile, remembered Amalfitano, and he also thought: fuck, he's describing the god of poets, the god of the poor, the god of the Comte de Lautréamont and Rimbaud.

The novel is moving along, said Padilla in the postcript, but the proofreading work was killing him. Too many hours comparing originals and proofs, soon he would probably need glasses. This last bit of news saddened Amalfitano. The only glasses that suited Padilla's face were sunglasses, and then only because of the unsettling effect produced when Padilla removed them with a flourish at once provocative and endearing.

In response, he listed all the reasons why Padilla should persist at all costs with *The God of Homosexuals*. When you finish, he suggested with false casualness, you can come visit us. They say that the north of Mexico is delightful. This letter received no response. For a while Padilla remained silent.

12

Soon after this, Amalfitano began to feel watched. There were other times in his life when he'd had the same feeling: that of the prey in the woods who scents the hunter. But it was so long ago that he'd forgotten the instructions and advice received in his youth, the proper way to behave in a situation like the one that now, rather than presenting itself, was gradually creeping up on him.

II. AMALFITANO and PADILLA

1

Padilla said tell me, tell me about the dangers you've seen, and Amalfitano thought of an adolescent on horseback, himself, achingly beautiful, and then he thought of a black blanket, the blanket he wrapped around himself early in the morning at the detention camp, first he thought of its color, then its smell, and finally its texture, how nice it felt to cover his face with it and let his nose, his lips, his forehead, his bruised cheekbones, come into contact with the rough cloth. It was an electric blanket, he remembered happily, but there was nowhere to plug it in. And Padilla said my love, let my lips be like your black blanket, let me kiss those eyes that have seen so much. And Amalfitano felt happy to be with Padilla. He said: Joan, Joan, Joan, here I am at last emerging from the tunnel, all that time wasted, all those days lost, and he also thought: if only I'd met you sooner, but he didn't say it, or rather he communicated it telepathically, so that Padilla couldn't say you idiot, sooner? when? in a time outside of time, thought Amalfitano as Padilla kissed him softly on the back, in an ideal time, when to be awake was to dream, in a country where men love men, isn't that the title of a novel? asked Padilla, yes, said Amalfitano, but I can't think of the name of the author. And then, as if he were riding the night in successive waves, he returned to the black electric blanket, with its little tail and its stains, and over the shouting, shouting that announced an impending hurricane, Padilla's voice rose like the captain of a sinking ship. This will end badly, thought Amalfitano, end badly, end badly, as Padilla's cock sank smoothly into his old ass.

Then, as always, came the madness. Padilla introduced him to a fat, blue-eyed adolescent, the poet Pere Girau, a wonderful kid, said Padilla, you have to hear him read, he's got a voice as rich and deep as Auden's. And Amalfitano listened to Pere Girau read his poems and then they went out for a drive, out for drinks at the Killer Trucker and the Brothers Poyatos, and the three of them ended up in Padilla's studio and in Padilla's bed, and Amalfitano, consumed by doubt, thought that this wasn't what he wanted, even though later he really did want it. But still, he would have liked a different kind of bond, spending evenings with Padilla discussing literature, for example, making time for intimacy and friendship.

And after the poet Pere Girau there were two others, classmates of Padilla, and Amalfitano's surprise upon meeting them and discovering the purpose of their meeting was huge. This was no longer a matter of attending dramatic readings. He was ashamed, he blushed, he tried to be casual and cold but failed. And Padilla seemed to enjoy his distress, seemed to change and grow, become suddenly old and cynical (he had always been foulmouthed), while Amalfitano grew progressively younger, more dazed, shyer. An adolescent in a foreign land. Don't worry, Óscar, they understand, they've been doing this since long before I popped your cherry, they like you, they say they've never had such a good-looking professor, they say it's incredible, considering how old you are, they wonder what you'd like to do tonight, said Padilla, laughing, thoroughly pleased with himself, master of his actions and his emotions, before the disease, before his encounter with the god of homosexuals.

Tell me, tell me the dangerous things you've done in your life, said Padilla. The most dangerous was sleeping with you, thought Amalfitano, but he was careful not to say it.

2

Amalfitano thought, too, about the last time he made love with Padilla. Days before he left for Mexico, Padilla called. Trembling all over, Amalfitano agreed to what he imagined would be their last date. An hour later a taxi dropped him off at the port and Padilla, with his black jacket buttoned up to the neck, strode toward him.

He really should stop smiling, thought Amalfitano as he gazed fixedly, spellbound, at Padilla's face, finding it haggard, paler, almost translucent, as if lately the sun never shone on it. Then, when he felt Padilla's lips on his cheek, brushing the corner of his own lips, he experienced a feeling for his former student that—the few times he stopped to think about it—disturbed him. A mixture of desire, paternal affection, and sadness, as if Padilla were the embodiment of an impossible trinity: lover, son, and ideal reflection of Amalfitano himself. He felt sorry for Padilla, for Padilla and his father, for the deaths in his life and his lost loves, which cast him in a lonely light: there, on that sad backdrop, Padilla was too young and too fragile and there was nothing Amalfitano could do about it. And while at the same time he knew with certainty—and most of the time this perplexed him—that there existed an invulnerable Padilla, arrogant as a Mediterranean god and strong as a Cuban boxer, the pity lingered, the sense of loss and impotence.

For a while they strolled aimlessly along narrow sidewalks, skirting terraces, fried-fish stands, and northern European tourists. The few words they spoke to each other made them smile.

"Do you think I look like a gay German?" asked Padilla as they wandered the port in search of a cheap hotel.

"No," said Amalfitano, "the gay Germans I know—and all my knowledge of them comes from books—are happy brutes like you, but they tend toward self-destruction and you seem to be made of stronger stuff."

Immediately he regretted his words; it's talk like that, he thought, that will destroy any kind of love.

3

About the plane trip Rosa remembered that in the middle of the Atlantic her father seemed sick or queasy and all of a sudden a stewardess appeared without being called and offered them a deep golden liquid, bright and sweet smelling. The stewardess was dark-skinned, of average height, with short dark hair, and she was wearing hardly any makeup but her nails were very well kept. She asked them to try the juice and then tell her what it was. She smiled with her whole face, like someone playing a game.

Amalfitano and Rosa, distrustful by nature, each took a sip.

"Peach," said Rosa.

"Nectarine," murmured Amalfitano, almost in unison.

No, said the stewardess, and her good-humored smile restored some of Amalfitano's lost courage, it's mango.

Father and daughter drank again. This time they took lingering sips, like sommeliers who are back on the right path. Mango: have you tried it before? asked the stewardess. Yes, said Rosa and Amalfitano, but we'd forgotten. The stewardess wanted to know where. In Paris, probably, said Rosa, in a Mexican bar in Paris, a long time ago, when I was small, but I still remember it. The stewardess smiled again. It's delicious, added Rosa. Mango, mango, thought Amalfitano, and he closed his eyes.

4

Shortly after classes began, Amalfitano met Castillo.

It was one evening, almost night, when the Santa Teresa sky turns from deep blue to an array of vermilions and purples that linger scarcely a few minutes before the sky turns back to deep blue and then black.

Amalfitano left the department library and as he crossed the campus he spotted a shape under a tree. He thought it might be a bum or a sick student and he went over to check. It was Castillo, who was sleeping peacefully and was awakened by Amalfitano's presence: when he opened his eyes he saw a tall, angular, white-haired figure, looking vaguely like Christopher Walken, with a worried expression on his face, and he knew right away that he would fall in love.

"I thought you were dying," said Amalfitano.

"No, I was dreaming," said Castillo.

Amalfitano smiled, satisfied, and made as if to leave but didn't. This part of the campus was like an oasis, three trees on a mound surrounded by a sea of grass.

"I was dreaming about the paintings of an American artist," said Castillo, "they were set along a wide street, in the open air, the street was unpaved, lined with houses and stores, all built of wood, and the paintings seemed about to melt away in the sun and dust. It made me feel very sad. I think it was a dream about the end of the world."

"Ah," said Amalfitano.

"The strangest thing is that some of the paintings were mine."

"Well, I don't know what to tell you, it is a strange dream."

"No it isn't," said Castillo. "I shouldn't be telling this to a stranger, but somehow I trust you: I really did paint some of them."

"Some of them?" asked Amalfitano as night fell suddenly over Santa Teresa and from a campus building, a building that seemed empty, came the music of drums and horns and something that might have or might not have been a harp.

"Some paintings," said Castillo. "I painted them myself, forged them."

"Oh, really?"

"Yes, that's how I make a living."

"And you tell this to the first person who walks by, or is it common knowledge?"

"You're the first person I've told, no one knows, it's a secret."

"I see," said Amalfitano. "And why are you telling me?"

"I don't know," said Castillo, "I really don't. Who are you?"

"Me?"

"Well, it doesn't matter, that was a rude question, never mind," said Castillo, in a protective tone that grated on Amalfitano's nerves. "You aren't Mexican, that's plain to see."

"I'm Chilean," said Amalfitano.

His reply and the expression on his face when he admitted where he was from were humble in the extreme. So far away, said Castillo. Then both of them were silent, standing there facing each other, Castillo a bit taller because he was up on the mound, Amalfitano like a bird or some hulking raptor sensing in every pore the coming of night, the stars that were beginning swiftly (and also *violently*, this Amalfitano noticed clearly for the first time) to fill the sky of Santa Teresa, standing there motionless, waiting for some sign under the sturdy trees that rose like an island between the literature department and the administration building.

"Shall we get some coffee?" asked Castillo finally.

"All right," said Amalfitano, grateful though he couldn't say why.

They circled around the center of Santa Teresa in Castillo's car, a yellow 1980 Chevy. Their first stop was at the Dallas, where they chatted politely about painting, forgeries, and literature, and then they left because Castillo decided there were too many students. Without speaking, they drove along streets unfamiliar to Amalfitano until they reached the Just Once, and then, strolling down brightly lit and shuttered streets where it was hard to park a car, they stopped at the Dominium of Tamaulipas and the North Star and later the Toltecatl. Castillo kept laughing and drinking more mescal.

The Toltecatl was a big, rectangular room, the walls painted sky blue. On the back wall, a six-foot-square mural featured Toltecatl, god of pulque and brother of the maguey goddess Mayahuel. Indian drifters, cowboys and herds of cattle, policemen and police cars, ominously abandoned customs stations, amusement parks on either side of the border, children on their way out of a school blazoned with the name—painted in blue on a whitewashed wall— Benito Juárez, distinguished son of the Americas, a fruit market and a pottery market, North American tourists, shoeshine men, singers of rancheras and boleros (the ranchera singers looked like gunmen, the bolero singers suicidal or like pimps, Castillo remarked), women on their way to church, and hookers talking, running, or gesturing mysteriously: this was the backdrop, while in the foreground the god Toltecatl, an Indian with a chubby face covered with welts and scars, laughed uproariously. The owner of the bar, Castillo told him, was a man by the name of Aparicio Montes de Oca, and in 1985, the year he bought the place, he had killed a man at the busiest time of day, in front of everyone. At the trial he got off by pleading self-defense.

When Castillo pointed out Aparicio Montes de Oca behind the bar, Amalfitano noticed how much the bar owner looked like the figure of Toltecatl painted on the wall.

"It's a portrait of him," said Amalfitano.

"Yes," said Castillo, "he commissioned it when he got out of jail."

Then Castillo took Amalfitano home with him to prove that he wasn't lying, he really was a forger.

He lived on the second floor of a dilapidated three-story

building on the edge of town. On the first floor hung the sign for a tool wholesaler; no one lived on the third floor. Close your eyes, said Castillo when he opened the door. Amalfitano smiled but didn't close his eyes. Go on, close your eyes, insisted Castillo. Amalfitano obeyed and ventured cautiously into the sanctum to which he was being granted access.

"Don't open them until I turn on the light."

Amalfitano opened his eyes immediately. In the moonlight coming in through the uncurtained windows, he got a glimpse of the contours of a large room plunged in a gray fog. At the back he could make out a big Larry Rivers painting. What am I doing here? wondered Amalfitano. When he heard the click of the switch he automatically closed his eyes.

"Now you can look," said Castillo.

The studio was much bigger than he had thought at first, lit by many fluorescent bars. In a corner was Castillo's spartan-looking bed; in another corner, a kitchen reduced to the bare essentials: hot plate, sink, a few pots, glasses, plates, cutlery. The rest of the furnishings, apart from the canvases stacked everywhere, consisted of two old armchairs, a rocking chair, two sturdy wooden tables, and a bookcase filled mostly with art books. Near the window and on one of the tables were the forgeries. Do you like them? Amalfitano nodded.

"Do you know who the artist is?"

"No," said Amalfitano.

"He's American," said Castillo.

"I can tell that much. But I don't know who he is. I'd rather not know."

Castillo shrugged.

"Do you want something to drink? I think I have everything."

"Whiskey," said Amalfitano, suddenly feeling very sad.

I've come here to make love, he thought, I've come here to take my pants off and fuck this naïve kid, this art student, this forger of Larry Rivers, early- or mid-career Larry Rivers, what do I know, a forger who brags when he should cringe, I've come to do what Padilla predicted I would do and what he surely hasn't stopped doing for even a moment, even a second.

"He's Larry Rivers," said Castillo, "an artist from New York."

Amalfitano took a desperate gulp of whiskey.

"I know," he said. "I know Larry Rivers. I know Frank O'Hara, so I know Larry Rivers."

"Why did you say you didn't, then? Are they that bad?" asked Castillo, not offended in the least.

"I can't imagine who buys them, frankly," said Amalfitano, feeling worse and worse.

"Oh, they sell, believe me." Castillo's voice was smooth and persuasive. "There's a Texan who buys them—short little guy, a real character, you have to meet him—and then he sells them to other filthy rich Texans."

"It doesn't matter," said Amalfitano. "Forgive me. We're here to go to bed, aren't we? Or maybe not. Again, forgive me."

Castillo sighed.

"Yes, if you want. If you don't, I'll take you home and we'll pretend nothing happened. I think you've had too much to drink."

"So do you want to?"

"I want to be with you, in bed or talking, it makes no difference. Or not much, anyway."

"Forgive me," murmured Amalfitano and he dropped onto a sofa. "I don't feel well, I think I'm drunk."

"No worries," said Castillo, sitting down beside him, on the floor, on an old Indian rug. "I'll make you coffee."

After a while the two of them lit cigarettes. Amalfitano told Castillo that he had a seventeen-year-old daughter. They talked, too, about painting and poetry, about Larry Rivers and Frank O'Hara. Then Castillo drove him home.

The next day, when he got out of his last class, Castillo was waiting for him in the hall. That same afternoon they slept together for the first time.

5

One morning a gardener stopped by Amalfitano's classroom and handed him a note from Horacio Guerra. Guerra wanted to see him in his office at two. Without fail. Guerra's office turned out to be hard to find. Guerra's secretary and another woman drew him a map. It was on the first floor of the department building, at the back, next to the little theater—hardly bigger than a classroom—where college actors put on plays once a month for students, family, teachers, and other Santa Teresa intellectuals. Horacio Guerra was the director, and next to the dressing room, in what must once have been the props room, he had set up his office. It was a space with no natural light, the walls papered with posters for old shows, a shelf of university press books, a big oak table stacked with papers, and three chairs in a semicircle, facing a black leather swivel chair.

When Amalfitano came in, the room was dark. He spied Guerra sunk low in the big chair and for an instant he thought the other man was asleep. When he turned on the light he saw that Guerra was wide awake: his eyes were unnaturally alert and bright, as if he were high, and there was a sly smile on his lips. Despite the manner of their meeting, they greeted each other formally. They talked about the school year, about Amalfitano's predecessors, and about the university's need for good professors. In the sciences the best people left for Monterrey or Mexico City, or made the leap to some American university. In the arts it's a different story, said Guerra, nobody pulls a fast one on me, but to make sure of it I have to be everywhere, supervise everything personally, it's a lot to handle. I can imagine, said Amalfitano, who had decided to tread with care. Then they talked about theater. Horacio Guerra wanted to revamp the department's drama program and in order to do so he needed the cooperation of everyone. Absolutely everyone. The department had two theater groups, but if he was to speak frankly both were undisciplined. Though the students weren't bad actors. Amalfitano wanted to know what he meant by undisciplined. Announcing the date of an opening and not opening, losing an actor and having no understudy, starting the show half an hour late, failing to stick to a budget. My task, explained Guerra, is to find the evil and root it out. And I've found it, my friend, and I've rooted it out. Do you want to know what it was? Yes, of course, said Amalfitano. The directors! That's right, those ignorant kids, ignorant but most of all undisciplined, who have no idea that a play is like a battlefield, complete with logistics, artillery, infantry, cavalry to cover the flanks (or light armored units, don't take me for some old fart, even air squadrons if you insist), tanks, engineers, scouts, etc., etc.

"Actually," said Guerra, "as you may have guessed, this isn't my office. My office has air and light and I take pride in the furniture, but good generals have to stand with their troops, so I moved here."

"I know," said Amalfitano, "your secretary told me."

"Have you been to my other office?"

"Yes," said Amalfitano, "that's where they told me how to get here. I guess it took me a while to find you. At first I got lost."

"Yes, yes, the same thing always happens. Even our theatergoers get lost on their way to our plays. Maybe I should put up signs pointing the way."

"Not a bad idea," said Amalfitano.

They continued their conversation about theater, although Guerra avoided asking Amalfitano what he thought about the repertory he had planned. The only authors Amalfitano had heard of were Salvador Novo and Rodolfo Usigli. The others sounded either like discoveries or yawning pits. All the while Guerra talked about his project as if he were planning a delicate repast that only a few would really attack with relish. Not a word was spoken about Amalfitano's job. When they parted, an hour later, Guerra asked whether he'd been to the Botanic Garden. Not yet, answered Amalfitano. Later, as he was waiting for a taxi to take him home, he wondered why Guerra had sent a gardener rather than an office boy to summon him. It seems a good sign, he thought.

6

The Texan; the people who bought the fake Larry Rivers paintings from the Texan; Castillo, who sincerely believed he was doing good work; the art market in New Mexico, Arizona, and Texas: all of them, thought Amalfitano, were ultimately like characters from an eighteenth-century philosophical novel, exiled on a continent like the moon, the dark side of the moon, the perfect spot for them to grow and be formed, innocent and greedy, singular and brave, dreamers and utterly naïve. How else to explain, he thought, that not only are these paintings commissioned and painted but even sold, that there are people who buy them, and no one exposes them and turns them in? The art spreads across Texas, thought Amalfitano, like a revelation, like a lesson in humility that bypasses the dealers, like a kind of goodness that redeems everything, even bad forgeries, and he immediately pictured those fake Berdies, those fake camels, and those extremely fake Primo Levis (some of the faces undeniably Mexican) in the private salons and galleries, the living rooms and libraries of modestly prosperous citizens, owners of nothing but their well-appointed houses and their cars and maybe a few oil stocks, but not many, just enough, he imagined them strolling through rooms cluttered with trophies and photographs of cowboys, casting sidelong glances at the canvases on the walls at each pass. Certified Larry Rivers. And then he imagined himself strolling around Castillo's nearly empty studio, naked like Frank O'Hara, a cup of coffee in his right hand and a whiskey in his left, his heart untroubled, at peace with himself, moving trustingly into the arms of his new lover. And superimposed on this image again were the fake Larry Rivers paintings scattered across a flat expanse, with big houses set far from one another, and in the middle, in the geometric and artificial yards, art, shaky and fragile as a forgery; Larry Rivers's Chinese horsemen riding across a field of roiling white horsemen. Fuck, thought Amalfitano in excitement, this is the center of the world. The place where things really happen.

But then he came back down to earth and cast a skeptical eye over Castillo's paintings and was assailed by doubt: either he had forgotten how Larry Rivers painted or the Texas art buyers were a bunch of blind raving lunatics. He thought, too, about the loathsome Tom Castro and said to himself that yes, maybe the authenticity of the canvases resided precisely in their failure to exactly replicate the Larry Rivers paintings, allowing them, paradoxically, to pass for originals. Through an act of faith. Because those Texans *needed* paintings and because faith is comforting.

Then he imagined Castillo painting—with such effort, such dedication—a beautiful boy blithely asleep on the university campus or wherever, dreaming about mixed-race exhibitions in which the authentic and the fake, the serious and the playful, the real work and the shadow, embraced and marched together toward destruction. And he thought about Castillo's smiling eyes, his laugh, his big white teeth, about his hands showing him the strange city, and despite everything he felt happy, lucky, and he even managed to appreciate the camels.

7

Once, after discussing the curious nature of art with Castillo, Amalfitano told him a story he had heard in Barcelona. The story was
about a recruit in Spain's Blue Division who had fought on the
Russian front in World War II, the northern front, to be precise,
in an area near Novgorod. The recruit was a little man from Se-
villa, thin and blue-eyed, who by some trick of fate (he was no
Dionisio Ridruejo or Tomás Salvador and when he had to give
the Roman salute he saluted, but he wasn't a real fascist, or even a
Falangist) had ended up in Russia. In Russia, someone said hey,
sorche, hey, recruit, come here, do this, do that, and the word *recruit* stuck with the Sevillan, but in the dark recesses of his mind
and in that vast place, with the passage of time and the daily ter-
rors, it turned into the word *chantre*, or cantor. So the Andalusian
thought of himself in terms of a cantor, with all the duties and
obligations of a cantor, though he didn't have any conscious idea
what the word meant, which was choir director at some cathedrals.
And yet somehow, by thinking of himself as a cantor he became
one: during the terrible Christmas of '41 he directed the choir
that sang carols while the Russians pounded the 250th Regiment. In general, he bore himself with courage, though as time
went by he began to lose his sense of humor. Soon enough he was
wounded. For two weeks he was at the hospital in Riga under the
care of the sturdy, smiling nurses of the Reich and some incredibly ugly Spanish volunteer nurses, probably sisters, sisters-in-law,
and distant cousins of José Antonio. When he was released, something happened that would have serious consequences for the

Sevillan: instead of being given a billet with the correct destination, he was given one that sent him to the quarters of an SS battalion stationed some two hundred miles from his regiment. There, surrounded by Germans, Austrians, Latvians, Lithuanians, Danes, Norwegians, and Swedes, all much taller and stronger than he, he tried to explain the mistake but the SS kept delaying their verdict and until the matter was settled they gave him a broom, a bucket of water, and a scouring brush and set him to sweep the barracks and scrub the huge, oblong wooden structure where all kinds of prisoners were interrogated and tortured. Without resigning himself entirely to the situation, but performing his new duties conscientiously, the Sevillan watched the time go by from his new barracks, eating much better than he had before and safe from any fresh threat. Then, in the dark recesses of his mind, the word *recruit* began to appear again. I'm a recruit, he said, a raw recruit, and I must accept my fate. Little by little, the word *cantor* vanished, though some evenings, under an endless sky that filled him with Sevillan longing, it still echoed, lost who knows where. And one fine day the inevitable happened. The barracks of the SS battalion were attacked and taken by a regiment of Russian cavalry, according to some, or a group of partisans, according to others. The result was that the Russians found the Sevillan hiding in the oblong building, wearing the uniform of an SS auxiliary and surrounded by the not exactly past-tense horrors perpetrated there. Caught red-handed, as they say. Soon he was tied to one of the chairs that the SS used for interrogations, one of those chairs with straps on the legs and the seat, and every time the Russians asked him a question, the Sevillan replied in Spanish that he didn't understand, he was just an underling there. He tried to say it in German, too, but he hardly spoke a word of the language, and the Russians didn't speak it at all. After beating him for a while, they went to get another Russian who spoke German and who was interrogating prisoners in one of the other cells in the oblong building. Before they came back, the Sevillan heard shots and realized that they were killing some of the SS, and he almost gave up hope; but when the shooting ended, he clung to life again with all his might. The German speaker asked him what he did there, what his duties and his rank were. The Sevillan tried to explain in German, but to no avail. Then the Russians opened his mouth and with a pair of pliers that the Germans used for other purposes they seized his tongue and yanked. The pain made tears spring to his eyes and he said, or rather shouted, the word *coño*, cunt. With the pliers in his mouth the exclamation was transformed, coming out as the word *kunst*. The Russian who spoke German stared at him in surprise. The Sevillan shouted *Kunst, Kunst,* and wept in pain. The word *Kunst*, in German, means art, and that was how the bilingual soldier heard it and he said that the son of a bitch was an artist or something. The soldiers who were torturing the Sevillan removed the pliers along with a little piece of tongue and waited, momentarily hypnotized by the discovery. *Art.* The thing that soothes wild beasts. And just like that, like soothed beasts, the Russians took a break and waited for some sign while the recruit bled from the mouth and swallowed his own blood mixed with big doses of saliva and choked and retched. The word *coño*, however, transformed into the word *art*, had saved his life. The Russians took him away with the few remaining prisoners, and later another Russian who spoke Spanish came to hear the Sevillan's story and he ended up in a prisoner-of-war camp in Siberia while his accidental comrades were shot. It was well into the 1950s before he left Siberia. In 1957 he settled in Barcelona. Sometimes he opened his mouth and told the story of his little war in great good humor. Other times, he opened his mouth and showed the piece of tongue he was missing. It was hardly noticeable. When people told him so, the Sevillan explained that over the years it had grown back. Amalfitano didn't know him personally, but when he heard the story the Sevillan was still living in the concierge quarters of some building in Barcelona.

8

At some point Castillo brought Amalfitano to see Juan Ponce Esquivel, art student and amateur numerologist, who lived in Aquiles Serdán, one of the poorest neighborhoods in Santa Teresa, west of Colonia El Milagro, near the old railroad tracks. The original idea was that Ponce would tell their fortunes, but when they got there they found him absorbed in a forecast of the nation's future. I think we're going to see the same heroes all over again, said Ponce as he served them tea. Carranza, for example, has already been born. He'll die in the year 2020. Villa too: right now he's a kid mixed up with narcos, hookers, and illegals. He'll be shot to death in 2023. Obregón was born in 1980 and will be killed in 2028. Elías Calles was born in 1977 and will die in 2045. Huerta was born in the year that the atomic bomb was dropped on Hiroshima and he'll die in 2016. Pascual Orozco was born in 1982 and will die in 2016. Madero was born in 1973, the year of Allende's fall, and he'll be killed in 2013. Everything will happen all over again. The Mexican people will watch spellbound as new rivers of blood are shed. I get a bad vibe from 2015. Zapata was born already, in 1983; he's still a kid playing out in the street, memorizing two or three Amado Nervo poems or four *poemínimos* by Efraín Huerta. He'll die in a hail of bullets in 2019. The numbers say that everything will repeat itself. Everybody will be born again, the heroes, the soldiers, the innocent victims. The most important ones and the ones who'll die first have already been born. But some are still missing. The numbers say that Aquiles Serdán will be killed again. Shit for luck, shit for fate.

Viva Mexico, said Castillo.

Amalfitano didn't say anything, but he had the sense that someone, a fourth person, was saying something from the next room or from a big chest that Juan Ponce Esquivel had at the back of the room: excuse me, is anyone there? excuse me, excuse me?

9

Between the medical school and the plain—a bare open space scarcely interrupted by yellow hills under a high and mobile sky, across which the highway ran east—was the famous Botanic Garden of the city of Santa Teresa, under the stewardship of the university.

"Come and take a good look around," said Professor Horacio Guerra.

There, tended by four bored gardeners, stood a small forest of no more than three specimens per species. The little dirt paths bordered by alluvial stones wound and unwound like snakes through the garden; in the middle rose a wrought-iron gazebo and every so often, in random spots, the visitor came upon limestone benches where he could sit. Little labels on stakes in the ground announced the name of each tree and plant.

Guerra moved like a fish in the water, his step quick. He didn't need to check the labels to tell Amalfitano what species a given tree was or what part of Mexico it came from. His sense of direction was unerring. He could walk the labyrinth of dark paths—which looked to Amalfitano like some crazed, baroque version of an English garden maze—with his eyes closed. That's right, he said when Amalfitano remarked upon this with some admiration, you can blindfold me with a handkerchief and I'll lead you straight out, never fear.

"There's no need for that, I believe you, I believe you," said Amalfitano, alarmed to see that Guerra was about to make good on his words and had pulled a bright green handkerchief emblazoned with the crest of the University of Charleston from his suit pocket.

"Blindfold me," bellowed Guerra, with a smile that said I can't help myself, don't worry, I haven't lost my mind.

Then he wiped the sweat from his brow with the handkerchief.

"Look at the plants and trees," he said with a sigh, "and you'll begin to understand this country."

"They're impressive," said Amalfitano as he wondered what kind of person Guerra was.

"Here you have all kinds of agave and mesquite, our native plant," said Guerra, making a sweeping gesture.

Amalfitano heard the song of a bird: it was a shrill sound, as if the bird were being strangled.

"Various species of cactus, like the giant pitahaya (*Cereus pitajaya*), the organ pipes, which are a different species of *cereus*, and the prickly pears, so delicious."

Guerra filled his lungs with air.

"That's a *Cereus pringlei* from Sonora, quite a night-bloomer if you look closely."

"Yes, indeed," said Amalfitano.

"There to the left is the yucca, beautiful without being showy, wouldn't you say? and here is the divine *Agave atrovirens*, the source of pulque, which is a brew you should try, though make sure you don't get hooked, sir, heh heh. Life is hard. Just think: if Mexico could export pulque, we'd give the whiskey, cognac, and wine makers of the goddamn world a run for their money. But pulque ferments too fast and can't be bottled, so there you have it."

"I'll try it," promised Amalfitano.

"That's the spirit," said Guerra, "one of these days we'll go to a pulquería. You'd better come with me. Don't even think of going alone, eh? No giving in to temptation."

A gardener went by with a sack of dirt and he waved to them. Professor Guerra began to walk backwards. Over there, he said, more species of agave, the *Agave lechuguilla*, source of istle, the *Agave fourcroydes*, source of henequen. The path zigzagged constantly. Bits of sky and small, fast clouds appeared through the branches. Every so often Guerra sought something in the shadows: dark eyes that he scrutinized with his brown eyes without bothering to offer Amalfitano any sort of explanation. Ah, he said, ah, and then he was silent and he gazed around the Botanic Garden with a scowl that flickered between displeasure and the certainty of having found something.

Amalfitano recognized an avocado tree and was reminded of the trees of his childhood. How far away I am, he thought with satisfaction. Also: how near. The sky, over their heads and over the tops of the trees, seemed to be put together like a puzzle. Occasionally, depending on how you looked at it, it sparkled.

"There's an avocado," said Guerra, "and a brazilwood and a mahogany tree and two red cedars, no, three, and a *Lignum vitae*, and there you have the quebracho and the sapodilla and the guava. Along this little path is the cocoyol palm (*Cocos butyracea*) and in that clearing there's amaranth, jicama, arborescent begonia, and spiny mimosa (*Mimosa comigera*, *plena* and *asperata*).

Something moved in the branches.

"Do you like botany, Professor Amalfitano?"

From where Amalfitano was standing, he could scarcely see Guerra. Guerra's face was completely obscured by shadows and a tree branch.

"I don't know, Professor Guerra, it's a subject on which I plead ignorance."

"Put it this way, do you appreciate the shapes, the external aspect of plants, their style, their spirit, their beauty?" Guerra's voice mingled with the song of the strangled bird.

"Yes, of course."

"Well, then, that's *something* at least," he heard Guerra say as the Mexican stepped off the visitors' path and into the garden.

After a brief hesitation, Amalfitano followed him. Guerra was standing by a tree, urinating. This time it was Amalfitano who paused, startled, in the shadows under the branches of an oak tree. That oak, said Guerra, still urinating, shouldn't be there. Amalfitano looked up: he thought he heard noises, little feet pattering in the branches. Follow me, ordered Guerra.

They came out onto a new path. Night was falling and the clouds that had been breaking up to the east were massing again and getting bigger. That's the sacred fir, said Guerra walking ahead of Amalfitano, and those are pines. That's a common juniper. When he came around a bend Amalfitano saw three gardeners taking off their overalls and putting away their tools. They're leaving, he thought as he followed Guerra into the garden, which was growing darker and darker. The man is going to smother me with hospitality, thought Amalfitano. Guerra's voice droned on, listing the gems of the Botanic Garden:

"The sacred fir. The common fir. Two shrubs, the guayule and the candelilla. Epazote (*Chenopodium ambrosioides*). The grass called *zacatón* (*Epicampes macroura*). Giant grass (*Guadua amplexifolia*). And here," said Guerra, stopping at last, "our national tree, or at least that's how I think of it, our dear, beloved *ahuehuete* (*Taxodium mucronatum*)."

Amalfitano gazed at Guerra and the tree and thought wearily but also with emotion that he was back in America. His eyes filled with tears that later he wouldn't be able to explain to himself. Ten feet from him, his back turned, Professor Guerra trembled.

10

In his next letter, Padilla talked about Raoul Delorme and the sect known as the barbaric writers, created by Delorme midway through the 1960s. While the future novelists of France were breaking the windows of their high schools or erecting barricades or making love for the first time, Delorme and the nucleus of the soon-to-be barbaric writers were shut up in tiny garrets, concierge quarters, hotel rooms, and the backs of stores and pharmacies, preparing for the coming of a new literature. For them, according to Padilla's sources, May of '68 was a period of creative retreat: they kept indoors (eating stockpiled provisions or fasting), talked only among themselves, and—singly and in groups of three—practiced new writing techniques that would astonish the world, attempting to predict the moment when they would burst onto the world scene, a moment that was first erroneously calculated be 1991 but upon further divining adjusted to 2005. The sources Padilla cited were magazines that Amalfitano had never heard of before: Issue 1 of the *Evreux Literary Gazette*, Issue 0 of the *Metz Literary Journal*, Issue 2 of the *Arras Journal of Night Watchmen*, Issue 4 of the *Literary and Trade Journal of the Grocers' Guild of the Poitou*. A "foundational elegy" by someone called Xavier Rouberg ("We salute a new literary school") had been printed twice, in the *Literary Gazette* and the *Literary Journal*. The *Journal of Night Watchmen* included a crime story by Delorme and a poem by Sabrina Martin ("The Inner and Outer Sea") preceded by an introductory note by Xavier Rouberg that was simply a shorter version of his "foundational elegy." Featured in the *Literary and Trade Journal* was the work of six poets

(Delorme, Sabrina Martin, Ilse von Kraunitz, M. Poul, Antoine Dubacq, and Antoine Madrid), each represented by a single poem— except Delorme and Dubacq with three and two, respectively— under the collective heading "The Barbaric Poets: When Pastime Becomes Profession." As if to confirm what amateurs the poets were, their day jobs were indicated in parentheses beneath their names, next to the passport-style photos. Thus the reader learned that Delorme owned a bar, that Von Kraunitz was a nurse's aide at a Strasbourg hospital, that Sabrina Martin worked cleaning houses in Paris, that M. Poul was a butcher, and that Antoine Madrid and Antoine Dubacq made a living tending newsstands. Regarding Xavier Rouberg, the John the Baptist of the barbarics, Padilla claimed to have done some sleuthing: he was eighty-six, his past was full of lacunae, he had spent time in Indochina, for a while he had been a publisher of pornographic literature, he had communist, fascist, and surrealist sympathies (he was a friend of Dalí, about whom he wrote a trifling little book, *Dalí For and Against the World*). Unlike the barbaric writers, Rouberg came from a well-to-do family and had been to university. Everything seemed to indicate that the barbarics were the last project to which Xavier Rouberg attached his hopes. Like almost all Padilla's letters, this one ended abruptly. No goodbye, no hasta pronto. Amalfitano read it in his faculty cubicle with mounting amusement and trepidation. For a moment he imagined that Padilla was serious, that such a literary group really existed, and—horrors—that Padilla shared or was prepared to embrace its interests. Then he changed his mind, and decided that neither the group nor much less the magazines existed (*Literary and Trade Journal of the Grocers' Guild of the Poitou!*), that it might all be part of *The God of Homosexuals*. Later, on his way out of class, he gave Padilla's letter some more thought and became sure of one thing: if Delorme and the barbaric writers were characters in Padilla's novel, it must be a very bad novel. That night, as he was walking with Castillo and a friend of Castillo's along what was both the leafiest and the darkest street in Santa Teresa, he tried to call Padilla from a public phone. Castillo and his friend got change for Amalfitano at a taco cart and chipped in all the coins they had in their pockets. But in Barcelona there was no answer. After a while he stopped trying and attempted to convince himself that everything was all right. He got home later than usual. Rosa was awake in her room, watching a movie. He called good night to her through the closed door and went straight to his desk and wrote a letter to Padilla. Dear Joan, he wrote, dear Joan, dear Joan, dear Joan, how I miss you, how happy and how miserable I am, what an incredible life this is, what a mysterious life, we hear so many voices over the course of a day or a life, and the memory of your voice is so lovely. Etc. He ended by saying that he'd really liked the story about Delorme, the barbaric writers, and all those journals, but that as he'd envisioned it (for no good reason, probably), there was nothing in *The God of Homosexuals* about any French literary school. You have to tell me more about your novel, he said, but also about your health, your financial situation, your moods. In closing, he begged him to keep writing. He didn't have long to wait, because the next day another letter arrived from Padilla.

11

As had become customary, Padilla didn't wait for Amalfitano to answer before he sent another letter. It was as if after putting a letter in the mail, a zeal for accuracy and precision compelled him to immediately send a series of explanations, particulars, and sources intended to shed further light on the missive already dispatched. This time Amalfitano found neatly folded photocopies of the covers of the *Literary Gazette*, the *Literary Journal*, the *Journal of Night Watchmen*, and the *Literary and Trade Journal of the Grocers' Guild*. Also: photocopies of the articles cited and of the poems and stories by the barbaric writers, which upon brief perusal struck him as horrible: a blend of Claudel and Maurice Chevalier, crime fiction and first-year creative writing workshop. More interesting were the photographs (appearing in the *Literary and Trade Journal*, which looked as if it were printed by professionals, unlike the *Journal* and the *Gazette*, surely put out by the barbarics themselves, not to mention the *Journal of Night Watchmen*, mimeographed in the manner of the 1960s and full of crossings-out, smudges, spelling mistakes). There was something magnetic about the faces of Delorme and his gang: first, they were all staring straight at the camera and therefore straight into Amalfitano's eyes, or the eyes of any reader; second, all of them, without exception, seemed confident and sure of themselves, especially the latter, light-years from self-doubt or a sense of their own absurdity, which—considering that they were French writers—might not have been so surprising, and yet it was, despite everything (let's not forget that they were amateurs, though maybe it was precisely because they were amateurs, thought

Amalfitano, that they were beyond any awkwardness, embarrass-
ment, or whatever, drifting in the limbo of the naïve); third, the
age difference wasn't just striking, it was unsettling: what bond—
let alone literary school—could unite Delorme, who was well into
his sixties and looked his age, and Antoine Madrid, who surely
had yet to turn twenty-two? Confident expressions aside, the faces
could be classified either as *open* (Sabrina Martin, who seemed to be
about thirty, and Antoine Madrid, though there was something
about him that spoke of the tight player, the man of reserve), or
closed (Antoine Dubacq, a bald man with big glasses who must have
been in his late forties, and Von Kraunitz, who might just as easily
have been forty as sixty), or *mysterious* (M. Poul, nearly skeletal,
spindle-faced, cropped hair, long bony nose, ears flat to the skull,
prominent and probably jumpy Adam's apple, maybe fifty, and
Delorme, by all lights the chief, the Breton of this writerly proletariat, as Padilla described him). Without Rouberg's notes, Amalfitano would have taken them for advanced students—or simply
eager students—of a writing workshop in some blue-collar subur-
ban neighborhood. But no: they had been writing for a long time,
they met regularly, they had a common writing process, common
techniques, a style (undetected by Amalfitano), goals. The information on Rouberg came from Issue 1 of the *Literary and Trade
Journal* of which he seemed to be the editor in chief, though his
name didn't appear on the masthead. It wasn't hard to imagine old
Rouberg—retired, though only spiritually, and under the stigma
of who can say what sins—in the Poitou. The journals, of course,
were from the collection of Raguenau, who each month received
copies from all over the world. And yet, added Padilla, when
asked about the four journals in question and the complete collection (Issues 1 through 5) of the grocers' organ, Raguenau admitted to Padilla and his nephew Adrià, who was digitizing his
library with the occasional assistance of Padilla, that he didn't subscribe to any of them. How, then, had they come into his power?
Raguenau couldn't remember, though he advanced a hypothesis:
perhaps he had bought them at an antiquarian bookshop or a book-
seller's stall on his last trip to Paris. Padilla affirmed that he had

subjected Raguenau to hours of interrogation before coming to the conclusion that he was innocent. What had attracted him to the magazines was probably their air of kitsch. And yet it was too much of a coincidence that all of them contained information on the barbaric writers and that Raguenau had bought them at random. Padilla ventured another hypothesis: that Raguenau had gotten them from one of the barbaric writers, working among the other stall keepers. But the interesting thing, the *truly* interesting thing about this business, was that Padilla (astounding memory, thought Amalfitano, more and more intrigued) had previously come across references to Delorme. His name was mentioned by Arcimboldi in an old interview dating back to 1970 published in a Barcelona magazine in 1991, and also by Albert Derville in an essay on Arcimboldi from a book on the contemporary French novel. In the interview Arcimboldi spoke of "a man named Delorme, an amazing autodidact who wrote stories near where I was living."

Later he explained that Delorme was the concierge of the building where he lived in the early 1960s. The context in which he referred to him was one of fear. Fears, frights, attacks, surprises, etc. Derville mentions him as part of a list of bizarre writers handed to him by Arcimboldi just before the publication of *The Librarian*. According to Derville, Arcimboldi confessed that he had grown afraid of Delorme, believing that he cast spells and performed Satanic rituals and black masses in his cramped concierge quarters, by means of which he hoped to improve his written French and the pacing of his stories. And that was all. Padilla promised that he would delve further and report back soon. Was Arcimboldi's disappearance related to the barbaric writers? He didn't know but he would keep up the investigation.

12

That night, after rereading the letter for the fourth or fifth time, Amalfitano had to get out of the house. He put on a light jacket and went for a walk. His steps led him to the center of the city, and after wandering around the plaza where the statue of General Sepúlveda stood with its back to the sculpture group commemorating the victory of the city of Santa Teresa over the French, he found himself in a neighborhood that, though only two blocks from the city center, displayed—even flaunted—every stigma, every sign of poverty, squalor, and danger. A no-man's-land.

The term amused Amalfitano, eliciting feelings of bitterness and tenderness; he too, over the course of his life, had known no-man's-lands. First the working-class neighborhoods and the industrial belts; then the terrain liberated by the guerrilla. Calling a neighborhood of prostitutes a no-man's-land, however, struck him as felicitous and he wondered whether those distant danger zones of his youth weren't simply giant prostitution belts camouflaged in Rhetoric and Dialectic. Our every effort, our long prison revolt: a field of invisible whores, the glare of pimps and policemen.

Suddenly he was sad and also starving. In blatant disregard of gastrointestinal prudence and caution, he stopped at a cart on the corner of Avenida Guerrero and General Mina and bought a ham sandwich and a hibiscus drink that in his fevered imagination was like the jasmine nectar or Chinese peach blossom juice of his childhood. The fucking insane wisdom, the discernment of these Mexicans, he thought as he savored one of the best sandwiches of his life: between two slices of bread, sour cream, black bean paste, avocado, lettuce, tomato, three or four slices of chipotle chile, and a thin slice of ham, which was what gave the sandwich its name and at the same time was the least important part. Like a philosophy lesson. Chinese philosophy, of course! he thought. Which reminded him of the following lines from the Tao Te Ching: "Mystery defines him. / And in that mystery / lies the gate of all that is most wonderful." What defines Padilla? he wondered, walking away from the stand toward a big floodlit sign in the middle of Calle Mina. The mystery, the wonder of being young and unafraid and then suddenly afraid. But was Padilla really afraid? or were the signs that Amalfitano interpreted as fear actually indications of something else? In big red letters, the sign announced Coral Vidal, singer of rancheras; a communicative striptease; and a magician, Alexander the Great. Under the marquee, amid a swarm of insomniacs, were vendors of cigarettes, drugs, dried fruit, magazines, and newspapers from Santa Teresa, Mexico City, California, and Texas. As he was paying for a Mexico City paper—any of them, the *Excélsior*, he told the vendor—a boy tugged at his sleeve.

Amalfitano turned. The boy was dark, thin, about eleven, wearing a yellow University of Wisconsin sweatshirt and running shorts. Come, sir, follow me, he insisted in the face of Amalfitano's initial resistance. A few people had stopped and were staring at them. Finally he decided to obey. The boy turned down a side street full of tenements that seemed on the verge of collapse. The sidewalks were lined with cars that had been sloppily parked or, to judge by their sorry state, abandoned by their owners. From inside some apartments came a cacophony of angry voices and televisions blaring at full volume. Amalfitano counted at least three signs for cheap hotels. Their names struck him as picturesque, but not as picturesque as the sign on Calle Mina. What did communicative striptease mean? Did the audience undress too or did the stripper announce the items that she was about to take off?

Suddenly the street fell silent, as if drawing in on itself. The boy stopped between two particularly dilapidated cars and met Amalfitano's eyes. At last, Amalfitano understood and shook his head. Then he forced a smile and said no, no. He took a bill out of his pocket and put it in the boy's hand. The boy took it and tucked it into one of his sneakers. When he bent down a ray of moonlight seemed to fall on his small, bony back. Amalfitano's eyes filled with tears. *Mystery defines him*, he remembered. Now what? asked the boy. Now you go home and go to bed, said Amalfitano, and immediately he realized how stupid his chiding was. As they walked back, this time side by side, he pulled out more money and gave it to him. Wow, thanks, said the boy. Get yourself something to eat this week, said Amalfitano with a sigh.

Before they left the street they heard sobbing. Amalfitano stopped. It's nothing, said the boy, it comes from over there, it's La Llorona. The boy pointed to the front door of a house in ruins. Amalfitano approached with hesitant steps. In the darkness behind the door, the sobs could be heard again. They came from above, from one of the upper floors. The boy stood next to him and pointed the way. Amalfitano took a few steps in the darkness but was afraid to follow the sound. When he turned he saw the boy standing there, balancing on a piece of rubble. It's some guy from around here who's dying of AIDS, he said glancing absentmindedly toward the upper floors. Amalfitano said nothing. On Calle Mina they parted ways.

13

A week later Amalfitano returned with Castillo to the street where he'd heard the sobs. He found the house without difficulty: by the light of day it didn't look as terrible as it had that night. In the entryway someone had tried to build a barricade. Inside, however, the building was in slightly better shape, though the windows had no glass and the hallways were a succession of rubble and holes.

Should we go in? asked Castillo, with a squeamish look on his face. Amalfitano didn't answer and began to poke around. In a room on the second floor he found a mattress and a couple of dirty blankets. This is it, come up, he called. In a corner was a kind of improvised brick hearth, and above it, dug into the wall, a rough niche holding a pot, a griddle, two soup spoons, and a plastic cup. At the foot of the mattress—on the floor but in relatively neat stacks—were movie magazines, everything from trash to art monographs, the latter in English but with lots of photographs. The spacing of the mattress, niche, and magazines conveyed a subtle and desperate sense of order holding at bay the chaos and ruin of the rest of the house.

Amalfitano knelt to get a better look at the objects. This is like reading a letter from a dying man, he said when he was done with his scrutiny. Castillo, leaning in the doorway, shrugged. What does the letter say? he asked grudgingly. I can't read it, it's in a foreign language, though sometimes I think I recognize one or two words. Castillo laughed. What words: love, loneliness, desperation, rage, sadness, isolation? No, said Amalfitano, nothing like that. The word I see gives me the shivers because I never would have thought I'd find it here. What is it, then, let's hear it. Hope, said Amalfitano, but so softly that at first Castillo didn't hear him. Hope, he repeated. Oh, that, said Castillo, and after a few seconds he added: I have no idea where you see it, there's more filth here than hope. Amalfitano stared at Castillo (Padilla would have understood) and smiled. Castillo returned the smile. When you're like this, when you smile like that, he said, you look like Christopher Walken. Amalfitano gave him a grateful look (he knew very well that he looked nothing like Christopher Walken, but it was nice to hear Castillo say he did) and went back to rummaging through the room. Suddenly it occurred to him to lift up the mattress. Underneath, as if put there to iron out the wrinkles, he found a Hawaiian shirt. The shirt was green with swaying palm trees and blue waves tipped with the purest white foam and red convertibles and white hotels and yellow cake and tourists dressed in Hawaiian shirts identical to the Great Hawaiian Shirt with swaying palm trees and blue waves and red convertibles as if infinitely repeated in a pair of facing mirrors. No, not infinitely, thought Amalfitano. In one of the reflections, one of the layers, the tourists would be unsmiling, their shirts black. The images on the shirt sprang from the floor and clung to the back of Amalfitano's troubled spirit. The rotting smell that suddenly swept over the room made him cover his nose and gag. The shirt was rotten. From the doorway Castillo made a face of disgust. Someone died here, said Amalfitano. Where's the body, Sherlock? asked Castillo. At the morgue, of course. Oh, you can be so negative, sighed Castillo.

When they emerged, the sun was beginning to drop behind roofs bristling with antennas. The sharp points seemed to puncture the bellies of the low-hanging clouds. On Calle Mina, the Teatro Carlota was advertising the same show. Amalfitano and Castillo stopped under the marquee and spent a long time reading the display while a big cloud passed overhead. Just then the box office opened. My treat, said Amalfitano. Are we going to see the communicative striptease? asked Castillo with a smile. Come on, keep me company, I want to see it, said Amalfitano. He was laughing too. If we don't like it we'll leave. All right, Castillo said.

14

The show at the Teatro Carlota began at eight and was repeated continuously until two in the morning, though closing time tended to vary depending on the size of the audience and the mood of the performers. If a spectator arrived at eight, one ticket bought him the right to see the show multiple times or to sleep until the usher kicked him out in the early morning hours. This was the habit of country folk on visits to Santa Teresa when they got tired of their cheap hotels, and, more frequently, the habit of the pimps who worked Calle Mina. Those who were there to see the show usually sat in the orchestra seats. Those who were there to sleep or do business sat in the gallery. The seats there were less tattered and the lighting was lower. In fact, most of the time the gallery was sunk in impenetrable darkness, at least as viewed from the orchestra seats, a darkness broken only when the lighting man flung the spotlights here and there for one of the danceable numbers. Then the beams of red, blue, and green light illuminated the bodies of sleeping men and interlaced couples, as well as the huddles of pimps and pickpockets discussing the events of the afternoon and evening. Below, in the orchestra seats, the atmosphere was radically different. People were there to have fun and they came in search of the best seats, the closest to the stage, bringing beer and assorted sandwiches and ears of corn that they ate—previously slathered with butter or sour cream and dusted with chile powder or cheese—skewered on little sticks. Though the show was in theory restricted to those over sixteen, it wasn't unusual to see couples with small children in tow. In the view of the box office, these children were so young that the show wouldn't compromise their moral integrity, and thus their parents, for lack of a babysitter, needn't be deprived of the miracle of Coral Vida singing rancheras. The only thing requested—of the children and their parents—was that they not run too much in the aisles while the acts were under way.

This season the stars were Coral Vidal and a magician, Alexander the Great. The communicative striptease, which was what had brought Amalfitano to the Teatro Carlota, was in fact something supposedly new, brainchild of a choreographer who happened to be a first cousin of the owner and manager of the Teatro Carlota. But it didn't work in practice, though its creator refused to admit it. In concept it was fairly simple. The stripper came out fully dressed and carrying an extra set of clothes, which, after much huffing and puffing, she crammed on over the clothes of a generally reluctant volunteer. Then she began to remove her garments while the spectator who had joined the act was invited to do the same. The end came when the performers were naked and the volunteer finally managed to rid himself, clumsily and sometimes violently, of his ridiculous robes and trappings.

And that was all, and if the great Alexander hadn't suddenly appeared—almost without transition and with no introduction whatsoever—Amalfitano and Castillo would have left disappointed. But Alexander was a different thing entirely, and there was something about the way he came out onstage, the way he moved, and the way he gazed at the spectators in the orchestra seats and the gallery (he had the stare of a sad old man but also the stare of an X-ray-eyed old man who understood and accepted everyone equally: the connoisseurs of sleight of hand, the working couples with children, the pimps plotting their desperate long-range schemes) that kept Amalfitano glued to his seat.

Good day, said Alexander. Good day and good evening, kind members of the audience. From his left hand sprouted a paper moon, some ten inches in diameter, white with gray striations. It began to rise on its own until it was six feet above his head. His accent, Amalfitano realized almost at once, wasn't Mexican or

Latin American or Spanish. Then the balloon burst in the air, re-
leasing a cascade of white flowers, carnations. The audience, which
seemed to know Alexander from previous shows and to respect
him, applauded generously. Amalfitano wanted to clap, too, but
then the flowers froze in the air and—after a brief pause in which
they remained still and trembling—re-formed in a five-foot ring
around the old man's waist. The burst of applause was even greater.
And now, esteemed and honorable members of the audience,
we're going to play some cards. So the magician was a foreigner,
not a native speaker of Spanish, but where is he from, wondered
Amalfitano, and how did he end up in this lost city, good as he is?
Maybe he's from Texas, he thought.

The card trick was nothing spectacular, but it managed to interest Amalfitano in a strange way that even he didn't understand.
Part of it was anticipation, but part of it also was fear. At first Alexander spoke from onstage—with a deck of cards in his right
hand one moment and in his left the next—on the qualities of the
cardsharp and the countless dangers that lie in wait for him. A deck
of cards, as anyone can see, he said, can lead a decent working
man to ruin, humiliation, or death. It can lead a woman to perdi-
tion, if you know what I mean, he said, winking an eye but never
losing his air of solemnity. He was like a TV evangelist, thought
Amalfitano, but the strangest thing was that the people listened to
him intently. Even up above, in the gallery, a few crime-hardened
and sleepy faces popped up, the better to follow the magician's
rounds. Alexander moved with increasing decisiveness around the
stage and then up and down the aisles of the orchestra level, talking always about cards, cards as nemesis, the great lonely dream of
the deck, poker-faced players and players who talk a big game, in
an accent that definitely wasn't Texan, while the eyes of the audience followed him in silence, uncomprehendingly, or so Amalfitano supposed (he didn't understand, either, and maybe there was
nothing to understand). Until suddenly the old man stopped in the
middle of an aisle and said all right, here we go, I won't take up
any more of your time.

What happened next left Amalfitano openmouthed in astonishment. Alexander approached a member of the audience and asked him to check his pocket. The man did as he was told, and when he removed his hand there was a card in it. Immediately the magician urged another person in the same row, much farther down, to do the same. Another card. And then a new card appeared in a different row, and one after another the cards—to the cheers of the audience—began to form a royal flush of hearts. When only two cards were left, the magician looked at Amalfitano and asked him to check his wallet. He's more than ten feet away, thought Amalfitano, if there's a trick it must be a good one. In his wallet, between a picture of Rosa at ten and a wrinkled, yellowing slip of paper, he found the card. What card is it, sir? asked the magician, fixing his eyes on Amalfitano and speaking in that peculiar accent that Amalfitano couldn't quite place. The queen of hearts, said Amalfitano. The magician smiled at him the way his father might have. Perfect, sir, thank you, he said, and before he turned he winked an eye. The eye was neither big nor small, brown with green splotches. Then he strode confidently—triumphantly, one might say—to a row where two children were asleep in their parents' arms. Do me the favor of removing your son's shoe, he said. The father, a thin, sinewy man with a friendly smile, removed the child's shoe. In it was the card. Tears rolled down Amalfitano's face and Castillo's fingers delicately brushed his cheek. The king of hearts, said the father. The magician nodded. And now the little girl's shoe, he said. The father removed his daughter's shoe and held another card up in the air, so that everyone could see it. And what card is that, sir, if you'll be so kind? The joker, said the father.

15

Amalfitano often had nightmares. His dream (one in which Edith Lieberman and Padilla had Chilean elevenses with tea, buns, avocado, tomato jam made by his mother, rolls and homemade butter nearly the color of a sheet of Ingres-Fabriano paper) opened up and let in the nightmare. There, in those lonely latitudes, Che Guevara strolled up and down a dark corridor and in the background huge diamond-crusted glaciers shifted and creaked and seemed to sigh as at the birth of history. Why did I translate the Elizabethans and not Isaac Babel or Boris Pilniak? Amalfitano asked himself, disconsolate, unable to escape the nightmare but still holding scraps of the dream (beyond the glaciers the whole distant horizon *was* Edith Lieberman and Padilla having their delicious elevenses) in his empty, frozen, nearly transparent hands. Why didn't I slip like Mighty Mouse through the bars of the Lenin Prizes and the Stalin Prizes and the Korean Women Collecting Signatures for Peace and discover what was there to be discovered, what only the blind couldn't see? Why didn't I stand up at one of those oh-so-serious meetings of leftist intellectuals and say the Russians the Chinese the Cubans are making a fucking mess of things? Why didn't I stand up for the Marxists? Stand up for the pariahs? March in step with history while history was being born? Offer silent assistance at its birth along the way? Somehow, Amalfitano said to himself from the depths of his nightmare, his tone scholarly and his voice unrecognizably hoarse, masochist that I am, I blame myself for crimes that were never committed: by 1967 I had already been expelled from the Chilean Communist Party, my comrades had run me down and turned me out, I was no longer well liked. Why do I blame myself, then? I didn't kill Isaac Babel. I didn't destroy Reinaldo Arenas's life. I wasn't part of the Cultural Revolution and I didn't sing the praises of the Gang of Four like other Latin American intellectuals. I was the simple-minded son of Rosa Luxemburg and now I'm an old faggot, in each case the object of mockery and ridicule. So what do I have to blame myself for? My Gramsci, my situationism, my Kropotkin (lauded by Oscar Wilde as one of the greatest men on earth)? For my mental hang-ups, my lack of civic responsibility? For having seen the Korean Women Gathering Signatures for Peace and not stoning them? (I should have buggered them, thought Amalfitano from the whirl of glaciers, I should have fucked those fake Koreans until their true identity was revealed: Ukrainian Women Gathering Wheat for Peace, Cuban Women Gathering Cockles in an Unremitting Latin American Twilight.) What am I guilty of, then? Of having loved and continuing to love—no, not of loving: of longing. Of longing for the conversation of my friends who took to the hills because they never grew up and they believed in a dream and because they were Latin American men, true macho men, and they died? (And what do their mothers, their widows, have to say about it?) Did they die like rats? Did they die like soldiers in the Wars of Independence? Did they die tortured, shot in the back of the head, dumped in the sea, buried in secret cemeteries? Was their dream the dream of Neruda, of the Party bureaucrats, of the opportunists? Mystery, mystery, Amalfitano said to himself from the depths of the nightmare. And he said to himself: someday Neruda and Octavio Paz will shake hands. Sooner or later Paz will make room on Olympus for Neruda. But we will always be on the outside. Far from Octavio Paz and Neruda. Over there, Amalfitano said to himself like a madman, look over there, dig over there, over there lie traces of truth. In the Great Wilderness. And he said to himself: it's with the pariahs, with those who have nothing at all to lose, that you'll find some justification, if not vindication; and if not justification, then the song, barely a murmur (maybe not voices, maybe only the wind in the branches), but a murmur that cannot be silenced.

16

The root of all my ills, thought Amalfitano sometimes, is my
admiration for Jews, homosexuals, and revolutionaries (true revolutionaries, the romantics and the dangerous madmen, not the
apparatchiks of the Communist Party of Chile or its despicable
thugs, those hideous gray beings). The root of all my ills, he thought,
is my admiration for a certain kind of junkie (not the poet junkie
or the artist junkie but the straight-up junkie, the kind you rarely
come across, the kind who almost literally gnaws at himself, the
kind like a black hole or a black eye, with no hands or legs, a black
eye that never opens or closes, the Lost Witness of the Tribe, the
kind who seems to cling to drugs in the same way that drugs cling
to him). The root of all my ills is my admiration for delinquents,
whores, the mentally disturbed, said Amalfitano to himself with
bitterness. When I was an adolescent I wanted to be a Jew, a Bol-
shevik, black, homosexual, a junkie, half-crazy, and—the crown-
ing touch—a one-armed amputee, but all I became was a literature
professor. At least, thought Amalfitano, I've read thousands of
books. At least I've become acquainted with the Poets and read
the Novels. (The Poets, in Amalfitano's view, were those beings
who flashed like lightning bolts, and the Novels were the stories
that sprang from *Don Quixote*). At least I've read. At least I can still
read, he said to himself, at once dubious and hopeful.

17

Amalfitano hardly ever thought about old age. Sometimes he saw himself with a cane, strolling along a bright tree-lined boulevard and cackling to himself. Other times he saw himself trapped, without Rosa, the curtains drawn and the door propped shut with two chairs. We Chileans, he said to himself, don't know how to grow old and as a general rule we make the most terrific fools of ourselves; ridiculous as we are, though, there's something courageous about our old age, as if when we grow wrinkled and fall ill we recover the courage of our rugged childhoods in the land of earthquakes and tsunamis. (Though what Amalfitano *knew* about Chileans was only supposition, considering how long it had been since he'd associated with any of them.)

18

In one of his classes, Amalfitano said: the birth of modern Latin American poetry is marked by two poems. The first is "The Soliloquy of the Individual," by Nicanor Parra, published in *Poemas y antipoemas*, Editorial Nascimento, Chile, 1954. The second is "Trip to New York," by Ernesto Cardenal, published in a Mexico City magazine in the mid-'70s (1974, I think, but don't quote me on that), which I have in Ernesto Cardenal's *Antología*, Editorial Laia, Barcelona, 1978. Of course, Cardenal had already written "Zero Hour," "Psalms," "Homage to the American Indians," and "Coplas on the Death of Merton," but it's "Trip to New York" that to me marks the turning point, the definitive fork in the road. "Trip" and "Soliloquy" are the two faces of modern poetry, the devil and the angel, respectively (and let us not forget the curious fact—though it may be rather more than that—that in "Trip" Ernesto Cardenal mentions Nicanor Parra). This is perhaps the most lucid and terrible moment, after which the sky grows dark and the storm is unleashed.

Those who disagree can sit here and wait for Don Horacio Tregua, those who agree can follow me.

19

Notes from a Class in Contemporary Literature: The Role of the Poet

Happiest: García Lorca.

Most tormented: Celan. Or Trakl, according to others, though there are some who claim that the honors go to the Latin American poets killed in the insurrections of the '60s and '70s. And there are those who say: Hart Crane.

Most handsome: Crevel and Félix de Azúa.

Fattest: Neruda and Lezama Lima (though I remembered—and with grateful resolve chose not to mention—the whale-like bulk of a Panamanian poet by the name of Roberto Fernández, keen reader and best of friends).

Banker of the soul: T. S. Eliot.

Whitest, the alabaster banker: Wallace Stevens.

Rich kid in hell: Cernuda and Gilberto Owen.

Strangest wrinkles: Auden.

Worst temper: Salvador Díaz Mirón. Or Gabriela Mistral, according to others.

Biggest cock: Frank O'Hara.

Secretary to the alabaster banker: Francis Ponge.

Best houseguest: Amado Nervo.

Worst houseguest: various and conflicting opinions: Allen Ginsberg, Octavio Paz, e. e. cummings, Adrian Henri, Seamus Heaney, Gregory Corso, Michel Bulteau, the Hermanitos Campos, Alejandra Pizarnik, Leopoldo María Panero and his older brother, Jaime Sabines, Roberto Fernández Retamar, Mario Benedetti.

Best deathbed companion: Ernesto Cardenal.

Best movie companion: Elizabeth Bishop, Berrigan, Ted Hughes, José Emilio Pacheco.

Best in the kitchen: Coronel Urtecho (but Amalfitano reminded them of Pablo de Rokha and read him and there was no argument).

Most fun: Borges and Nicanor Parra. Others: Richard Brautigan, Gary Snyder.

Most clearsighted: Martín Adán.

Least desirable as a literature professor: Charles Olson.

Most desirable as a literature professor, though only in short bursts: Ezra Pound.

Most desirable as a literature professor for all eternity: Borges.

Greatest sufferer: Vallejo, Pavese.

Best deathbed companion after Ernesto Cardenal: William Carlos Williams.

Most full of life: Violeta Parra, Alfonsina Storni (though Amalfitano pointed out that both had killed themselves), Dario Bellezza.

Most rational way of life: Emily Dickinson and Cavafy (though Amalfitano pointed out that—according to conventional wisdom— both were failures).

Most elegant: Tablada.

Best Hollywood gangster: Antonin Artaud.

Best New York gangster: Kenneth Patchen.

Best Medellín gangster: Álvaro Mutis.

Best Hong Kong gangster: Robert Lowell (applause), Pere Gimferrer.

Best Miami gangster: Vicente Huidobro.

Best Mexican gangster: Renato Leduc.

Laziest: Daniel Biga. Or, according to some, Oquendo de Amat.

Best masked man: Salvador Novo.

Biggest nervous wreck: Roque Dalton. Also: Diane Di Prima, Pasolini, Enrique Lihn.

Best drinking buddy: several names were mentioned, among them Cintio Vitier, Oliverio Girondo, Nicolas Born, Jacques Prévert, and Mark Strand, who was said to be an expert in martial arts.

Worst drinking buddy: Mayakovsky and Orlando Guillén.

Most fearless dancer with American death: Macedonio Fernández.

Most homegrown, most Mexican: Ramón López Velarde and Efraín Huerta. Other opinions: Maples Arce, Enrique González Martínez, Alfonso Reyes, Carlos Pellicer, fair-haired Villaurrutia, Octavio Paz, of course, and the female author of *Rincones románticos* (1992), whose name no one could remember.

Questionnaire

Question: Why would you want Amado Nervo as a houseguest?

Answer: Because he was a good man, industrious and resourceful, the kind of person who helps set the table and wash the dishes. I'm sure he wouldn't even hesitate to sweep the floor, though I wouldn't let him. He would watch TV shows with me and discuss them afterward, he would listen to my troubles, he would never let things get blown out of proportion: he would always have the right thing to say, the appropriate levelheaded response to any problem. If there were some disaster—an earthquake, a civil war, a nuclear accident—he wouldn't flee like a rat or collapse in hysterics, he would help me pack the bags, he would keep an eye on the children so that they didn't run off in fear or for fun or get lost, he would always be calm, his head firmly on his shoulders, but most of all he would always be true to his word, to the decisive gesture expected of him.

Readings

Poems by Amado Nervo (*Los jardines interiores*; *En voz baja*; *Elevación*; *Perlas negras*; *Serenidad*; *La amada inmóvil*). Laurence Sterne, *A Sentimental Journey* (Colección Austral, Espasa Calpe). Matsuo Basho, *Narrow Road to the Interior* (Hiperión).

20

Of all the habits, remembered Amalfitano, Padilla defended smoking. The one thing ever to unite Catalonians and Castilians, Asturians and Andalusians, Basques and Valencians, was the art, the appalling circumstance of communal smoking. According to Padilla, the most beautiful phrase in the Spanish language was the request for a light. Beautiful, soothing phrase, the kind of thing you could say to Prometheus, full of courage and humble complicity. When an inhabitant of the peninsula said "¿tienes fuego?" a wave of lava or saliva gushed anew in the miracle of communication and loneliness. Because for Padilla the shared act of smoking was basically a staging of loneliness: the tough guys, the talkers, the quick to forget and the long to remember, lost themselves for an instant, the length of time it took the cigarette to burn, an instant in which time was frozen and yet all times in Spanish history were concentrated, all the cruelty and the broken dreams, and in that "night of the soul" the smokers recognized each other, unsurprised, and embraced. The spirals of smoke were the embrace. It was in the kingdom of Celtas and Bisontes, of Ducados and Rexes, that his fellow countrymen truly lived. The rest: confusion, shouting, the occasional potato tortilla. And as for the repeated warnings of the Department of Health: rubbish. Though every day, it was said, people smoked less and more smokers switched to ultra-light cigarettes. He himself no longer smoked Ducados, as he had in his adolescence, but unfiltered Camels.

There was nothing strange, he said, about a condemned man being offered a cigarette before he was executed. As a popular rite of faith, the cigarette was more important than the prayers and blessing of the priest. And yet those who were executed in the electric chair or the gas chamber weren't offered anything: it was a Latin custom, a Hispanic custom. And he could go on and on like this, dredging up an endless string of anecdotes. The one that Amalfitano remembered most vividly and that struck him as most significant—and premonitory, in a way, since it was about Mexico and a Mexican and he had ended up in Mexico—was the story of a colonel of the Revolution who had the misfortune to end his days in front of a firing squad. His last wish was for a cigarette. The captain of the firing squad, who must have been a good man, granted his request. The colonel found a cigar and proceeded to smoke it, not saying a thing to anyone, gazing at the barren landscape. When he had finished, the ash still clung to the cigar. His hand hadn't trembled; the execution could proceed. That man must be one of the patron saints of smokers, said Padilla. So what was the story about, the colonel's nerves of steel or the calming effects of smoke, the communion with smoke? Padilla, remembered Amalfitano, couldn't say and didn't care.

21

Sometimes Amalfitano meditated on his relatively recent homosexuality and sought literary affirmation and examples as consolation. All that came to mind was Thomas Mann and the kind of languid, innocent fairyhood with which he was afflicted in his old age. But I'm not that old, he thought, and Thomas Mann was probably gaga by then, which isn't the case for me. Nor did he find consolation in those few Spanish novelists who, once past the age of thirty, suddenly discovered that they were queer: most of them were such jingoistic butches that when he thought about them he became actively depressed. Sometimes he remembered Rimbaud and drew convoluted analogies: in "Le cœur volé," which some critics read as the detailed account of the rape of Rimbaud by a group of soldiers while the poet was on his way to Paris to join the dream of the Commune, Amalfitano, turning over in his head a text that could be read many different ways, saw the end of his heterosexuality, stifled by the absence of something he couldn't put his finger on, a woman, a heroine, a superwoman. And sometimes, instead of just thinking about Rimbaud's poem, he recited it aloud, which was a habit that Amalfitano, like Rosa, had inherited from Edith Lieberman:

> *Mon triste cœur bave à la poupe,*
> *Mon cœur couvert de caporal:*
> *Ils y lancent des jets de soupe,*
> *Mon triste cœur bave à la poupe:*
> *Sous les quolibets de la troupe*

Qui pousse un rire général,
Mon triste cœur bave à la poupe,
Mon cœur couvert de caporal!

Ithyphalliques et pioupiesques
Leurs quolibets l'ont dépravé!
Au gouvernail on voit des fresques
Ithyphalliques et pioupiesques.
Ô flots abracadabrantesques,
Prenez mon cœur, qu'il soit lavé!
Ithyphalliques et pioupiesques
Leurs quolibets l'ont dépravé!

Quand ils auront tari leurs chiques,
Comment agir, ô cœur volé?
Ce seront des hoquets bachiques
Quand ils auront tari leurs chiques:
J'aurai des sursauts stomachiques,
Moi, si mon cœur est ravalé:
Quand ils auront tari leurs chiques
Comment agir, ô cœur volé?

It all made sense, thought Amalfitano, the adolescent poet de-
graded by brutish soldiers just as he was heading—on foot!—
toward an encounter with the Chimera, and how strong Rimbaud
was, thought Amalfitano (he had given up any idea of consolation and was filled with excitement and astonishment), to write
this poem almost immediately afterward, with a steady hand, the
rhymes original, the images oscillating between the comic and
the monstrous . . .

22

What Amalfitano would never know was that the corporal of "mon cœur couvert de caporal," the son of a bitch who raped Rimbaud, had been a soldier in Bazaine's army in the Mexican adventure of Maximilian and Napoleon III.

In March 1865, unable to learn anything about the fate of Colonel Libbrecht's column, Colonel Eydoux, commander of the plaza of El Tajo, which served as supply depot for all of the troops operating in that part of the Mexican northeast, sent a detail of thirty horsemen toward Santa Teresa. The detail was under the command of Captain Laurent and Lieutenants Rouffanche and González, the latter a Mexican monarchist.

The detail arrived in Villaviciosa on the second day of March. It never made it to Santa Teresa. All the men—except for Lieutenant Rouffanche and three soldiers who were killed when the French were ambushed as they ate at the only inn in town—were taken prisoner, among them the future corporal, then a twenty-two-year-old recruit. The prisoners, gagged and with their hands bound with hemp rope, were brought before the man acting as military boss of Villaviciosa and a group of town notables. The boss was a mestizo addressed alternately as Inocencio and El Loco. The notables were country folk, most of them barefoot, who stared at the Frenchmen and then withdrew to a corner to confer. Half an hour later, after a bit of hard bargaining between two evidently opposed groups, the Frenchmen were taken to a covered corral where, after being stripped of their clothes and shoes, they were raped and tortured by a group of captors for the rest of the day.

At midnight Captain Laurent's throat was cut. Lieutenant González, two sergeants, and seven soldiers were taken to the main street and forced to play chasing games by torchlight. They all died, either run through or with their throats slit by pursuers on the backs of the soldiers' own horses.

At dawn, the future corporal and two other soldiers managed to break their bonds and flee cross-country. Only the corporal survived. Two weeks later he reached El Tajo. He was decorated and remained in Mexico until 1867, when he returned to France with Bazaine, who retreated with his army, abandoning the emperor to his fate.

23

Sometimes Amalfitano saw himself as the Prince of Antioch or the homesick Knight of Tyre, the King of Tarsus or the Lord of Ephesus, adventurers of the Middle Ages once upon a time read or misread—with equal enthusiasm—by a luckless God-fearing lord in the midst of pandemonium and exile and untold confusion, accompanied by a beautiful daughter and an aura intensified by the ravages of time. As in the story by Alfonso Reyes (God rest his soul, thought Amalfitano, who truly loved him), "The Fortunes of Apollonius of Tyre," from *Real and Imaginary Portraits*. A dethroned king, he thought, wandering the Mediterranean islands painted by that so-called Michelangelo of comic strips, the creator of *Prince Valiant*, those divine and infernal islands where Valiant met Aleta, but also where the Knight of Epirus bewailed his unjust persecution, and the giddy vagabond of Mytilene told the story of his misfortunes, these characters who, as Reyes noted, sprang from the Greek or Roman depths of our memory, and this was precisely what was false about it all, what was disturbing and revelatory: the vagabond prince was a stand-in for Ulysses and the Baron of Thebes was a stand-in for Theseus, though both were God-fearing knights who prayed morning and night. In this masquerade, Amalfitano discovered unknown regions of himself. In the Greek king who fled with his daughter from monastery to monastery, from desert island to desert island, as if he were traveling backward from the year 1300 to 500 and from 500 to 20 B.C. and onward, ever deeper in time, he saw the futility of his efforts, the basic naïveté of his struggle, his spurious role as scrivener monk. Now all I need is to go blind, with Rosa as my cherished guide leading me from classroom to classroom, he thought gloomily.

24

When Amalfitano learned that his daughter had disappeared with
a black man, he thought randomly of a line from Lugones that he
had come across years—many years—ago. Lugones's words were
these: "It is well known that youth is the most intellectual stage of
an ape's life, as it is of the Negro's." What a brute, that Lugones!
And then he remembered the story, Lugones's plot: a man, a neu-
rotic, the narrator, labors for years to teach a chimpanzee to talk.
All his efforts are in vain. One day the narrator senses that the ape
can talk, that he has learned to talk but hides it cleverly. Whether
he hides it out of fear or atavism, Amalfitano can't remember.
Probably fear. So unrelenting is his master that the ape falls ill. His
sufferings are almost human. The man cares for him as devotedly
as he might care for his own child. Both feel the pain of their imminent separation. At the final moment, the ape whispers: Water,
master, my master, my master. This was where the Lugones story
ended (for a second, Amalfitano imagined Lugones shooting himself in the mouth in the darkest and coolest corner of his library,
swallowing poison in an attic strung with cobwebs, hanging himself from the highest beam of the bathroom, but could Lugones's
bathroom possibly have had beams? where had he read that or
seen it? Amalfitano didn't know), giving way—one ape leading to
another—to the story by Kafka, the Chinese Jew. What different
viewpoints, thought Amalfitano. Good old Kafka puts himself
without hesitation into the skin of the ape. Lugones sets out to
make the ape speak; Kafka gives him voice. Lugones's story, which
Amalfitano thought extraordinary, was a horror story. Kafka's

story, Kafka's incomprehensible text, also took wing through realms of horror, but it was a religious text, full of black humor, human and melodramatic, unyielding and inconsequential, like everything that is truly unyielding, in other words like everything that is soft. Amalfitano began to weep. His little house, his parched yard, the television set and the video player, the magnificent northern Mexico sunset, struck him as enigmas that carried their own solutions with them, inscribed in chalk on the forehead. It's all so simple and so terrible, he thought. Then he got up from his faded yellow sofa and closed the curtains.

25

So what did Amalfitano's students learn? They learned to recite aloud. They memorized the two or three poems they loved most in order to remember them and recite them at the proper times: funerals, weddings, moments of solitude. They learned that a book was a labyrinth and a desert. That there was nothing more important than ceaseless reading and traveling, perhaps one and the same thing. That when books were read, writers were released from the souls of stones, which is where they went to live after they died, and they moved into the souls of readers as if into a soft prison cell, a cell that later swelled or burst. That all writing systems are frauds. That true poetry resides between the abyss and misfortune and that the grand highway of selfless acts, of the elegance of eyes and the fate of Marcabrú, passes near its abode. That the main lesson of literature was courage, a rare courage like a stone well in the middle of a lake district, like a whirlwind and a mirror. That reading wasn't more comfortable than writing. That by reading one learned to question and remember. That memory was love.

26

Amalfitano's sense of humor tended to go hand and hand with his sense of history and both were as fine as wire: a skein in which horror mingled with a gaze of wonderment, the kind of gaze that knows everything is a game, which might explain why after these rare outpourings Amalfitano's inner self, forged in the rigors of dialectical materialism, was left stricken, somehow ashamed of itself. But this was his sense of humor and there was nothing he could do about it.

Once, when he was teaching in Italy, he somehow found himself in the middle of an informal dinner attended by new-fledged Italian patriots, the same people who years later would form the New Right.

The dinner was held at a celebrated Bologna hotel and between the dessert course and the after-dinner drinks there were speeches. At a certain point, clearly as the result of a misunderstanding, it was Amalfitano's turn to speak. To sum it up in a few words, his short speech—delivered in a passable Italian flavored by what more than a few listeners thought was a real or faked central European accent—was about the mystery of so-called great civilizations. In two lines he dispatched the Romans and the princes of the Renaissance (with a tossed-off mention of the tragic fate of the Orsini, probably referring to Mujica Láinez's Orsini), arriving rapidly at the subject of his toast: World War II and the role of Italy. A role that was distorted by history and obscured by Theory: the ersatz exploits, forged in mystery, of the brave Alpini and the gallant Bersaglieri. Immediately, and without putting too fine a point on it, he asked what the French of the Charlemagne Brigade had achieved, what the Croats or the Austrians or the Scandinavians of the Viking Division, the Americans of the 82nd Airborne Division or the 1st Armored Division, the Germans of the 7th Panzer Division or the Russians of the 3rd Guards Tank Army had *really* accomplished. Shreds of glory, he mused aloud, deeds that pale alongside the countless hardships of old Badoglio's Greek Campaign or the Libyan campaign of bold Graziani, the anvil on which Italian identity was forged and the well from which the strategists of the future will drink when the mystery is uncovered at last. The desert raids, he said, and he raised a finger skyward, the bitter fight to hold the forts, the fixed-bayonet charges of the brave men of the Littorio (a tank division) still rouse the ardor of this patient and peaceful nation. Next he spoke in commemoration of the generals, old and young, the most skilled and steadfast that the palm groves and huts of Africa (he said the word *huts*, or *bohíos*, in Spanish, to the bafflement of his audience, except for a professor of Latin American literature who understood the term but was left even more in the dark) had ever seen. Then he argued that the glory of the Germans obscured the memory of Gariboldi, for one, who, to make matters worse, was dogged by a nagging error: in nearly every country's history books, except those of Italy, France, and Germany—meticulous in this regard—he was referred to as Garibaldi, but history, Amalfitano confided, was rewritten daily, and, like a humble and virtuous seamstress, constantly stitched up any holes. He warned that Africa should strive to be worthy of Sicily's stubborn resistance or the hard fighting on the steppes that had earned Italy the admiration of the Slavs. At this point, those who weren't whispering to each other or staring off into space with cigars in their mouths realized that he was pulling their leg and the uproar and shouting began. But Amalfitano refused to be cowed and he continued to hold forth on the matchless courage of those who fought to the last on the peninsula, the San Marco Regiment, the Monte Rosa, the Italia, the Grenadiers of Sardinia, the Cremona, the Centauro, the Pasubio, the Piacenza, the Mantua, the Sassari, the Rovigo, the Lupi de Toscana, the Nembo. The betrayed Army, fighting at a disadvantage, and yet still, at some point, like a miracle or an annunciation, laughing in the faces of the arrogant pups from Chicago and the City.

The end was quick. Blood, Amalfitano asked himself, to what end? What justifies it, what redeems it? And he answered himself: the awakening of the Italian colossus. The colossus that everyone since Napoleon has tried to anesthetize. The Italian nation, which has yet to speak its final word, its brilliant final word. Its radiant final word, in Europe and the world. (Punches, shoves, shouts of foreigner go home, the applause of two vaguely anarchist professors.)

27

Sitting on the porch of his Mexican house at dusk, Amalfitano thought that it was strange that he hadn't read Arcimboldi in Paris, when the books were closer at hand. As if the writer's name had been suddenly erased from his mind when the logical thing would have been to go in search of all his novels and read them. He had translated *The Endless Rose* at a moment when no one outside of France, except for a few Argentinean readers and publishers, had shown any interest in Arcimboldi. And he had liked it so much, it had been so thrilling. Those days, he remembered, the months before the birth of his daughter, were perhaps the happiest of his life. Edith Lieberman was so beautiful that sometimes she seemed to glow with a dense light: lying in bed, on her side, naked and smooth, her knees drawn up a little, the serenity of her closed lips disarming, as if she passed straight through every nightmare. Forever unscathed. He would stand there watching her for a long time. Exile, with her, was an endless adventure. His head swarmed with projects. Buenos Aires was a city on the edge of the abyss, but everyone seemed happy, everyone was content to live and talk and plan. *The Endless Rose* and Arcimboldi were—he realized then, though later he forgot—a gift. A final gift before he and his wife and daughter entered the tunnel. What could have made him fail to seek out those words? What could have lulled him like that? Life, of course, which puts the essential books under our noses only when they are strictly essential, or on some cosmic whim. Now that it was too late, he was going to read the rest of Arcimboldi's novels.

III. *ROSA AMALFITANO*

1

For the first week they stayed at the Sinaloa Motel, on the edge of Santa Teresa, off the northbound highway. Each morning Amalfitano called a taxi to take him to the university. An hour or two later Rosa followed suit and spent the rest of the morning wandering the streets of Santa Teresa. When it was time for lunch they met at the university cafeteria or at a cheap restaurant discovered by Rosa called The King and the Queen, which served only Mexican food.

They spent the afternoons looking for a place to live. They hired a taxi and visited apartments and houses downtown or in other neighborhoods, but none of them satisfied Rosa, either because they were awful or too expensive or the neighborhoods weren't to her liking. As they went back and forth by taxi, Amalfitano read and prepared for his new job and Rosa stared out the window. In their own way, father and daughter were living in another world, a happy, enchanted, provisional world.

Until at last they found a three-bedroom house with a big, sunny living room, a bathroom with a bathtub, and an open kitchen in Colonia Mancera, a middle-class neighborhood in the south of the city.

The house had a small front yard that had once been well tended but was now full of weeds and burrows, as if inhabited by moles. There was a front porch with a tiled floor and wooden railings that promised rocking chairs and peaceful afternoons. There was a smaller backyard, too, about two hundred square feet, and a junk room filled to the rafters with useless objects. It's the perfect house, Dad, said Rosa, and there they stayed.

Amalfitano took the biggest bedroom. In addition to the bed, the bedside table, and the wardrobe, Rosa found a writing table, moved in a chair from the dining room, and hired a carpenter to build two big bookcases for the books that had been sent by boat from Barcelona and would still be a while in coming. In the room that she chose for herself Rosa put a smaller bookcase and after filling it hastily with the old belongings of her nomadic childhood she painted the walls, taking all the time in the world: two the shade of tobacco and two a very pale green.

When she wanted to give Amalfitano's walls the same treatment, he refused. He liked white walls and it distressed him to see his daughter dressed in a T-shirt and old pants all day doing work that he should ostensibly be doing himself.

They had never lived in a house with an open kitchen, and the first few nights, dazzled by the novelty, they cooked together, talking and moving constantly from the kitchen to the living room, wiping the counter, watching each other cook, and then eating, one of them perched on a stool while the other served, as if they were at a bar, taking turns being waiter and customer.

2

When life returned to normal, Rosa had time to fall in love with the streets of Santa Teresa, cool streets, streets that in a secret way spoke of a field of transparencies and Indian colors, and she never took a taxi again.

Accustomed as she was to the colorful, perfectly demarcated streets of Barcelona or the perfectly fussy streets of the Casco Antiguo—the streets of a civilization, or in other words real streets—the streets of Santa Teresa seemed somehow newborn, streets with a secret logic and aesthetic, streets with their hair down, where she could walk and feel alive walking, on her own and not *a part of.*

And also, she discovered in surprise, they were streets shooting outward, urban and at the same time open to the country, a country of great mysterious spaces that crept in during the first hours of dusk down streets shaded by stunted or powerful trees, in a system she couldn't explain to herself, as if Santa Teresa were interleaved with even the humblest of the nearby hills, viewed from an impossible perspective. As if the streets were the barrels of multiple telescopes trained on the desert, on the planted fields, on the scrubland and pastures, or on the bare hills that on moonlit nights seemed to be made of bread crumbs.

3

Rosa Amalfitano and Jordi Carrera began to write to each other a
week after the Amalfitanos arrived in Mexico. The first to write
was Jordi. After a strange week in which he could hardly sleep
a wink, he decided to do something that in all his seventeen years
he had never done before. After much hesitation, he bought what
seemed to him the most appropriate postcard, a panel from a
comic strip by Tamburini and Liberatore (one of the two of them,
he thought he remembered, but everything was so hazy, had died
of an overdose), and after writing a couple of sentences that seemed
stupid to him, I hope you're well, we miss you (why the fucking
plural?), he put it in the mail and tried in vain to forget her.

Rosa's typed response was three pages long. It said, more or
less, that she was advancing by forced marches into adulthood and
that the feeling this gave her was wonderful and exciting at first,
though later, as always, one got used to it. She also talked about
Santa Teresa and how pretty some of the colonial buildings were:
a church, a porticoed market, and the house of the bullfighter
Celestino Arraya, now a museum, that she had visited soon after
arriving, as if magnetically drawn. Not only was this Celestino
handsome, he was a local luminary killed in the flower of his youth
(here Rosa went on to make various half-comprehensible and not
quite successful jokes about the flower of desire and the flower of
sin), and there was an impressive statue of him in the Santa Teresa
cemetery that she planned to visit later on. She sounds like a sculptor or an architect, thought Jordi despondently after reading the
letter for the tenth time.

It took him twenty days to answer. This time he sent her an extra-large postcard of a Nazario comic. Faced with the impossibility of telling her what he really needed to say, he launched into a garbled but scrupulously truthful account of his latest basketball game. It's like an absurdist poem, thought Rosa when she read the postcard. The game was described as a series of electrokinetic and electromagnetic instants, bodies moving in a rapid blur, the ball sometimes too big or too small, too bright or too dark, and the shouts of the crowd—which Jordi compared enthusiastically (for once) to the cries at a Roman circus—like a metronome behind his ribs. I hope I'm not overdoing it, he thought. As for himself, he insinuated that he had played badly, inattentively, listlessly, and by this he meant that he was feeling down and he missed her.

This time Rosa's response was only two pages long. She wrote about her English classes, the exploratory walks she took around the neighborhoods of Santa Teresa, the solitude she deemed a precious gift and that she spent reading and getting to know herself, Mexican food (here in passing she mentioned Catalan white beans with sausage in a way that Jordi found derogatory and unfair), some of which she had already tried to make for her father, chicken with red mole sauce, for example, which was relatively easy, she said, all you had to do was boil a chicken or a couple of chicken breasts and make the mole (an earthen red powder that was bought premixed, from a bin or in jars) in a frying pan with a little oil and then a little water, ideally the broth left over from boiling the chicken, and in a separate pot, of course, you boiled a little rice, which was served with the chicken and plenty of mole sauce. It was a hot, strong-flavored dish (maybe a little too intense for her father—not her—to eat *at night*), but she had loved it from the start and now she couldn't do without it. It's possible, she said, that I've become a chicken mole fanatic, which traditionally should really be turkey mole, or *mole de guajolote*, as they call it here.

In a nutshell, she wrote at the end of the letter, she was happy and life couldn't be better. In this sense, she confessed, I'm a little like Candide, and my teacher, Pangloss, is this fascinating part of

Mexico. My father, too—though actually no, my father is nothing at all like Pangloss.

Jordi read the letter in the subway. He had no idea who Candide and Pangloss were, but it seemed to him that his friend was at the gates of paradise while he was stuck permanently in purgatory.

4

At night, after they had watched a movie together on TV, he asked his father who Candide and Pangloss were.

"Two characters from Voltaire," said Antoni Carrera.

"Yes, but who are they," asked Jordi, to whom *Voltaire* sounded vaguely like some cabaret or rock band.

"The characters in a philosophical novel," said Antoni Carrera, "but you should know that by now. Is this for some school project?"

"No. It's personal," said Jordi, feeling that his house was suffocating him. The furniture, the TV, the yard with the lights on, everything was suddenly oppressive.

"Candide is the quintessential innocent, and Pangloss is, too, more or less."

"Pangloss is his teacher?"

"Yes. He's a philosopher. The classic optimist. Like Candide, except that Candide is an optimist by nature and Pangloss argues rationally for optimism. He's a moron, basically."

"And is the novel set in Mexico?"

"No, I don't think so. Pangloss teaches theology, metaphysics, cosmology, and nigology, and don't ask me what that is because I don't know."

"Nigology. Huh," said Jordi.

That night he looked up *nigology* in the *Dictionary of the Royal Spanish Academy*. He couldn't find it. Those fucking professors, he thought angrily. The closest thing was *nigola*: (*Naut.*) Lengths of thin line strung between the shrouds of a sailing ship to make a ladder; ratline. To sail amid the rigging and the topsails! There was also *nigromancia*, or necromancy, the meaning of which Jordi knew thanks to role-playing games, and also *nigérrimo*, ma. (Del lat. *Nigerrimus*.) adj. sup. de *negro. Negrísimo*, very black.

Nor was it in the *Ideological Dictionary of the Spanish Language* by Julio Casares or in the *Pompeu I Fabra*.

Much later, while his parents were sleeping, he got out of bed naked, and with measured steps, as if he were on a phantom basketball court, he headed for his father's library and searched until he found a Spanish translation of *Candide*.

He read: "It is clear," said Pangloss, "that things cannot be otherwise than they are, for since everything is made to serve an end, everything necessarily serves the best end. Observe: noses were made to support spectacles, hence we have spectacles. Legs, as anyone can plainly see, were made to be breeched, and so we have breeches. Stones were made to be shaped and to build castles with; thus My Lord has a fine castle, for the greatest Baron in the province should have the finest house; and since pigs were made to be eaten, we eat pork all year round. Consequently, those who say everything is well are uttering mere stupidities; they should say everything is for the best."

For a while he knelt there on the rug in the library, rocking slightly back and forth with his five senses elsewhere. Have I fallen in love with you? he thought. Am I falling in love? And if I am, what can I do about it? I don't know how to write letters. I'm doomed. Then, stricken, he whispered: fuck, Rosa, fuck, it's so unfair, so unfair . . .

5

Around this time Jordi Carrera dreamed that he was playing for Barcelona at the Palau Sant Jordi alongside the stars of Catalan basketball. The opposing team was Real Madrid, but it wasn't the usual Real Madrid. The only player he recognized was Sabonis, but this Sabonis was much older and slower and his hands shook when he caught the ball. The rest of the Madrid players were strangers, and not only were they strangers, even their bodies were indistinct. Their legs were legs, but at the same time there was something about them that was uncharacteristic of a pair of limbs, as if they were constantly coming in and out of focus. The same was true of their arms and faces, which never seemed to settle into a fixed expression or firm outline, though this strange phenomenon didn't seem to bother the other Barcelona players. The Palau was full to bursting and the shouting of the spectators was so loud that for a moment Jordi thought he would pass out. Without much surprise he realized that he was playing point guard, not center. The Madrid players soon began to commit fouls and almost all of them were against him. He didn't know the score. So focused was he on the game that he never lifted his head to glance at the electronic scoreboard. In fact, he had no idea where the scoreboard was, but he suspected that his team was winning, and this made him incredibly happy. When he noticed that he was bleeding from the nose, the brow, and the upper lip, the scene underwent a radical shift.

Now he wasn't on the Palau court but in a dark locker room with raw cement walls and long, damp benches and a constant noise of water, as if a river were running above the changing room. He wasn't alone. A shadowy figure was watching him from a corner. Jordi felt his bloody face and cursed the shadow in Catalan. He said *son of a bitch* in Catalan, then he said *bastard*, though the word was the same in Spanish. The shadowy figure quivered like a broken fan. Jordi told himself that he should take a shower, but the ominous presence in the corner made it an ordeal to undress. Feeling cramps in both legs, he sat down and covered his face with his hands. Incomprehensibly, he saw his father, his mother, and Amalfitano drinking whiskey in the yard one fall afternoon, happy, with no problems on the horizon. The afternoon, the sky, and the rooftops of the neighboring buildings were heartrendingly beautiful. Where is Rosa? he asked longingly, careful not to disturb the equilibrium of the scene, which he sensed was precarious. But his parents didn't seem to hear him. He soon realized that they were in another dimension. Then the dream lifted, drifting away in a balloon or on a cloud, and below, in the streets of Barcelona, Catalan nationalists fought house to house against the Spanish army. Jordi knew the name of the army without being told: it was the King's Army, the National Army, and it fought with commendable tenacity against him and his compatriots. But this time it wasn't just the Castilian soldiers whose faces and limbs were blurred. The Catalan militiamen also grew hazy amid the rubble and even the cries of the wounded or the leaders ordering their men to advance or retreat took on the same quality, blurring in the air, fleeing the Catalan and Spanish languages for a kingdom where words were like electrocardiograms, where voices were like Tartar dreams.

In the last image of his dream Jordi saw himself huddled in a corner, hugging his knees as hard as he could and thinking of Rosa, Rosa, Rosa, so far away.

6

Celestino Arraya, whose house Rosa Amalfitano visited on the third day after her arrival in Santa Teresa, was born in Villaviciosa in 1900 and died at a cantina called Los Primos Hermanos in 1933, a few months after Hitler came to power. Little information is available about his childhood: legend has him as a brave young soldier with Pancho Villa when the reality is that he spent the Villa years hiding away on a ranch where his friend Federico Montero—an eminent politician and landowner who managed to navigate the turbulent years of the Revolution with courage and unerring instinct—bred fighting bulls. It was the Piedras Negras bullring that saw his first triumph, in 1920. After that, successful appearances followed in other border cities and towns: Ojinaga, Nogales, Matamoros, Nueva Rosita. These were some of the rings from which he emerged raised aloft, clutching tail and ears in his hands like a shipwrecked sailor frozen stiff with cold. He was extremely adept in the art of killing. His final anointing occurred at the Monterrey bullring and, in 1928, in Mexico City, where he was acclaimed in the ring and feted on public thoroughfares. He was tall and slender—cadaverous, according to some—and always sharply dressed, whether in bullfighting attire or civilian clothes. The elegance with which he moved in the ring, though, became a mannered stride in everyday life, the strut of a preening gangster. Along with Federico Montero and other friends, he belonged to a bachelor's club, The Cowboys of Death, which was officially gastronomic and harmless, though of terrible memory. Death, the real thing, came to him at the hands of a sixteen-year-old boy who for motives that remain unknown came looking for him at the cantina Los Primos Hermanos and with his old rifle put two bullets in his head before being shot in turn by the bullfighter's comrades. The statue that stands guard over his mausoleum was erected at the initiative of Montero and other friends, who bore the full cost themselves. The sculptor was Pablo Mesones Sarabia (1891–1942), of the Potosí school of Maestro Garabito.

7

The sculpture group titled *Victory of the Town of Santa Teresa over the French*, situated in the Plaza del Norte one hundred feet from the statue of General Sepúlveda, hero of the Revolution, and created by Pedro Xavier Terrades (1899–1949) and Jacinto Prado Salamanca (1901–1975), both sculptors of the Potosí school of Maestro Garabito, presented a kind of inaccuracy or basic historical error. The work in itself was nothing to sneeze at: composed of five wrought-iron figures, it possessed the characteristic élan of the Potosí school, a quality of the sublime or of transfiguration, its frenzied figures contorted, one might say, by the breath of History. The life-size group included a Santa Teresa militiaman pointing southeast toward something that the spectator might guess were the retreating enemy troops. The face of the militiaman, lips clenched and features twisted in a scowl of pain or rage, is partly obscured by a too-big bandage around his head. In his left hand he carries a musket. Behind, at his feet on the ground, lies a dead Frenchman. The Frenchman's arms are flung wide and his hands are gnarled as if by fire. His face, nevertheless, has the thing that artists of old called the repose of death. To one side, a soldier of the irregular forces dies in the arms of a girl no older than fifteen. The gaze of the soldier—eyes of a madman, eyes of a visionary—turns to the sky, while the eyes of the girl, part Madonna and part Goya Gypsy, remain gravely and piously shut. The left hand of the dying man clutches the girl's right hand. And yet these are not two hands together; not at all. They are two hands that reach for each other in the dark, two hands that repel each other, two hands that recognize each other and flee in despair. Finally, there is an old man, half turned to the side, his head lowered as if he'd rather not see what's happened, his lips puckered in an expression that might be of pain, but might also signify the act of whistling (and that's what the children who play in the square call him: the Whistler). The old man is frozen, his right hand over his heart but not quite resting on his breast, the left hanging to one side, as if rendered useless. The sculpture group was commissioned in 1940 and finished in 1945. According to some critics, it is Terrades and Prado Salamanca's masterpiece, and the last piece on which they worked together. Be that as it may, the work's flaw is in its title. There was never a battle against the French for the simple reason that the men against whom the town of Santa Teresa fought under José Mariño and Amador Pérez Pesqueira weren't French but Belgian. The campaign and subsequent battle, according to the well-documented book *Benito Juárez vs. Maximilian: The Fall of Europe*, by the Mexican historian Julio V. Anaya, proceeded like this: in August 1865 a battalion of four companies of one hundred men each, made up of volunteers from the Belgian Legion and led by Colonel Maurice Libbrecht, tried to take Santa Teresa, which at that time was undefended by Republican troops. The column came first to Villaviciosa, where it encountered no resistence. After revictualing, it set out from Villaviciosa, leaving behind a garrison of twenty men. An alert was raised and in Santa Teresa preparations for the defense of the city were rapidly made under the leadership of Señor Pérez Pesqueira, mayor of the city, and Don José Mariño, wealthy local landowner and liberal with a reputation as an adventurer and eccentric, who recruited any man who could bear arms to swell the ranks of the militia. On August 28, at noon, Libbrecht's Belgians reached the edge of town and after sending out a scouting party—which returned with the news that the city's defenses were nonexistent and that three horsemen had been lost in a skirmish—it was decided to give the troops an hour of rest and then launch a direct assault. The battle was one of the worst disasters to befall the invading army in the northeast of Mexico. The militiamen of Santa Teresa were waiting for the Belgians in the

center of the city. A few snipers on the edge of town who immediately retreated and even some flower-bedecked balconies draped
with banners made from sheets, reading "Long Live the French"
or "Long Live the Emperor," were enough to cause the unsuspect-
ing Libbrecht to fall into the trap. The battle was fierce and both
sides fought without seeking or granting mercy. The Belgians
made their stand in the Central Market and in the streets leading
to the Plaza Mayor. The militiamen made theirs at the Town Hall
and the Cathedral, as well as in the streets between the Belgian
position and the fields outside of town, the ochre fields that—
except for Libbrecht's few supply troops and some shepherds who
moved across foreground and background, through pastures and
over hills, like figures in a Flemish painting—bore empty and as if
fear-struck witness to the din and the cannon blasts that resounded
in the city, an abstract entity within which there unfolded a battle
of wills and agonies. By night, with the Belgians demoralized after various attempts to break the siege, José Mariño's militiamen
launched the final attack. Libbrecht fell in the onslaught and shortly
afterward the Belgians surrendered. Among them was Captain
Robert Lecomte, of Bruges, who would later marry the daughter
of Don Marcial Hernández, in whose house he spent the rest of
the war, more as a guest than as a captive. In his memoirs, published in four installments in the *Bruges Monitor,* Lecomte hints
that the defeat owed to Libbrecht's overconfidence and ignorance
of Mexican idiosyncracies. His story is almost entirely consistent
with that of J. V. Anaya, who draws upon it: the battle was cruel
but remained within the bounds of chivalry and gallantry; most
of the prisoners were taken to Piedras Negras, where the division
of General Arístides Mancera was stationed; their treatment at
the hands of the Mexicans was exquisite. Nor does it differ from
the memories of another extraordinary witness, José Mariño, patron of the arts and man of the world, who in 1867, as the guest
of General Mariano Escobedo, was present at the Battle of Queré-
taro and the subsequent shooting of the Emperor; in his *Memoirs,*
New York, 1905, Mariño gives an extensive account of the preparations for the battle and a succinct description of the battle

itself. Mariño's book is full of so many things—battles, affairs of honor, political intrigues, romances, ties to great poets (he was a personal friend of Martí and Salvador Díaz Mirón, some of whose letters are woven into the eight-hundred-plus-page volume)— that the episode of the Battle of Santa Teresa necessarily plays a minor role, included only, one might say, in order to once again demonstrate the personal initiative and battle-tested courage of its author. Nevertheless, Mariño devotes nearly four full pages to the pursuit that was launched soon after the conclusion of the battle, a pursuit in which he played no part. Who was pursued? The troops who didn't enter Santa Teresa and the few soldiers who managed to escape the siege. A certain Emilio Hernández (son of Don Marcial Hernández?) led the chase. First to be pursued were the men who escaped Santa Teresa; they put up little resistance. Next were the supply troops with their gear; they surrendered without a fight. Warned of the presence of "French" troops in Villaviciosa, Emilio Hernández returned prisoners and captured equipment to Santa Teresa, and with only thirty horsemen headed off to liberate Villaviciosa. He arrived in the early hours of the following day and found no "Frenchmen" or Belgians. Some villagers had left town and scattered through the neighboring fields. Others were asleep in their low, dark houses and wouldn't rise until past noon. When they were asked, the peasants said that the soldiers had gone. Where, which way? inquired Emilio Hernández. Home, said the peasants. Though dauntless, Emilio Hernández's men—half of them ranchers and gentlemen, the other half cowboys and hired men—grew uneasy, feeling watched, as if they were on the threshhold of something better ignored (this is made plain by José Mariño, an excellent narrator of boudoir scenes and opera finales and an amateur translator of Poe). But Emilio Hernández refused to give up and sent half of his men after the soldiers while with the others he set out to comb the town. The first group found a horse hacked to death by machete. The second found only sleeping people, children with a dazed look, and women washing clothes. As the afternoon wore on, a smell of decay crept into everything.

At dusk, Emilio Hernández decided to return to Santa Teresa. The Belgians of Villaviciosa had vanished into thin air. Concludes Mariño: "the town seemed one thousand, two thousand years old, the houses like tumors blooming from the earth; it was a lost town and yet it was haloed with the invincible nimbus of mystery . . ."

8

In Mariño's telling of the story, in what might be called a curious aside, there is something that stands out.

Mariño describes Emilio Hernández's conversation—his labored conversation—with the town elders. Hernández, impatient and ill at ease, doesn't dismount. His horse prances in front of the doorway where the old men of Villaviciosa are taking shelter from the sun. The old men speak with indifference and reserve. They speak of time, the seasons, the harvest. Their faces seem carved from stone. Hernández, meanwhile, shouts and erupts with ambiguous threats that even he doesn't understand. Mariño hints that Hernández is afraid. His face is covered in sweat and dust from his long ride. His pistol remains holstered, but several times he moves as if to draw it. The old men spook him. He's tired and he's young and he's impetuous. Still, a glimmer of caution tells him that it's best not to back himself into a corner. His men reluctantly search the town for something vague, hampered by the villagers' passivity and absolute lack of cooperation. Hernández admonishes the villagers for their attitude. We've come to help you, he says in reproach, and this is how you repay us. The old men are like turtles. Then Mariño puts the following question in Hernández's mouth, simple and unambiguous: what do you want? And the old men respond: we want to *improve ourselves*. That's all. The elders of Villaviciosa have spoken and their words will go down in history: they want to improve themselves.

9

Her mother instilled in her a love of the French poets. Rosa remembered her sitting in a green armchair, a book in her hands (long, thin, very white hands, almost translucent), reading aloud. She remembered a window and the silhouettes of three modern buildings, her parents knew the names of the architects, behind which lay the beach and the sea. The three architects hated each other fiercely and her parents joked about it. When the sun went down her mother would sit in the chair and read French poems. Rosa couldn't remember the names of the books but she could remember the names of the poets. Sometimes her mother cried. The tears rolled down her cheeks and then she left the book open on her lap, smiled at Rosa (who was next to her, sitting on a pouf or lying on the rug, drawing), dried her tears with a handkerchief or with the sleeve of her blouse, and for a few seconds, not crying anymore, sat quietly gazing at the silhouettes of the three buildings and the rooftops of the lowest buildings. Then she picked up the book and began to read again as if nothing had happened. The poets were Gilberte Dallas, Roger Milliot, Ilarie Voronca, Gérald Neveu . . .

When they left Rio they abandoned the books, except for Neveu's *Fournaise obscure*. In Paris (or Italy?) she came across the poets again: they were all in the anthology *Poètes maudits d'aujourd'hui: 1946–1970*, by Pierre Seghers. A bunch of suicide victims and failures, alcoholics and head cases. Her mother's poets.

True, her mother also read her the poems of Éluard, Bernard Nöel (whom she liked very much and who often made her laugh),

Saint-John Perse, even Patrice de la Tour du Pin, but it was the *maudits d'aujourd'hui* whom she remembered or thought she remembered with the most disquiet, names that were mostly unknown in Brazil or Argentina or Mexico and that made Edith Lieberman cry, reminding her perhaps of another life, of her break with that other life, when she was a student at the Collège Français and she dated boys from the Jewish neighborhood, when she listened to Brahms and didn't miss a single Audrey Hepburn movie. Perhaps her mother, from that Rio apartment, saw herself as another French *maudit* poet, and liked—as only the *maudits* like—to contemplate scenes of a happiness spurned but in the end sadly lost. And Rosa thought: lost at the moment when the man who would be my father appeared with his proletarian vanguard and his wildly ambitious plans. And if he hadn't appeared, would she and her mother be in Chile now, living in Santiago without a care in the world, happy as can be, sharing their little news each night, always together? But the louse of the proletarian vanguard had suddenly appeared, as if teleported in by fate. That was a fact, and now nothing could be changed. Probably they wouldn't be in Chile, anyway, and besides, the little she knew about the country horrified her. Even the Chilean accent, which so many years later her father still hadn't lost, was jarring, unpleasant, affected. She, of course, didn't talk like that. Once she wondered what accent she had, and she came to the conclusion that she had none: she spoke a United Nations Spanish. Of the *maudits*, Gilberte Dallas was her favorite. Her mother liked Gérald Neveu or Ilarie Voronca, but Gilberte Dallas, La Gilberte, was the best. She imagined her tall and bony, her face like Greta Garbo's but with two scars on each cheek like the women of some African tribes. Sometimes she didn't smile and seemed sad, but as a rule she was cheerful, her gestures abrupt and her tongue swift. Very elegant: what suited her best were gauzy dresses, silk tunics, feathered hats, and sporting attire. When, years later, she read Anne Clancier's introduction to the poems of Gilberte H. Dallas, 1918–1960, she realized that she had been fated to love her. Anne Clancier: *"Une fillette de dix ans, allongée dans une barque, flotte sur la mer, à midi. Elle essaie de fixer le soleil, attendant de ses rayons la mort et la délivrance. Elle se croit mal aimée, abandonnée de tous, elle éspère retrouver au-delà de la mort la mère à jamais perdue. Lorsqu'on découvre l'enfant, après des heures de recherches, elle est inconsciente, frappée par l'insolation; on réussit à la sauver et il lui faut poursuivre sa route. Ce souvenir d'enfance nous livre la clef de la vie et de l'œuvre de Gilberte Dallas. Perpétuellement à la recherche d'une mère disparue précocement, désespérant de trouver un contact sécurisant avec un père malade . . ."*

Poets whom children should be forbidden to read. At the age of fifteen she found her own *maudits*. First Sophie Podolski and *Le pays où tout est permis*, then Tristán Cabral, then Michel Bulteau and Matthieu Messagier. At sixteen she grew tired of them and returned to Gilberte Dallas. The sound of the words reminded her of her mother. She read her aloud, alone, when her father had gone out or was in class, and the strains of Gilberte brought back the green armchair in Rio and her mother gazing out the window at the three rival silhouettes and the treetops of the Paseo Marítimo and the sea a few yards beyond. And then her mother told her stories about what she was like as a baby and what she would be like when she was grown-up and beautiful. And she no longer needed to read Gilberte because the kisses they exchanged and her eyes closing were more powerful and soothing than words.

10

Rosa Amalfitano discovered that her father slept with men a month after she arrived in Santa Teresa, and the discovery worked on her like a stimulant. What a bitter pill! she said to herself, unconsciously quoting the heroine of a Bioy Casares story that she was reading. Then she began to tremble like a leaf and hours later, at last, she was able to cry. Earlier, Amalfitano had bought a TV set and video player in which she had shown no interest. From that day on, as if under an evil spell, Rosa stopped reading books and began to go through two or even three movies a day. Amalfitano, who tried to speak freely with his daughter on any subject, had done his best to warn her. In a long and chaotic conversation before they left for Mexico, using an allegory that even he didn't understand and logic that later struck him as weak at best and idiotic at worst, he tried to explain to her that sexual tastes aren't fixed, or at least not necessarily. At the root of his argument was an attempt to console himself—and also, hypothetically, his daughter—by reasoning that if the Eastern Bloc could crumble, so, too, could his thus far unequivocal heterosexuality, as if the two phenomena were linked or as if one were the logical consequence of the other. A kind of domino effect on the plane of affective inclinations, though an odd one, since Amalfitano was always critical of actual socialism. But Rosa literally didn't hear him, being distractable by nature and used to her father's long soliloquies, so that she had to discover for herself the activities to which he devoted himself while she was in school when one afternoon she returned earlier than usual. And though Amalfitano realized in horror that his daughter had seen him, and Rosa knew that he knew, they never discussed it. That same night, Amalfitano tried to explain who Castillo was, what had happened in Barcelona, what was happening inside of him, but Rosa was categorical. About this there could be no discussion. Saddened, Amalfitano obeyed and as the days went by, in his own way, he forgot or liked to think he had forgotten the incident. Rosa couldn't.

For a few nights she had nightmares in which she was sure she was dying. She stopped eating and for a few days she ran a temperature. She felt betrayed: by her father and by the world in general. Everything disgusted her. Then she began to dream again about her mother, who had died of cancer eight years before. She dreamed that Edith Lieberman was walking the dusty streets of Santa Teresa and that she, behind the wheel of a black Ford Falcon, was rolling along behind. Her mother looked the way she did in her photographs: dressed up, though in outmoded finery. In her dream Rosa was afraid that her mother would head to the house and discover her father in bed with that boy, but Edith Lieberman's steps led her straight to the cemetery.

The Santa Teresa cemetery was big and as white as homemade yogurt. Rosa thought that her mother would get lost in its labyrinthine streets, flanked by twenty-foot walls of neglected niches, but her mother seemed to know the place better than she did and without difficulty she came to a little square where water taps and the statue of the bullfighter Celestino Arraya rose.

They've turned me out of my grave, the dead woman announced flatly, and Rosa understood. Finding himself in financial and bureaucratic straits, Amalfitano hadn't been able to cremate his wife's body and had been forced to rent a niche in the working-class cemetery of Rio de Janeiro. Before he was able to pay the first installment, Amalfitano had left Brazil with his daughter, harried by the police, creditors, and colleagues accusing him of various heterodoxies. And Edith Lieberman's remains? Father and daughter were well aware of what had befallen them and had resigned themselves to it. Debtors were fated to end up in a potter's field. Sometimes Rosa dreamed of an imaginary Brazil divided into two self-contained parts: the jungle and the potter's field. The jungle teemed with copulating people and animals. The potter's field was like an empty opera house. Both led down a long tunnel to the ossuary. She usually woke up crying despite the fact that it didn't bother her at all to know that her mother's remains lay scattered together with the bones of countless anonymous Brazilians. Like her father, Rosa was an atheist, and as an atheist she believed that she shouldn't care where a person was buried.

"I've been turned from my grave like an old homeless woman," whispered her mother in the dream.

"It doesn't matter, Mama, you'll be freer that way."

"I have nothing of my own anymore. I live in squalor and chaos. I asked to be cremated, my ashes scattered over the Danube, but your father is a fickle soul who doesn't know how to keep his word."

"I knew nothing about any of that."

"Never mind, dearest. At last my soul is about to achieve concentric happiness."

"Concentric happiness?"

"Yes, classic generosity."

"What does that mean, Mama?"

"It means I'm turning into a guardian spirit. And it means that I'll spend a while longer beside this horrible statue and I'll protect you in the dangerous days to come."

Then her mother, turning away from her, began to speak in French. She seemed to be addressing the statue.

When she awoke, the fragments of a poem still echoed in her head. Verses that her mother had recited to her when she was little:

> *Des soleils noirs*
> *Les soleils noirs*
> *Millions de soleils noirs*
> *Girent dans le ciel*
> *Dévorent le ciel*
> *S'abattent sur les pavés*

Eventrent les églises du Bon Dieu
Eventrent les hôpitaux
Eventrent les gares . . .

A poem by Gilberte Dallas! she remembered with melancholy.

Soon afterward she stopped reading books and became a video addict.

11

Rosa's education, it's worth mentioning here, was practical and rational, at times progressive and occasionally sublime. Her constant changes of school and country played a part. Despite everything, she was a diligent student. At ten she could speak Spanish, Portuguese, and French with some fluency. At twelve, English—though more labored—could be added to the list. About her teachers the least that can be said is that they were touching figures. Seventy percent of them had at some point in their lives written or tried to write critical essays, monographs, or reviews of Makarenko, A. S. Neill, Freinet, Gramsci, Fromm, Ferrer i Guardia, Paulo Freire, Peter Taylor, Pestalozzi, Piaget, Suchodolski, and Johann Friedrich Herbart. One of them, a shy Nicaraguan, a teacher at the only Active School in Managua, had written a book on Hildegart Rodríguez and her terrible mother, Aurora, titled *The Fallacies of Education* (Mexico, Pedagogía Libre, 1985), that in its day gained some renown: it postulated a life outdoors, far from classrooms and libraries, as the ideal school for children and adolescents; one of its preconditions, however, was the destruction of cities, something that the author called the Great Return and that was ultimately a kind of wild-eyed and millenarian Long March. Another of her teachers published a book called *The School of Parricides* (Brazil, Actas del Sur, 1980). And even her most beloved teacher, Miss Agnès Rivière of the Active School of Montreal, was a specialist in Paulo Freire, about whom she regularly wrote essays and appreciations for various Canadian and American journals of pedagogy. Those who weren't education theorists—that is, the remaining thirty percent—were fanatical devotees of Art. Before she was thirteen, Rosa had a teacher who was a believer in the healing properties of the dance of Merce Cunningham and Martha Graham, a teacher convinced of the prophetic qualities of the poetry of Rimbaud and Lautréamont, a teacher who was an enthusiast of the coded messages of Klee. In other words: apostles, leftists, pacifists, ecologists, anarchists cooped up in small progressive schools that almost no one had heard of—or at least no one hardworking and normal. Small sanctuaries like fringe churches or those arrogant English clubs where the offspring of those who had lost the Revolution (the exquisite few) were readied for the joys and sorrows of the world.

IV. *J.M.G. ARCIMBOLDI*

1

Works of J.M.G. Arcimboldi (Carcasonne, 1925)

NOVELS

The Enigma of the Cyclists of the Tour de France—Gallimard, 1956.
Vertumnus—Gallimard, 1958.
Hartmann von Aue—Gallimard, 1959.
Sam O'Rourke's Search—Gallimard, 1960.
Riquer—Gallimard, 1961.
Railroad Perfection—Gallimard, 1964.
The Librarian—Gallimard, 1966.
The Endless Rose—Gallimard, 1968.
The Natives of Fontainebleau—Gallimard, 1970.
Racine—Gallimard, 1979.
Doctor Dotremont—Gallimard, 1988.

ESSAYS

The Downtrodden: Articles and Notes on Literature—Gallimard, 1975.
   (Collection of critical texts written between 1950 and 1960 for
   newspapers and literary magazines.)

PLAYS

For Lovers Only—Gallimard, 1975. (Dated 1957 and performed
   for the first time by the Little Theater of Revolutionary Action,
   Carcassonne, 1958.)
The Spirit of Science Fiction—Gallimard, 1975. (Dated 1958 and
   performed for the first time by the Colombian Company of
   Rebels and Toilers, Cali, 1977.)

POETRY

Railroad Perfection; or, The Fracturing of the Pursued—Pierre-Jean Oswald, 1959.

Doctor Dotremont; or, The Paradoxes of Illness—Le Pont de l'Epée, 1960.

TRANSLATIONS

Songs of Hartmann von Aue—Millas Martin, 1956. (Selection, translation, prologue, and notes on the oeuvre of Von Aue, minnesinger.)

2

Two Arcimboldi Novels Read in Five Days
Hartmann von Aue (Gallimard, 1959, 90 pages)

At first glance, *Hartmann von Aue* is an examination of moments from the life of the German minnesinger, but the central character is really someone else: Jaufré Rudel.

Rudel, according to legend, fell in love with the Countess of Tripoli after hearing her praises sung by pilgrims returning from Antioch. He wrote some poems about her that were admired by all and increased his fame. But none of this was enough for the Prince of Blaye, and one day, driven by the desire to meet his beloved, he became a crusader and embarked for the Holy Land. During the voyage he fell gravely ill. As fate had it, he was still alive when the ship docked and he was taken to a Tripoli hospital. The countess heard the news and came to see him. Surprisingly, Jaufré Rudel regained consciousness, praised God for allowing him to set eyes on his beloved, and immediately thereafter died in her arms. He was buried at the house of the Knights Templar. Soon afterward, the countess entered a convent.

Von Aue listens over and over to this story and reflects on love and death. At moments he envies the Prince of Blaye and at moments he dimly despises him. He is a nobleman and a soldier and Rudel's fate seems to him unworthy, almost a betrayal. But the next moment, Rudel crossing the seas and dying in the arms of his beloved appears bathed in the most seductive light. Von Aue dreams of such a fate for himself. He tries to fall in love with

Spanish women who live in faraway places, but the very attempt strikes him as banal. Von Aue is incapable of action.

In the novel there are references to other minnesingers: the best known is Heinrich von Morungen, who, along with Von Aue, takes part in the Fourth Crusade. During the voyage, the Swabian knight and the Thuringian knight compete in feats of arms, hunting, music, and poetry. Fatefully, Von Aue shares the story of Jaufré Rudel with Von Morungen. Von Morungen is seized by excitement: the passion of Jaufré Rudel that Von Aue transmits to him changes his plans and his fealties and sets him on a new path. In Von Aue's vague memories, the figure of Morungen, ardent and unhinged, continues on to the East, to India. The fragile figure of Jaufré Rudel blazes like a torch: he is the Cross of the World.

With the years, the soldier gives way to the poet and the poet to the scholar: Von Aue, taking refuge in castle or forest, famed as the poet and adapter of Chrétien de Troyes's *Erec* and *Yvain*, bids farewell to the world without ever deciphering the transparent mystery of the Prince of Blaye.

Vertumnus (Gallimard, 1958, 180 pages)
The novel is set in an unspecified country in the Americas that sometimes resembles Argentina, sometimes Mexico, sometimes the American South. It is also set in France: Paris and Carcassonne. Time period: the end of the nineteenth century. Alexandre Maurin, landowner and man of strong character, orders his son to return to France. André, his son, objects, arguing that he was born in these lands and that his duty is to remain by his father's side in times of trouble. Over the course of an endless afternoon with great black clouds hanging overhead, Alexandre Maurin warns André of the danger he faces if he stays. For some time now the local strongmen have been scheming to kill them all. André inquires about the fate of the seven boys who live with them, in the same house, sharing the same table, orphans or vagabonds whom Maurin has gathered up and raised in his own way. In a sense André considers them his brothers. Maurin smiles: they aren't your brothers, he

says, you have no brothers or sisters, at least as far as I know. The orphans will suffer the same fate as their father, that's what Maurin has decided, but André, his only son, must be saved. Finally André's departure is settled. Maurin and the seven orphans, by now armed to the teeth, accompany the youth to the railroad station: their parting is cheerful, the orphans brim with confidence and boast of their weapons, they assure him that he can go with his mind at ease, no one will touch a hair on his father's head. The train trip is long and lonely. André doesn't speak to anyone. He thinks about his father and the boys and believes that he has made an unforgivable mistake leaving them there. He has a dream: as death rains down all around them, his father and the orphans ride and shoot their rifles at a mass of enemies who stand motionless, gripped by fear. Then André reaches a port city, has an encounter with a woman in a hotel on a hill, boards a ship, is bored during the long crossing, arrives in France. In Paris he meets his mother, in whose house he lives for the first few days. His relationship with his mother is distant and formal. Later, with the money he's brought from America, he rents a little house and begins his university studies.

For months he has no news of his father. One day a lawyer appears and informs him of the existence of a bank account opened in his name, an account with enough money in it for him to live on, finish his degree, and tour Europe. The account is replenished each year with a remittance from America. Your father, says the lawyer, is a man of means. An example for young people. Before he leaves he hands him a letter. In it, Alexandre Maurin provides more or less the same explanation and urges him to finish his degree quickly and to lead a healthy, virtuous life. The boys and I, he says, are holding down the fort. After two years, André meets a traveler at a party who has been to the part of America where his father lives. The traveler has heard talk of him: a Frenchman surrounded by American boys, some of them wild and dangerous, who has the local authorities in a chokehold; the owner of vast grazing and croplands, orchards, and a couple of gold mines. He lived, it was said, in the exact center of his possessions, in a big single-story house of adobe and wood, its courtyards and passageways labyrinthine. About the wards of the Frenchman, who ranged in age from eight to twenty-five, it was said that they were many, though probably not more than twenty in number, and that some of them had already claimed various lives. These words cheer and trouble André. That night he can learn nothing else, but in the following days he obtains the traveler's address and pays him a visit. For weeks, on every sort of pretext, André smothers the traveler with attentions, his seemingly limitless generosity touching his new friend. At last he invites him to spend a few days at the family seat in Carcassonne, which he has yet to visit. The traveler accepts the invitation. The train trip from Paris to Carcassonne is pleasant: they talk of philosophy and opera. The ride from Carcassonne to the family seat is by stagecoach and along the way André is silent. He's never been there before and he's assaulted by a kind of irrational and nameless fear. The house is empty but a neighbor and some servants inform them that old M. Maurin has been there. André realizes that they mean his grandfather, who he'd thought was dead. Leaving the traveler settled at the house, he sets out in search of his grandfather. When he finds him, in a village near Carcassonne, the old man is very ill. According to the family that has taken him in, death won't be long in coming. André, who is about to complete his medical degree, treats and cures him. For a week, forgetting all else, he remains by the old man's bedside: in his grandfather's face, ravaged by illness and hard living, he seems to glimpse his father's features, his father's fierce joy. When the old man recovers he brings him back to the house, over his protests. The traveler, meanwhile, has struck up friendships with a few of the neighbors, and when André arrives he reveals that he knows why he was invited. André admits that at first his motives were selfish, but now he feels true friendship. With the arrival of fall, the traveler leaves for Spain and the north of Africa and André remains in Carcassonne, caring for his grandfather. One night he dreams of his father: surrounded by more than thirty boys, adolescents and children, Maurin crosses a field of flowers on horseback. The horizon is vast and of a dazzling blue. When he wakes, André decides to return to Paris. The years go by. André receives his degree and starts a practice in an elegant quarter of Paris. He marries a pretty young woman from a good family. He has a daughter. He is a professor at the Sorbonne. He stands for Parliament. He buys property and speculates on the stock exchange. He has another daughter. Upon the death of his grandfather—at the age of ninety-three—he has the family seat restored and spends his summers in Carcassonne. He takes a lover. He travels around the Mediterranean and the Near East. One night, at the Monte Carlo Casino, he sees the traveler again. He avoids him. The next morning the traveler shows up at his hotel. He has lost everything, and he asks for a loan in the name of their old friendship. Silently, André Maurin hands him a more-than-generous check. The traveler, moved and grateful, tells him that he's spent five years in America and that he's seen his father. André says that he doesn't want to know anything about him. He no longer even touches the account that his father adds to each year without fail. But this time, says the traveler, I saw him in person, I spoke to him about you, I spent seven days at his house, I can give you all sorts of detail about his life. André says that none of that interests him anymore. Their parting is cold. That night, on his way back to Paris, André Maurin dreams of his father: all he sees are children and weapons and terrified faces. By the time he reaches Paris, he's forgotten everything.

3

An Arcimboldi Novel Read in Four Days

The Natives of Fontainebleau (Gallimard, 1970, 140 pages)

A painter by the name of Fontaine returns to the city of his birth in the south of France after thirty years of absence. The first part of the book, briefly: the return trip by train, the view from the windows, the silence or loquacity of the other passengers, their conversations, the train corridor, the restaurant car, the step of the ticket inspector, assorted opinions on politics, love, wine, the nation, then night on the train, the countryside in the dark, and the moon. In the second part we see Fontaine two months later, settled on the edge of town in a little three-room house by a stream, where he lives in dignity and poverty. He has only one friend left: Dr. D'Arsonval, whom he has known since he was a child. D'Arsonval, who is well-off and fond of Fontaine, tries to help him financially but Fontaine refuses his help. Here we are given our first description of Fontaine: he's short and lamb-like, with dark eyes and brown hair, his expression occasionally intense and his movements clumsy. During his absence he's been all over the world but he prefers not to talk about it. His memories of Paris are happy and bright. In his youth Fontaine was a painter of whom great things were expected. Once (D'Arsonval remembers as he sets off on horseback for Fontaine's little house), he was accused of imitating Fernand Khnopff. It was a trap set with malice and craft. Fontaine didn't defend himself. He knew Khnopff's work, but he preferred that of another Belgian: Mellery, the delightful Xavier Mellery, like himself the son of a gardener. That was the beginning of the end of his career. D'Arsonval visited him three years later: Fontaine's time was devoted to the reading of Rosicrucian literature, to drugs, and to friendships that contributed little to his physical or mental well-being. He made a living by working some mysterious job at a big warehouse. He hardly painted at all, though once D'Arsonval was back working as a doctor in the Roussillon, he received invitations for various shows, presumably sent by Fontaine himself, from a group of painters who called themselves "The Occults"—shows that, as might be supposed, D'Arsonval did not attend. Soon afterward Fontaine disappeared. The third and last part of the novel is set in D'Arsonval's library, after a long and lavish dinner. The mistress of the house has gone to sleep, and D'Arsonval's four guests are single men: in addition to Fontaine, there is Clouzet, widower and fabulously wealthy merchant, an aficionado—like the host—of poetry, music, and the fine arts; the young painter Eustache Pérol, on the eve of his second and de-finitive trip to Paris, where he plans to stay and forge a career with the initial support of D'Arsonval and Clouzet; and finally the par-ish priest, Father Chaumont, who confesses himself ignorant of the delights of art. The postprandial conversation goes on until dawn. Everyone talks. Sometimes the discussion is calm, other times it is impassioned. Chaumont pokes fun at D'Arsonval and Clouzet. Eustache Pérol treats the priest like a spiritual outlaw. They bring up Michelangelo. D'Arsonval and Clouzet have been to the Sistine Chapel. Chaumont speaks of Aristotle and then of Saint Francis of Assisi. Clouzet recalls Michelangelo's *Moses* and sinks into something that might be nostalgia or silent desperation. Eustache Pérol speaks of Rodin, but no one pays any attention to him: he's reminded of *The Burghers of Calais*, which he's never seen, and grits his teeth. D'Arsonval puts his hand on Clouzet's shoulder and asks if he remembers Naples. Clouzet quotes Bergson, whom they met in Paris, and he and D'Arsonval laugh. *Pape Satàn, pape Satàn aleppe*, whispers the priest. Soon the subject changes to Perol's impending trip. Chaumont asks after his lady mother. Eustache Pérol confesses that she is beside herself. Clouzet says a few words about a mother's love. D'Arsonval laughs in a corner of the library. They open another bottle of cognac. The only one who has done nothing but drink thus far is Fontaine. At four in the morning, when everyone is drunk (Father Chaumont dozes in an armchair and the others stroll around the library in shirt-sleeves), he is moved to speak. He remembers his mother. He recalls his departure and his mother's tears the night before as she packed his bag. He speaks of the joy of work. Of sublime visions. Of the monotony of life. Of his inability to decipher its mystery. Days in Paris, he says without rising from his seat and staring at the floor, are swift. But swift like what? like the wind? like amnesia? He speaks of women and sunsets, of terrible daybreaks and of blank, demonic faces. A heedless gesture, a word, and you're sunk, the consequences will be unforeseeable, he says in a soft voice. He speaks of the death of his mother, of painters and of bars. He speaks of the Rosicrucians and the cosmos. One day, pressed by debt, he took a job in the colonies. He didn't paint anymore—he had given it up, you might say—and in this new enterprise his rise was meteoric. No one could have been more surprised than he. In just a few years, he found himself in a position of responsibility that required constant travel. Yes, he had been all over Africa and even to India. Surprising countries, he says in response to the expectant looks of D'Arsonval and Clouzet and the dolorously skeptical gaze of Eustache Pérol. At a certain point, he says, a series of stupid mistakes obliged me to spend a month at a trading post in Mada-gascar. This was early in the year 1900. Life on the plantation and in the village was deadly boring. In three days his work was done and time passed with exasperating slowness. At first he occupied himself devising projects that might improve the living conditions of the natives, but he soon gave up the effort, thwarted by their passivity. Their lack of interest was universal. After their labors on the plantation, none of them wanted to do extra work. The apa-thy of the natives piqued Fontaine's interest, and he decided to paint them. At first everything was exciting: with materials taken from nature, he made the colors and brushes. An employee of the company supplied him with the canvases: an old sheet and pieces of sacking and burlap. He began to paint; far now, he says, from the symbolist school, from the visionaries and the wretched Occults. Now it was his eye, his naked eye, that guided his hand. The divine innocence of the company man, he says. From the start, the painting escaped his control. He began with the sacking and burlap and saved the sheet for the grand finale. One night, as he gazed at the sacking by the light of an oil lamp, he realized that he had turned that poor Madagascar village into a vast, sumptuous palace crowded with passageways, stairs, and hidden corners. Like Fontainebleau, he says, though he had never been there. The next day he tackled the sheet. It took him eight days to finish it, painting around the clock: by day in the open air and by night in the dilapidated company offices. He went without food and sleep. On the ninth day he packed up his things and didn't set foot outside his room. On the tenth day he departed in the ship that had come for him. A year later, settled in a small, friendly African city, he decided at last to take another look at his paintings. There were twenty small canvases and one big one, and together he called them *The Natives of Fontainebleau*. In the paintings, the village had, in fact, become a palace. The occupations of the natives had become the occupations of courtiers. The grand salons, their patterns of light and shadow, the statues, the mirrors, the murals, the heavy draperies: all seemed equally sunk in an unspecified illness. The floor oozed fever, the rugs seemed about to founder. In this setting, in an atmosphere at once oppressive and gay, his black subjects moved about, casting sidelong glances at the painter, at the future spectators of the painting, as if they were out in the open air. Fontaine seemed to hear again—to hear for the first time— the sounds of that village to which he would never return, sounds that he had mistakenly confused with those of any other African village. Now, thousands of miles away, he heard and saw it for the first time, and was horrified and amazed. The paintings, of course, were lost, adds Fontaine, except for the old sheet, which had accompanied him like an act of penitence each time he moved. After a long silence the voice of Chaumont, whom everyone had thought was asleep, is heard: you speak of sin, he says. D'Arsonval and Clouzet, suddenly full of unease, send for the carriage in order to set out immediately for Fontaine's house to see this extraordinary painting. Pérol has fallen asleep, his face now peaceful and innocent. D'Arsonval and Clouzet each take Fontaine by an arm and go out into the courtyard, where the servant has already hitched up the horses. There, as day begins to dawn, they are served steamed milk, bread, cheese, cold meats. Fontaine stands and gazes up at the sky as he drinks a glass of wine. Father Chaumont joins them. The carriage traverses the sleeping town, crosses a bridge, enters a forest. At last they come to Fontaine's little house: he takes the canvas from a chest, spreads it on the bed, and, without looking at it, steps away toward the window. From there he hears the exclamations of D'Arsonval and Clouzet, the murmurs of Chaumont. Soon afterward, as summer nears its end, he dies. When D'Arsonval clears out his few belongings, he searches for the painting but can't find it.

4

Two Arcimboldi Novels Read in Three Days

The Librarian (Gallimard, 1966, 185 pages)

The protagonist's name is Jean Marchand. He's young, from a good family, and wants to be a writer. He has a manuscript, *The Librarian*, on which he's been working for a long time. A publishing house, recognizable as Gallimard, hires him as a reader. Overnight, Marchand finds himself buried in hundreds of unpublished novels. First he decides to set his book aside for a while. Then he decides to give up his literary aspirations (the practice of writing, if not his passion for it) to devote himself to the careers of other writers. He sees himself as a doctor at a leper colony in India, a monk pledged to a higher cause.

He reads manuscripts, has long discussions with writers, gives them advice, calls them on the phone, inquires after their health, lends them money. Soon there's a group of about ten whom he can consider his own, whose novels he's been involved with. Some—a few—find publishers. Parties are thrown and plans made. The rest come imperceptibly to swell the ranks of a collection of unpublished manuscripts guarded jealously by Marchand. Among these manuscripts by others is his own novel, *The Librarian*, unfinished and perfectly typed, neatly bound, a beauty among grubby, smudged, crumpled, dirty originals; a lady cat among tomcats. Marchand dreams that in one magical and endless night the rejected manuscripts make love every way possible with his abandoned manuscript: they sodomize it, rape it orally and genitally, come in its hair, on its body, in its ears, in its armpits, etc., but when morning comes his manuscript hasn't been fertilized. It's sterile. In that sterility, Marchand believes, lies its uniqueness, its magnetism. He also dreams that he's the leader of a gang that scavenges metal from mines and that the mountain they must plunder by the light of the moon is hollow, empty. His prestige at the publishing house grows, as it must. He has recommended the publication of a young writer who is the hit of the season. Marchand knows that for every writer he allows to breathe, there are five who endure with him (with the best Marchand, the most improbable) the airlessness and darkness of their labyrinthine works.

Eventually, one of his writers kills himself. Another turns to journalism. Another, of independent means, writes a second and a third novel that only Marchand will read and praise. Another is published by a small regional press. Another becomes an encyclopedia salesman. By this point Marchand has abandoned any scruples, any hesitation: not only does he maintain steady relationships with the writers but in more than one case he has become acquainted with their families (dear M. Marchand), their girlfriends and wives, their generous grandmothers, their best friends. In his imagination, his manuscript lives on in the novels that he stores at his house: the character of *The Librarian* enters the lives of the other characters— the characters from the other books—just as he works his way into the lives of the writers. Of the first ten, only one takes the tempestuous world of publishing by storm (and even so, Marchand controls him to the point of making him write stories that only he will read, rewrite novels whose discarded fragments only he will possess); as the years go by, the others find new interests, stop writing, readapt themselves, grow up. But the flow of new manuscripts is unceasing: Marchand takes on another ten writers, then another ten, and so on until his library is filled with manuscripts— strange ones, bad ones sometimes; surprising ones, delightful ones, dark ones sometimes—that he personally takes care to see are rejected by publishers. There comes a moment when Marchand reads only unpublished works: the novel gives brief plot summaries of about forty.

Marchand has dreams: a great fire in his building, described by Arcimboldi with the precision of an architect and a firefighter; the appearance of a thundering Messiah who publishes all the filched manuscripts and condemns him to burn in hell, the Librarian's greatest fear; the hatching of a generation of novelists who are as quick as lightning and whom he'll coddle and lead, step by step, into his library of rejected writers. The novel ends abruptly. Marchand dies of a heart attack. Present at his burial, along with the employees of the publishing house, are many former writers. A moving truck transports his collection of manuscripts to a warehouse. Arcimboldi describes the warehouse in great detail.

Racine (Gallimard, 1979, 140 pages)
A fragmented biography, divided into cold and seemingly unconnected bits; perhaps a collection of prose poems, as one critic notes. Scenes from the life of Racine, following one after another like closed and stifling rooms: the death of the girl Jeanne-Thérèse Olivier, recounted with evident pain despite the chilliness—the purported objectivity—of the prose; the death of Jeanne Sconin, mother of the poet, two years after the poet's birth; the death of Marquise Du Parc, the poet's lover, in the year of the publication of *Andromaque*; work with Boileau, the head of Boileau, his profile; friendship with Molière and their subsequent falling-out; the death of Jean Racine, the poet's father; early mornings in 1644 when the poet was a five-year-old orphan living with his grandparents; the unfinished and lost tragedies, the incalculable spent energy; life in Uzès, the birds of Languedoc, the poet's uncle Antoine Sconin; the lie that surrounds him like a barbed and dirty cloud; marriage to Catherine de Romanet; the accusation that he poisoned Marquise Du Parc for her jewels; the study of Latin; the premiere of *Andromaque* with Marquise Du Parc in the leading role; the period when Marquise Du Parc worked with Molière; La Champmeslé's bed; children; life in Versailles; the great blocks of ice of the seventeenth century; the music of Lully and Port-Royal.

5

Two Arcimboldi Novels Read in Seven Days

Sam O'Rourke's Search (Gallimard, 1960, 230 pages)

At first, this sad and rambling novel most resembles a plagiarized version of James Hadley Chase's *No Orchids for Miss Blandish*, or at best an adaptation. Despite the unremitting description of objects (beds, curtains, camp beds, guns, chairs, boxes of crackers, bottles, plates), very much in the style of the *nouveau roman*, the arc of James Hadley Chase's story impresses itself with great force: some small-time crooks kidnap the daughter of a tycoon; before long, the bungling kidnappers lose their captive to another gang; the brains behind the new gang is a fat, surly woman (Mona); Mona's deputies are her son (Chuck) and her godson (Jim, a.k.a. Kansas Jim). That same night—the night of the double kidnapping—we learn that Chuck is a dangerous psychopath and that he's about to fall for the beautiful heiress, and that Jim is handsome and clever and hates the heiress with a passion: his reasons, explained at great length, fluctuate between a very personal sense of class struggle and an appreciation of the charms and natural camaraderie of chorus girls, whom he clearly prefers.

The rest of the gang consists of four drab and ruthless individuals: a black man, two ex-farmers, and a fifty-five-year-old Polish dancer. The daily existence of these characters is something that seems to fascinate Arcimboldi: their routines, their hideouts, their interests, their obsessions, the ease with which they "slide through cracks in time." We soon learn all kinds of things about them: their favorite foods, their dreams, their favorite subjects of conversation, their hopes, their dark loves, their dark fates (cf. Victor Hugo, *Les Miserables*). Chuck and the kidnapped girl are like a kind of diabolical Romeo and Juliet, with Mona and the Pole (who sleep together once every two weeks, though almost without touching, masturbating each other from opposite sides of the bed with hands like insect antennae) as their antithesis: the old couple has attained or is about to attain wisdom, the state of a celestial Romeo and Juliet. Standing between the two couples in a space where everything is antagonism are the godson, the black man, sometimes the two ex-farmers: they are the spectators of love, the chorus that gives life and takes it away, that licenses it.

The two cities where the first part of the novel is set are described with seeming objectivity (another cascade of details), revealing glimpses of a dream landscape: clouds that hang incredibly low, at nearly the level of lightning rods; twisted, solitary trees (that Arcimboldi, for reasons unknown, calls Oklahomas) loaded with birds and rodents, greenish-black specters in desolate fields; illicit all-night gambling dens; seedy hotels with four beds to a room; farmhouses with barred doors and windows; cowboys who scan the valley from afar without dismounting. Down in the valley, the two cities glitter in the sun; up on the mountain, the cowboy smokes and smiles with an air of sadness, striking the same relaxed, careless pose that we've seen in so many movies.

Between the end of the first part of the novel and the start of the second, a washroom door is opened by someone unknown to reveal a dwarf brushing his teeth at a dwarf-sized sink. It's at precisely this point that the second part begins: a private detective (Sam O'Rourke) kneels at a dwarf-sized sink brushing his teeth and staring at himself in the mirror—which is also dwarf-height—with an expression of infinite sadness on his face. Someone opens the door (presumably the same person who opened the door earlier and found the dwarf) and orders him to go in search of the missing heiress. The image of the detective on his knees brushing his teeth is one to which Arcimboldi will return over and over again: a man shrunk to his true size; the description of the washroom tiles (Hardee-Royston, green and gray flowers on a matte surface); the description of the single lightbulb hanging naked over the mirror; the shadow of the door as it opens; the bulky form in the doorway and the eyes of the stranger, invisible to O'Rourke but in which he intuits a gleam of surprise and fear; the gaze of O'Rourke, first in the mirror (in which he sees only the reflection of the stranger's legs) and then upon turning to seek the face; voices that echo with strange limpidity; the water that runs in the chipped sink and trickles between the tiles.

O'Rourke's search is limited to the two cities and the network of farms scattered between them. A single city, concludes Arcimboldi, is by its very nature unfathomable; two cities are an infinity. O'Rourke navigates this infinity with American simplicity and integrity. The senseless deaths (despite the author's efforts to demonstrate—by the enumeration of causal events—that everything has a hidden meaning as unyielding as fate) follow upon one another with horrifying monotony. O'Rourke's inquiries lead him to a church, an orphanage, the charred shell of a farm, a brothel. During the investigation, which is like a voyage, he makes new friends and enemies, reencounters forgotten lovers, is nearly killed, kills, loses his car, makes love with his secretary. The conversations that O'Rourke has with policemen, pickpockets, thugs, night watchmen, gas station attendants, informers, whores, and dealers are reproduced in full and concern the existence of God, progress, mathematics, life after death, the reading of the Bible, fallen women and saintly wives, flying saucers, the role of Christ on strange planets, the role of man on earth, the advantages of life in the country over life in the city (clean air, fresh vegetables and milk, guaranteed daily exercise), the ravages of time, miracle drugs, the secret recipe for Coca-Cola, the choice to bring children into this mixed-up world, work as a social good.

As might be expected, the search for the heiress never ends. The cities, A and B, increasingly resemble each other. Mona's gang, once the ransom is collected, tries to flee but something nameless (and ominous) stands in the way. They end up settling in B, where they buy a nightclub in the suburbs. The nightclub is described as a castle or a fortress: from a secret room the heiress and Chuck watch the sunsets and the Oklahomas stretching into infinity. O'Rourke loses himself doubly: in the cities and in momentous and futile conversations. And yet, at the end of the novel, he has a dream. He dreams that Mona's entire gang is climbing a flight of stairs. Mona is in the lead and Kansas Jim brings up the rear. In the middle is the kidnapped heiress with Chuck's arm around her waist. They climb slowly but with steady and unfaltering steps—the stairs are wooden and uncarpeted—until they come to a hallway, dark or faintly lit by a yellowish bulb covered with fly droppings. There's a door. They open it. They see a dwarf sink. Kneeling at the tiny sink is O'Rourke, brushing his teeth. They remain on the threshhold without greeting him. O'Rourke turns, still on his knees, and gazes at them. The novel ends a few lines later with some disquisitions on love and repentance.

Railroad Perfection (Gallimard, 1964, 206 pages)
Novel consisting of ninety-nine apparently unrelated two-page dialogues. All the dialogues take place aboard a train. But not the same train, or even during the same time period. Chronologically, the first dialogue (page 101) takes place in 1899, between a priest and a clerk for a foreign company; the last (page 59) in 1957, between a young widow and a retired cavalry captain. Following the order in which they appear in the book, the first dialogue (page 9) takes place in 1940, between a landscape painter and a surrealist painter whose nerves are shot, presumably on a train to Marseille; the last (page 205) takes place in 1930, between a woman traveling with two children and an old woman who is deathly ill but who never dies, among other reasons because the dialogue, like those that precede it, is interrupted: in general, the reader encounters conversations that he doesn't see begin (and whose beginnings he can't even imagine) and that after two pages will inevitably be cut off. Still, the careful reader will find clues that occasionally explain how a conversation started, what motivated it, the reasons behind it. Although most, at least on the surface, arise from the monotony of the trip, some have a more specific origin: a remark about the crime novel that a passenger is reading,

a significant political or social event, a third person who has attracted the attention of two passengers. Each dialogue is given a short title that sometimes informs us of the profession of the speakers or their marital status or the destination of the train or the year or the age of the travelers, but not always, so that some chapters begin simply with a notation of the time: 3 a.m., 9 a.m., 11 p.m., etc. In addition, the careful reader will soon realize (though a second or third reading is often required) that this isn't a collection of stories or of ninety-nine fragments connected solely by train travel: as if this were a mystery novel, we learn to recognize at least two travelers through the fragments of dialogue, two ambiguous characters who, despite changes of job, age, and sometimes even sex (but then the young woman who works as a secretary at a chocolate factory in the Jura is no such young woman), are the same person, and both are fleeing, or chasing each other, or one is chasing and the other is hiding. It's also possible to piece together the clues to solve a crime, though the order in which the dialogues are presented tends to muddy the waters (conversation between the prefect of Narbonne and the Turkish intellectual, page 161; conversation between the train conductor and the sailor from Toulon, page 95; conversation between the proofreader whose mother has died and the town architect of Brest, page 51; conversation between the Italian immigrant and the watchmaker from Geneva, page 87; conversation between the fifty-year-old whore and the twenty-year-old whore, page 115); it's possible to spin a comic tale (conversation between the bride and groom off on their honeymoon, page 27; conversation between the man of independent means and the owner of vineyards in the Roussillon, page 77; conversation between the vaudeville performer and the highway engineer—or is he a German spy? or a Strasbourg bohemian?—page 109); a story of devotion (conversation between the elderly baker and the elderly country doctor, page 153; conversation between the soldier on leave and the woman of mystery, page 163; conversation between the stutterer from Lille and the Paris taxi driver, page 171); the story of a trip—to Spain, the Maghreb?—that ends in the death of the traveler (conversation between the professor of medieval literature and the traveling salesman, page 143; conversation between the woman of mystery and the married woman, page 69; conversation between the twenty-year-old athlete and the twenty-eight-year-old college graduate, page 181; conversation between the bridge player and the Englishwoman of a certain age, page 197); and the story of a house that burned down (conversation between the gravedigger from the south and the gravedigger from the north, page 39; conversation between the housewife who likes to write poetry but doesn't like to read it and the proofreader whose mother has died, page 119; conversation between the man who has never taken trains and the old man who was an only child, page 191). But the truly important story, the one that somehow encompasses and obliterates and supplants all the others, is the story of the chase. From the beginning, the reader is presented with a number of questions: is the pursuer motivated by love or hatred? is the pursued motivated by love or fear? how much time elapses from the start of the chase until the present day? at the end of the book is the chase still on or has it imperceptibly ceased at some point between 1899 and 1957? is the pursuer a man and the pursued a woman, or is it the other way around? what is the story and what are its outgrowths, elaborations, offshoots?

6

Friendships of Arcimboldi

Raymond Queneau, whom he considered to be his mentor and with whom he quarreled at least ten times. Five times by letter, four times over the phone, and twice in person, the first time with curses and insults, and the second time with scornful gestures and glares.

Georges Perec, whom he admired deeply. Once he remarked that Perec must surely be the second coming of Christ.

Raoul Duguay, Quebecois poet, with whom he maintained a relationship based on mutual hospitality: when Duguay was in France he stayed with Arcimboldi, and when Arcimboldi traveled to Canada or taught college classes he stayed with Duguay. On the subject of Duguay's working life: he might be a professor at a Texas university for three months and a waiter at a bar in Vancouver for the next three months. Which is something that might seem perfectly normal in America but that never failed to astonish Arcimboldi.

Isidore Isou, whom he saw mostly between 1946 and 1948, and with whom he broke ties upon the appearance of the book *Réflexions sur M. André Breton* (Lettristes, 1948). As far as Arcimboldi was concerned, Isou was a "Romanian fuck-stick."

Elie-Charles Flamand, whom he knew between 1950 and 1955. By this time the young Flamand was already extremely interested in esotericism, which in 1959 got him excommunicated by the surrealists. He and Arcimboldi shared a taste for certain poetic and

kabbalistic interpretations of texts. According to Arcimboldi, Flamand was so unobtrusive that when he sat down it was practically
as if he had remained standing. (This observation of Arcimboldi's
can be found in an Agatha Christie story.)

Ivonne Mercier, librarian from Caen, whom he saw from 1952
to 1960. He met Miss Mercier while on holiday in Normandy.
For a year their contact was strictly epistolary, though frequent,
consisting of two or even three letters a week. At the time, Miss
Mercier was engaged and hoped soon to be married. The sudden
death of her fiancé brought them closer. Ivonne Mercier traveled
to Paris an average of six times a year. Arcimboldi, meanwhile,
made only one more trip to Caen in his lifetime, in the summer of
1959, the year of the publication of the novel *Hartmann von Aue*
and the poetry collection *Railroad Perfection; or, The Fracturing of the
Pursued*. In 1960 Ivonne Mercier married a builder from the Normandy coast and broke off her visits to Paris. They continued to
write for a few years, though very sporadically.

René Monardes, childhood friend from Carcassonne whom
Arcimboldi always visited on his trips back to town. Monardes,
a wine wholesaler, remembered Arcimboldi as a sincere and big-
hearted person. He had never read any of his books, though he kept
some on the bookshelf in the dining room. Even after Arcimboldi
had left France, Monardes claimed that he occasionally came back
to visit. Once every two years. He comes, we have a glass of wine,
maybe eat some figs under the arbor, I fill him in on the news, not
that there's much of it these days, and then he leaves. He's still a
nice guy. Not a big talker, but a nice guy.

7

Epistolary Relationships of Arcimboldi

Robert Goffin, ten letters dated between 1948 and 1951. Subjects: eroticism, painting, motoring, the weather, Belgian and French cyclists, scams and great scam artists.

Achille Chavée, fifteen letters, 1953 to 1960. Various subjects. Literature, as they say, is noticeable for its absence. In the letters, Chavée rallies Arcimboldi: courage, young man, courage.

Cecilia Laurent, of the Center for Atomic Energy Research, Paris. Forty letters, postcards, telegrams, all dated 1960. In one postcard Arcimboldi confesses that he wants to kill her. In the next letter he takes it back: what I really want to do is make love with you. To penetrate you = to kill you. That same afternoon he sends her a telegram: never mind, forget what I said, I didn't mean it.

Dr. Lester D. Gore, of the Nuclear Energy Institute, Pasadena, California. Ten letters, dated 1962 to 1966, of a pseudoscientific nature. From one of them it may be deduced that Arcimboldi tried to visit Gore during a trip to the United States in 1966, but that in the end they were only able to speak by phone. (Was he trying to gather material for a scientific novel, as he explains in a subsequent letter?)

Dr. Mario Bianchi, head of the Plastic Surgery Department, St. Peter's Hospital, Orlando, Florida. Eight letters, dated 1964 to 1965, of a pseudoscientific nature. Arcimboldi expresses an interest in techniques of facial surgery, in nerve elongation, in techniques for bone implants, in "photographs of the inside of the face, the inside of the hands." And he explains: "color photographs, of course." Dr. Bianchi expresses an interest in knowing whether any of Arcimboldi's novels have been translated in the United States, and mentions an upcoming trip to Paris with his wife and son during which they might meet in person.

Jaime Valle, professor of French literature at the Universidad Nacional Autónoma of Mexico. Five letters dated between 1969 and 1971. Subjects relating to the purchase of real estate, oceanfront properties, cabins in Oaxaca, hippies, peyote, María Sabina. Regarding Mexican literature: surprisingly, Arcimboldi has read only Mariano Azuela's *Los de abajo*, in Anne Fontfreda's translation, Paris, 1951. And a bit of Sor Juana Inés de la Cruz. It's life in Mexico that interests me, not Mexican literature, he says. The last letter is a long defense of B. Traven, scorned by Jaime Valle as popular and facile.

Renato Leduc, whom he meets through a mutual friend, the exiled Panamanian Roberto Dole, black, homosexual, and pacifist. Ten letters dated between 1969 and 1974. Subjects: life in Mexico, the desert, the tropics, the places where it rains most and least. Leduc's responses are clear and to the point. He goes so far as to send Arcimboldi photographs and maps, newspaper clippings and tourist pamphlets. He even presents him with a copy of his book *Fábulas y poemas*, 1966, and Arcimboldi promises to translate it, though nothing further is heard of the project.

Dr. John W. Clark, plastic surgeon, Geneva, Switzerland. Twenty letters between 1972 and 1975. Subjects: skin grafts, *The Island of Dr. Moreau*, the ultimate facelift.

Dr. André Lejeune, Lacanian psychoanalyst. Eighteen letters between 1963 and 1974. Discussions of literature from which it may be deduced that Dr. Lejeune is a reader to be reckoned with, as well as a shrewd and mordant critic. The final letters contain veiled threats. Arcimboldi discusses killings, people who talk about killings, blood, and silence.

Amelia De León, Mexican professor of French literature whom Arcimboldi meets on a brief trip to Oaxaca in 1976. Ten letters, all with some exotic postmark, like Mauritania or Senegal; all dated 1977. In them, Arcimboldi makes constant though oblique references to age, to the joys of being twenty-nine and about to turn thirty, which was the case of Professor De León in 1977. Her letters are cold and academic: Stendhal, Balzac, etc.

8

Hobbies and Training

The piano. Arcimboldi learned to play the piano when he was forty-five. His teachers were Jacques Soler and Marie Djiladi. He never had a piano at home or felt the need for one. And yet when he went out at night and came upon a piano at a bar or a friend's house he would do anything to be allowed to play it. Then he would sit down and run his fingers over the keys and although he played very badly he forgot everything and sang—in a cracked and barely audible voice—blues, ballads, love songs.

Magic. From the time he was very young he was interested in magic tricks. His apprenticeship was anarchic and ad hoc. He never followed any particular method. At the age of fifty he decided to apply himself to the School of Thought, which should really be called the School of Hidden Words, and involves guessing the objects that an audience member is carrying in his or her purse or wallet. For this trick it's necessary to have an assistant who uses coded language to inquire after the objects. But it can also be performed without an assistant, according to the magician Arturo De Sisti, by working solely from a person's external appearance, an alphabet that leads via unexpected yet clear channels to the things he keeps in his pockets. In this case the hidden words aren't those uttered by an assistant but those spoken by a tie, a handkerchief, a shirt, a hat, a dress, a necklace: words barely whispered, concise words that hardly ever lie. This is not, let it be said, a matter of judging by appearances, but rather of establishing a correlation, a continuity, between what is in plain sight and what—by virtue of its small size or for the sake of convenience—is tucked away. He also developed an interest in the art of making people disappear. Theories on this tricky maneuver were developed by many schools, from the Chinese to the Italian and the Arab to the American (which was itself divided into two schools: the classic school that made people disappear and the modern school that made trains disappear). It's not known which school interested Arcimboldi. No one ever saw him make a person disappear, though with some friends he talked about it quite a bit.

9

Sworn Enemies of Arcimboldi

Lisa Julien, whom he met in 1946 and with whom he lived from 1947 to 1949. Their breakup was violent: Arcimboldi, in a conversation recorded in 1971, acknowledged having slapped Miss Julien *twice*, first with his open palm and then with the back of his hand. Between the first and second blows there were punches (Arcimboldi ended up with a black eye), kicks, scratches, and strong words that the writer describes as a limit experience. From beneath the hail of blows, he says, he managed to catch a curious and distracted glimpse of pure nothingness. Miss Julien's hatred was lasting: in a rare interview conducted in 1992 by a pseudoliterary scandal sheet as part of a feature titled "The Long-Suffering Companions of Creative Men," she referred to the writer as "that loathsome, impotent dwarf."

Arthur Laville, reader for Gallimard and art critic for various European and American trade publications, who saw the main character of *The Librarian* as a malicious portrayal of himself. Laville, in an uncharacteristic fit of rage, launched a feud with Arcimboldi that lasted from 1966 to 1970. He was also presumably the author of a number of anonymous death threats and countless phone calls during which he showered the writer with insults and mockery or was silent, breathing heavily and noisily. At the end of 1970, Laville's anger subsided as abruptly as it had arisen. In 1975 they ran into each other in a hallway at Gallimard and exchanged civil remarks.

Charles Dubillard, patriotic poet, huckster, and inveterate Pétain supporter. In 1943 he gave a public thrashing to the young Arcimboldi, who, it's worth mentioning, had done nothing to avoid the fight, assuring the friends who tried to talk him out of it that nothing in the world would deprive him of the pleasure of bashing out the brains of that fascist pig Dubillard. In 1947 they met again, this time in Paris, at a poetry reading at which Dubillard, converted to Gaullism, read a poem about the hills of Languedoc, the traces of time, and the light of the motherland (according to Arcimboldi every messiah of fascism got his start and finish under the rustling petticoats of the motherland). The fight, this time, was at the back door of the hall. Arcimboldi was alone, which meant that no one tried to stop him. Dubillard was accompanied by three college friends, one of whom ended his brilliant career as a socialist minister in the eighties, and together they tried to convince Arcimboldi, first, that times had changed, and second, that Dubillard was much stronger and bigger than he and therefore, objectively speaking, it wasn't a fair fight. They fought anyway, and Arcimboldi lost again. Their next encounter was in 1955, at a well-known Paris restaurant. Dubillard had given up literature and become a businessman. This time all they did was shove each other and shout insults, until Arcimboldi's friends broke things off by taking him away. Their final encounter was in the fall of 1980. Dubillard was out for a walk with his grandson and his grandson's nanny and they ran into Arcimboldi. The latter considered spitting at the boy but he thought better of it and contented himself with spitting at a wheel of the baby carriage. Dubillard showed no reaction. They never saw each other again.

Raoul Delorme, concierge of the building where Arcimboldi lived from 1959 to 1962. Amateur writer of poems about horses and meticulous crime stories in which the killer is never caught. For a while Arcimboldi tried to convince some magazines to publish his work. According to him, Delorme might have been an extraterrestrial boy scout, or perhaps just a telepath. There soon sprang up between them a cool and contained hatred. Delorme, according to Arcimboldi, performed Black Masses in his cramped concierge quarters: he defecated on books by Gide, Maupassant, pissed on books by Pierre Louÿs, Mendès, Banville, shot his wad between the pages of books by Barbusse, Hugo, Chateaubriand, all with the sole intent of improving his French.

Marina Libakova, architect, literary agent, and poet. One month of passion and five years of hard feelings. One night, according to Madame Libakova, in her house in Thézy-Glimont where they were spending the weekend, Arcimboldi, without provocation or explanation, tossed into the fire a poetry manuscript that she had kindly and eagerly presented for his consideration. 1969–1973. She also admits that Arcimboldi asked her forgiveness for his stupidity something like three hundred times over the course of those five years. No letters were preserved.

v. KILLERS of SONORA

1

Pancho Monje was born in Villaviciosa, near Santa Teresa, in the state of Sonora.

One night, when he was sixteen, he was woken up and led half-asleep to the Monte Hebrón, a bar where Don Pedro Negrete, the police chief of Santa Teresa, was waiting for him. He had heard of him but never seen him. Accompanying Don Pedro were two old women and three old men from Villaviciosa, and lined up before him were ten boys about the same age as Pancho, waiting for Don Pedro's decision.

The superintendent was sitting in a high-backed chair like a throne, though it was covered in frayed fabric, different from all the other chairs at the Monte Hebrón, and he was drinking whiskey from a bottle that he had brought from home, because no one at the Monte Hebrón drank whiskey. Behind the chief and the old men, in the shadows, was another man who was also drinking. But he wasn't drinking whiskey, he was drinking Los Suicidas mescal, a rare brand that couldn't be found anywhere anymore, except in Villaviciosa. The mescal drinker's name was Gumaro and he was Don Pedro's driver.

For some time, without getting up from his chair, Don Pedro examined the boys with a critical eye while every so often the old men whispered in his ear. Then he called Pancho and ordered him to step forward.

Pancho was still half-asleep and he didn't understand the order.

"Me?" he asked.

"Yes, you, idiot, what's your name?"

"Francisco Monje, at your service," said Pancho.

One of the old men whispered again in Don Pedro's ear.

"What else," said Don Pedro.

"What else?" asked Pancho.

"Francisco Monje what, boy," said Don Pedro.

"Francisco Monje Expósito," said Pancho.

Don Pedro stared at him and, after consulting with the old men, made his choice. The other boys went home and Pancho was ordered to wait outside.

The sky was full of stars and it was as bright as day. It was cold, but Don Pedro's Ford was still warm and Pancho put his two hands on the hood. Inside the Monte Hebrón, Don Pedro handed out money and inquired about people's health, whether the family was well, whether so-and-so had died or so-and-so had disappeared, then he said good night, ladies and gentlemen, and hurried out, followed by his driver who looked asleep.

Pancho and Don Pedro sat in the backseat and the Ford rolled slowly along the dark streets of Villaviciosa.

"Damn it, Gumaro," said Don Pedro, "I forgot all about the streetlights for this shithole town."

"What lights, boss?" said Gumaro without turning.

That night Pancho slept at the house of Don Gabriel Salazar, a Santa Teresa businessman, in one of the rooms built onto the gardener's house, a room with four bunks and the smell of sweat and tobacco. Don Pedro turned him over to an American called Pat Cochrane and left without a word. The American asked him a few questions and then gave him a Smith & Wesson and told him how it worked, how much it weighed, how to engage and disengage the safety, how many clips he should carry in his pocket at all times, when he should draw it, and when he should only pretend to draw it.

That night, the first that Pancho had spent away from Villaviciosa, he slept with the pistol under his pillow, and his sleep was fitful. At five in the morning he met one of his roommates, who came in drunk and stared at him for a long time, muttering incomprehensibly while Pancho, huddled in the upper bunk, pretended to be asleep. Later he met the other one. They didn't like him, and he didn't like them.

One was tall and fat and the other was short and fat and they were always seeking out each other's eyes, exchanging glances as if to confer silently about each new situation. They were from Tijuana and they were both named Alejandro: Alejandro Pinto and Alejandro López.

The job was to protect Don Gabriel Salazar's wife. They were her private bodyguards; that is, bodyguards of the second rank. More seasoned men were on call for the protection of Don Gabriel, gunmen who came and went with a swagger, men better dressed than Pancho and the pair from Tijuana. Pancho liked the work. He didn't mind waiting for hours while the mistress visited her friends in Santa Teresa, or leaning on the white Nissan, waiting for her to emerge from a boutique or a drugstore flanked by his two comrades, who on such occasions, out in the field, tended to confer with their eyes even more than usual.

Of the other bodyguards—the boss's—he had only a vague impression: they played cards, drank tequila and vodka, were laid-back and swore a lot, at least one of them smoked weed. Their jokes were delivered like remarks about the weather, as if they were discussing the chaparral, the rain, relatives crossing the border. Sometimes, too, they talked about illnesses, all kinds of illnesses, and there no one could match the two tubs from Tijuana. They knew everything, from the different kinds of flu and adult-onset measles to AIDS and syphilis. They talked about dead or retired friends or comrades, afflicted by all kinds of ailments, and the sound of their voices didn't match their faces: their voices were soft, bereaved, at times murmuring like a river that flows over sandstone and aquatic plants; their gestures, however, were broad and self-satisfied, they smiled with their eyes, their pupils shone, they winked complicitly.

One of the bodyguards, a Yaqui Indian from Las Valencias, said that death was no laughing matter, much less death from illness, but no one paid any attention to him.

The bodyguards' evenings stretched on almost until dawn. Sometimes Pat Cochrane, who spent his nights at the main house, would show up at the gardener's house to gauge morale, offering words of encouragement when spirits were low, and if he was in a good mood he would even put on water for coffee. In the mornings almost no one talked. They listened to Cochrane or to the birds in the yard and then they went into the kitchen, where Don Gabriel's old cook made them dozens of fried eggs.

Though Pancho didn't trust his two comrades from Tijuana, he soon got used to his new life. One of the gunmen from the big house told him that every so often Don Pedro Negrete supplied new recruits to certain local outfits or power brokers. The food was good and they were paid each Friday. It was Cochrane who assigned tasks, arranged life in the gardener's house, scheduled guard shifts and escort duties, and paid them at the end of the week. Cochrane had white hair down to his shoulders and was always dressed in black. From one moment to the next, depending whether it was sunny or cloudy, he could seem like an old hippie or a gravedigger. His men said he was tough and they treated him with familiarity, but also with respect. He wasn't Irish, as some thought, but American, a gringo, and Catholic.

Every Sunday morning, Don Gabriel Salazar's wife brought in a priest to say Mass at the private chapel on the other side of the big house. And Cochrane was the first to arrive, nodding to the mistress of the house and sitting in the first row. Next came the domestic staff, the cook, the maids, the gardener, and some bodyguards, though not many of them, since they preferred to spend Sunday mornings at the gardener's house, playing cards, cleaning their guns, listening to the radio, thinking or sleeping. Pancho Monje never attended the service.

Once Alejandro Pinto, who didn't go to Mass, either, asked whether he believed in God or whether he was agnostic. Alejandro Pinto read occultist magazines and knew the meaning of the word *agnostic*. Pancho didn't, but he guessed it.

"Agnostic? That's for faggots," he said. "I'm an atheist."

"What do you think comes after death?" asked Alejandro Pinto.

"After death? Nothing."

The other bodyguards were surprised that a boy of seventeen should be so sure about what he believed.

2

In 1865 a thirteen-year-old orphan was raped by a Belgian soldier in an adobe house in Villaviciosa. The next day the soldier's throat was cut and nine months later a girl was born, named María Expósito. The young mother died of childbed fever and the girl grew up in the same house where she was conceived, as the ward of the farmworkers who lived there. In 1880, when María Expósito was fifteen, on the feast day of St. Dismas, a drunken stranger rode off with her on his horse, singing at the top of his lungs:

> *Qué chingaderas son éstas*
> *le dijo Dimas a Gestas.*

On the slope of a hill that the country folk, with inscrutable humor, called the Hill of the Dead and that, seen from town, looked like a shy and curious dinosaur, he raped her several times and vanished.

In 1881 María Expósito had a daughter whom she baptized María Expósito Expósito and who was the wonder of the town of Villaviciosa. From the time she was very small she showed herself to be clever and spirited and although she never learned to read or write she was known as a wise woman, learned in the ways of herbs and medicinal salves.

In 1897, after she had been away for six days, the young María Expósito appeared one morning in the plaza, a bare space in the center of town, with a broken arm and bruises all over her body.

She would never explain what had happened to her, nor did the Villaviciosa officials insist that she tell. Nine months later a girl was born and given the name María Expósito, and her mother, who never married or had any more children or lived with any man, tried to initiate her into the secret art of healing. But the only thing the young María Expósito had in common with her mother was her good nature, a quality shared by all the María Expósitos of Villaviciosa (though some were quiet and others liked to talk), along with a natural ability to forge bravely ahead through periods of violence or extreme poverty.

The childhood and adolescence of the last María Expósito, however, were more carefree than her mother's and grandmother's had been. In 1913, at sixteen, she still thought and behaved like a girl whose only duties were to accompany her mother once a month in search of herbs and medicinal plants and to wash the clothes behind the house, in an old oak trough rather than the public washtubs that the other women used.

This was the year that Colonel Sabino Duque (who in 1915 would be executed for cowardice) came to town looking for brave men—and the men of Villaviciosa were famous for being something more than brave—to fight for the Revolution. Several boys from the town enlisted, selected by the town officials. One of them, whom until then María Expósito had thought of only as an occasional playmate, the same age as she and seemingly as naïve, decided to declare his love the night before he went to war. For the purpose he chose a grain shed that no one used anymore (since the people of Villaviciosa had little left to store) and when his declaration only made the girl laugh he proceeded to rape her on the spot, desperately and clumsily.

At dawn, before he left, he promised he would come back and marry her, but seven months later he died in a skirmish with federal troops and he and his horse were swept away by the Río Sangre de Cristo, also known as Hell River because it ran brownish-black. Though María Expósito waited for him, he never returned to Villaviciosa, like so many other boys from the town who went off to war or found work as guns for hire, boys who were never heard of again or who cropped up here and there in stories that might or might not have been true.

And nine months after his departure María Expósito Expósito was born and young María Expósito, suddenly a mother herself, set to work selling her mother's potions and the eggs from her own henhouse in the neighboring towns, and she did fairly well.

In 1917, there was an unusual development in the Expósito family: María got pregnant again and this time she had a boy.

His name was Rafael and he grew up amid the tumult of the new Mexico. His eyes were green like those of his distant Belgian great-grandfather and his gaze had the same strangeness about it that outsiders noted in the gaze of the townspeople of Villaviciosa: it was opaque and intense, the stare of a killer. The identity of his father was never revealed. He might have been a revolutionary soldier, or a federal soldier, since they, too, were seen around town at the time, or he might have been some random local who preferred to remain in prudent anonymity. On the rare occasions when she was asked about the boy's father, María Expósito, who had gradually adopted her mother's witchlike language and manner (though all she did was sell the medicinal brews, fumbling among the little rheumatism flasks and the drafts for the curing of melancholy), answered that his father was the devil and Rafael his spitting image, and despite what one might imagine, the inhabitants of Villaviciosa weren't ruffled in the slightest by this reply, since all the local boys, some more than others and some less, might have been the sons of Pedro Botero.

In 1933, during a Homeric bender, the bullfighter Celestino Arraya and his comrades from the club The Cowboys of Death arrived early one morning in Villaviciosa, the bullfighter's hometown, and took rooms at the Valle Hebrón bar, which at the time was also an inn, and shouted for roast goat, which they were served by three village girls. One of those girls was María Expósito. They left the next morning at eleven and four months later María Expósito confessed to her mother that she was going to have a baby. Who's the father? asked her brother. The women were silent and the boy set out to retrace his sister's steps on his own. A week later Rafael Expósito borrowed a rifle and set off on foot for Santa Teresa.

He had never been in such a big place and he was so struck by the bustle of the streets, the Teatro Carlota, and the whores that he decided to spend three days in the city before carrying out his mission. The first day he spent searching for Celestino Arraya's haunts and a place to sleep for free. He discovered that in certain neighborhoods night was the same as day, and he pledged simply not to sleep. On the second day, as he walked up and down the main street of the red-light district, a short, shapely Yucatecan girl with jet-black hair down to her waist and the look of a woman to be reckoned with took pity on him and brought him home with her. There, in a hotel room, she made him rice soup and then they spent the rest of the day in bed.

It was the first time for Rafael Expósito. When they parted the whore ordered him to wait for her in the room or, if he wanted to go out, at the entrance to the hotel. The boy said he was in love with her and the whore went off happily, laughing to herself. On the third day she brought him to the Teatro Carlota to hear the ballads of the Dominican troubador Pajarito de la Cruz and the rancheras of José Ramírez, but what the boy liked best were the chorus girls and the magic numbers by Professor Chen Kao, a Chinese conjurer from Michoacán.

At dusk on the fourth day, well fed and at peace with himself, Rafael Expósito said goodbye to the whore, retrieved the rifle from the vacant lot where he'd hidden it, and headed resolutely to the bar Los Primos Hermanos, where he found Celestino Arraya. Seconds after he shot him he knew without a shadow of a doubt that he had killed him and he felt avenged and happy. He didn't shut his eyes when the bullfighter's friends emptied their revolvers into him. He was buried in a pauper's grave in Santa Teresa.

In 1933 another María Expósito was born. She was shy and sweet and so tall that even the tallest men in town looked short next to her. From the time she was eight she spent her days helping her mother and grandmother to sell her great-grandmother's remedies and going along with her grandmother at dawn to gather herbs. Sometimes the peasants of Villaviciosa saw her silhouette against the horizon and it struck them as extraordinary that such a tall, long-legged girl could exist.

She was the first in her family to learn to read and write. At the age of seventeen she was raped by a peddler and in 1950 a girl was born whom they called María Expósito. By then there were five generations of María Expósitos living together outside Villaviciosa, and the little farmhouse had grown, with rooms added on any old way around the big kitchen with the hearth where the eldest prepared her brews and medicaments. At night, when it was time for dinner, the five always sat down together, the girl, her lanky mother, Rafael's melancholy sister, the childlike one, and the witch, and often they talked about saints and illnesses, about money, about the weather, and about men, whom they considered a scourge, and they thanked heaven that they were only women.

In 1968, while the students of Paris were taking to the streets, the young María Expósito, still a virgin, was seduced by three students from Monterrey who were preparing, or so they said, for a revolution of the peasantry, and whom after one thrilling week she never saw again.

The students lived in a van parked at a bend in the road between Villaviciosa and Santa Teresa and every night María Expósito would slip out of bed to go and meet them. When her great-grandmother asked who the father was, María Expósito remembered a kind of delicious abyss and had a very clear vision: she saw herself, small but mysteriously strong, able to take three men at once. They hurl themselves on me panting like dogs, she thought, from in front and behind so that I can hardly breathe and their cocks are enormous, they're the cocks of Mexico's peasant revolution, but inside I'm bigger than them all and they'll never conquer me.

By the time her son was born the Paris students had gone home and many Mexican students had stopped existing.

Against the wishes of her family, who wanted to baptize the boy Rafael, María Expósito called him Francisco, after Saint

Francis of Assisi, and decided that the first half of his last name wouldn't be Expósito, which was a name for orphans, as the students from Monterrey had informed her one night by the light of a campfire, but Monje, Francisco Monje Expósito, two different last names, and that was how she entered it in the register at the parish church despite the priest's reluctance and his skepticism about the identity of the alleged father. Her great-grandmother said that it was pure arrogance to put the name Monje before Expósito, which was the name she'd always had, and a little while later, when Pancho was two and running naked along the sand-colored streets of Villaviciosa, she died. And when Pancho was five the other old woman, the childish one, died, and when he turned fifteen, Rafael Expósito's sister died. And when Don Pedro Negrete came for him the only ones left were the lanky Expósito and Pancho's mother.

3

"We saw them from the distance and right away we knew who they were and they knew we knew it and they kept coming. I mean: we knew who they were, they knew who we were, they knew that we knew who they were, we knew that they knew that we knew who they were. Everything was clear. The day had no secrets! I don't know why, but the thing I remember best about that afternoon are the clothes. Their clothes, especially. The one who was carrying the Magnum, who was going to make sure that Don Gabriel's wife died, was wearing a sharp white guayabera with stitching on the front. The one carrying the Uzi was in a green serge jacket, maybe two sizes too big."

"*Ay*, the things you know about clothes, darling," said the whore.

"I was wearing a white short-sleeved shirt and some drill pants that Cochrane had bought for me and already taken out of my weekly pay. The pants were too big and I had to wear a belt to keep them up."

"You've always been on the skinny side, sugar," said the whore.

"All around me it was the different outfits that were moving, not the flesh-and-blood people. Everything was clear. The afternoon had no secrets! But at the same time, everything was out of whack. I saw skirts, pants, shoes, white tights and black tights, socks, handkerchiefs, jackets, ties, a whole store's worth of clothes, I saw cowboy hats and straw hats, baseball caps and hair ribbons, and all the clothes flowed along the sidewalk, flowed through the arcade, completely removed from the reality of the pedestrians, as if the flesh they sat on repelled them. Happy people, is what I should have been thinking. I should have envied them. Wanted to be them. People with money in their pockets or not, but glad to be on their way to the movie theater or the record store or anywhere, people going to eat or drink beer, or on the way home after a walk. But what I thought was: all those clothes. All those clean, new, useless clothes."

"You were probably thinking about the blood, darling," said the whore.

"No, I wasn't thinking about the bullet holes or the blood splattering everything. I was thinking about clothes, that's all. About the motherfucking pants and shirts going back and forth."

"Don't you want me to go down on you, sugar?" asked the whore.

"No. Stay where you are. Don Gabriel's wife, I didn't see her clothes. I saw her pearl necklace. Like a solar system. And I saw everything about the couple of fat slobs who were with me: the way they looked at each other, the shiny jackets, the dark ties, the white shirts, and the shoes, how to describe them, leather shoes that weren't old but weren't new, either, shoes for jerk-offs and scum, shoes for losers, with creases where you can see the pathetic celebrations and fears of men who've sold out everything and still think they can be happy or at least hold on to some kind of happiness, some dinner every once in a while, a Sunday with the family and the kids, the poor brats stuck in the desert, the crumpled photos good for squeezing out a couple of tears, tears that stink of shit. Yes, I saw their shoes and then I saw the parade of clothes in the air and I said to myself look at the waste, look at the wealth in this city of sin."

"Now you're exaggerating, love," said the whore.

"No, I'm not. It happened exactly the way I'm telling you. Don Gabriel's wife didn't even realize that death was on top of her. But the slobs from Tijuana and I saw it and right away we knew what we were seeing. The killers walked like movie stars. Like a weird cross between movie stars and clerks. They walked slowly, not bothering to really hide their guns and never taking their eyes off us for a second. I guess that was when my buddies decided they'd had enough. Those looks, they were thinking, beat the looks they'd been exchanging and after a second, they just spun around and went running, no, not running, trotting like draft horses, swinging past the crowds of people on the sidewalk and the arcade. They didn't say a thing to me. And I had no time to yell assholes, cowards, faggots."

"The worst kind of trash, darling," said the whore.

"I stood there motionless, next to the señora, who didn't know what was going on, why we had stopped, noticing how my white shirt and drill pants were shivering, too big, if my belt hadn't been pulled tight they would've fallen down and lain there shivering on the ground. But I also had time to get a look at the killers. One of them, the one with the Magnum, walked on as if he hadn't noticed a thing, and the other one smiled at the sight of my two buddies running off, as if to say life is funny isn't it, as if to say running away isn't cowardice, it just means you're light on your feet. I noticed the one with the Magnum: he reminded me of someone from Villaviciosa. There was something sad and serious about him and he wasn't so young anymore, or that's how it seemed to me. Not the other one, I'm sure the other one was from the city. Then people began to back away, probably because they saw the guns or because all of a sudden they realized that there was going to be a shoot-out or because they got a look at the señora and me and thought we looked like goners."

"I can imagine how scared you must have been, love," said the whore.

"I wasn't afraid. I waited until they were just fifteen feet away and when I had them there, before anyone could scream, I pulled my gun out nice and easy, no sudden movements, and took them both down. The assholes never got a shot out. The one with the Uzi died with a look of surprise on his face. Then I turned, angrily, since rage was all I felt then, and I emptied the rest of the clip at the slobs from Tijuana trotting away, but they were already too far. I think I wounded a bystander."

"You're a real son of a bitch, darling," said the whore.

"They held me for five hours at the General Sepúlveda police station. Don Gabriel's wife told the police that I was her body-guard but they didn't believe her. Before they put me in the patrol car I told her to call her husband and then go to some coffee shop to wait for him and not come out, and if there was a way to lock herself in the bathroom at the coffee shop, she should go ahead and do it. Then they cuffed me, put me in the patrol car, and took me to the station."

"I'm sure they knocked you around, love," said the whore.

"I had to answer all kinds of questions. The police wanted to know whether I knew either of the dead men, whether I knew the wounded pedestrian, why I fired at the slobs, whether I was high and what drugs I consumed on a regular basis, whether it was me who killed Pérez Delfino, Juan Pérez Delfino, Virgilio Montes's right-hand man, whether I knew any traffickers from Arizona, whether I had ever been to some fucking bar in Hermosillo, the Adiós, Mi Lupe, where I'd gotten the gun, whether I was friends with Robert Alvarado, whether I had ever been to prison and what prison and why and how many times. I've never been locked up, I told them. I wasn't shivering anymore and my brain was reg-istering people instead of clothes, people with an interest in me, people who wanted to hear what I had to say, people who wanted to sucker-punch me, people having fun or bored of it all, people doing their jobs. But I didn't say a word. Where did you learn to shoot? asked those flesh-and-blood people, do you have a permit? where the hell do you live? And I just kept my mouth shut, call Don Gabriel Salazar, he'll tell you whatever he thinks you need to know."

"You took it like a man, darling," said the whore.

"Five hours later Don Pedro Negrete arrived and the police-men stood to attention. Don Pedro came in with a smile on his face and his hands in his pockets, like he had all the time in the world and he didn't mind coming in to the station on a Saturday night. Who put this boy in the tank? he asked without raising his voice. The deputies who were questioning me pissed themselves they were so scared. Me, boss, said one. *Ay*, Ramírez, you really

fucked up this time, said Don Pedro, and Ramírez almost threw
himself at his feet to kiss them, no, Don Pedro, it was just routine,
I swear, Don Pedro, we never laid a finger on him, ask him, for
the love of God, Don Pedro, and Don Pedro looked down at the
ground, looked at me, looked around at the other policemen, *ay*,
Ramírez, Don Pedro laughed, *ay*, Ramírez, and everyone except
for me started to laugh, too, they were starting to recover, relax,
and they laughed, they laughed at poor Ramírez, man, you're in
the shit now and Ramírez gave each of them a look, one by one,
like he was saying have you all gone crazy? and then even I laughed,
and that poor dumbshit Ramírez finally laughed a little too. And
now that I think of it, the laughing sounded strange, it was laughing but it was something else too. You've never heard a bunch of
cops laughing at another cop in an interrogation room. It was a
kind of onion laugh. The bad boy inside each of them laughed and
the onion burned away little by little. The laughs echoed off the
damp walls. The onions were small and fierce. And to me it felt
like a welcome or a celebration."

"I like to hear one cop laugh, not a lot of cops all together,
sugar," said the whore.

"Gumaro, who was leaning in the doorway and who I hadn't
noticed until then, laughing. Don Pedro Negrete laughing, which
was like the laughter of God and smelled like whiskey and expensive cigarettes. And all the laughing from the men who were about
to be my crew, finding it honest-to-God funny, the beating that
son of a bitch Ramírez was going to take."

"I think I know the Ramírez you're talking about, love," said
the whore.

"I don't think so, Ramírez died before you got here. He tried
to get Don Gabriel Salazar to hire him, but it didn't work. Don
Gabriel wanted me, but Don Pedro Negrete told him he couldn't
have me, he'd had his chance and now he'd lost it, he'd put me
with two faggots who weren't worth even a bullet in the back of
the head, his man Pat Cochrane was worthless, and I wouldn't be
coming back. I gave you the boy, Gabriel, he said, and you almost
got him killed. This time I'm keeping him. That was how I quit

working for Don Gabriel Salazar. Don Gabriel wasn't too happy with Don Pedro's explanation, but when he said goodbye to me he gave me an envelope of money, from his wife, he said, who'd been a wreck for a week but who was still grateful for my services. With the money, I bought myself clothes and rented an apartment in Colonia El Milagro, on the south side of Santa Teresa."

"You've never invited me to your apartment, sugar," said the whore.

"It was my first place and it's still the only place I've ever had. It's on the third floor and it has a dining room, a kitchen, a bathroom, and a bedroom. It doesn't get any light, which for me is an advantage because I usually sleep during the day and I like the dark. When I turned eighteen I bought myself a '74 Ford Mustang. It was an old car, but it was pretty and the engine had been tuned. You could say that it was almost a gift. One good turn deserves another, Pancho, they told me, and I said okay."

4

Pedro and Pablo Negrete were born in Santa Teresa in 1930. To the surprise of their family and the amusement of the neighbors they turned out to be monozygotic twins. Until they were sixteen they were identical and only their mother could tell them apart. Then life changed the brothers radically, though beneath the surface a keen student of human physiognomy could see that their physical differences were like the reaction of each to the other. Thus, Pedro's mustache and Pedro's eyes, his strong hands, his steady pulse, his gut, the belly of a man who likes his food and drink, found their perfect counterpart, their ultimate elucidation, in the bloodless lips and thick glasses that Pablo had been stuck with since his sixteenth birthday, his manicured hands and his flat and ulcer-plagued stomach. Until well into adolescence both were of medium height, thin, dark, mild-looking. Then Pablo grew two inches taller than his brother and acquired a perennial expression of perplexity. Pedro, in contrast, remained the same height—in fact, as he got fatter he seemed to shrink—but his features grew stronger and his face filled out and his meekness was exchanged for an effortless congeniality, a deceptive congeniality that actually inspired respect or fear. By the time they were seventeen they were completely different. Pablo decided that he wanted to go to college and Pedro joined the Santa Teresa police force, thanks to the good offices of an uncle who was a sergeant. It was the first time that the twins had been apart.

Pedro, shoehorned into a shiny blue uniform, spent his days wandering Colonia Juárez, especially Calle Mina, home to streetwalkers and the strangest stores in the city: hardware shops that looked like gunsmiths' shops, gunsmiths' shops that looked like jails, doctors' offices that cured impotence and all kinds of venereal diseases, tiny bookstores where mystery novels, romance novels, and books about World War II overflowed onto the sidewalk, taxidermists' shops that displayed leopards and eagles on their high, dark shelves, cantinas and pulquerías frequented by shady-looking characters.

Pablo, meanwhile, embarked on the study of law and at night he washed dishes at an Italian restaurant on Calle Veracruz, between Colonia Escobedo and Colonia Juárez. The owner was a former teacher of his, a professor of rhetoric, and the restaurant was the only Italian spot in Santa Teresa, at least in those days. Later there were pizzerias and hamburger joints and even soda fountains, everything to suit the tastes of a modern city, but back then there was only one Italian restaurant, one Basque-French restaurant, and three Chinese holes-in-the-wall. Everywhere else the food was Mexican.

The first years weren't easy. A certain tendency toward melancholy and a reasonably happy childhood did nothing to prepare the two brothers for the world of work, but at the core they were tough and they soldiered on. Little by little they got ahead and managed to adapt to their circumstances. Although Pablo Negrete soon realized that the law bored him more than it interested him, a small amount of scheming got him his degree and a scholarship to study philosophy in the capital. Pedro, meanwhile, furnished sufficient proof of his courage as a police officer and a man, but most of all of his exquisite nose and tactful handling of the people who mattered. Quietly he rose through the ranks of the Santa Teresa police department. His superiors respected him and his subordinates half loved and half feared him. It was around this time that all kinds of gossip about him began to spread. It was said that he had slit the throat of a whore in her hotel room, that he had killed a leader of the railroad union (though the train didn't pass through Santa Teresa), that for the benefit of a local rancher he had engineered the disappearance of five seasonal workers clamoring for what they were owed. But nothing could ever be proved.

Pablo completed his philosophy degree with a thesis titled *Heidegger and Mexican Thought*, which some fellow students and professors judged to be in the great critical tradition and that was actually tossed off in twenty-five days, plagiarized from all kinds of sources, by the Michoacán poet Orestes Gullón, who three years later would die of cirrhosis of the liver. Gullón, reporter for *El Nacional*, author of slanderous palindromes and acrostics, as well as poems occasionally published in a few Mexico City journals and provincial newspapers, was Pablo Negrete's one friend during his profitable and happy time in the capital; serious-minded and polite, he knew how to avoid making enemies, but his only real friend was Gullón. With the latter he spent time at Café La Habana, on Calle Bucareli, and at the bar La Encrucijada, on Bucareli at Victoria, and at some dubious dance halls on Avenida Guerrero.

The northerner and his friend from Michoacán were an odd couple. Gullón was a talker, cultivated and self-centered. Pablo Negrete was reserved, not too busy grooming his ego—though he did put a lot of care into his attire—and his knowledge of the Greek classics left much to be desired. He was interested in German philosophy. Gullón professed an Olympic disdain for it: he said that the only decent German philosopher was Lichtenberg, who was less a philosopher than the ultimate jokester and clown. He liked Montaigne and Pascal. And he could recite from memory bits of Empedocles, Anaxagoras, Heraclitus, Parmenides, and Zeno of Elea, to the delight of Pablo, who grew fonder and fonder of him as time went by.

Unlike his brother, Pedro Negrete had many friends. Being a policeman made it easier. A policeman, he discovered without being taught, could be friends with anyone he wanted. The cultivation of friendship, an art previously foreign to him, became his favorite pastime. As a boy, friendship had struck him as mysterious, sometimes risky, even reckless. When he was older he understood that friendship—the essence of friendship—resided in the guts, not the brain or the heart. Everything boiled down to the play of mutual interests and a way of touching people (touching them physically, hugging them, slapping them on the back) with confidence. And it was precisely in the police force where this art was most vigorously practiced.

In 1958, at the age of twenty-eight, he was named detective. Shortly afterward Pablo returned to Santa Teresa and obtained a post at the university. They had no money but they had wiles and they continued to rise in their careers. In 1977 Pedro Negrete was promoted to police chief of Santa Teresa. In 1982, after his predecessor became embroiled in a scandal, Peblo Negrete took the rector's chair.

Shortly after meeting Amalfitano—seven hours later, in fact— Pablo called Pedro. The call was prompted by a premonition. This is how it happened: that afternoon, the new philosophy professor had stopped by his office to introduce himself, and that night, in the quiet of his library, with a whiskey and the third tome of Guillermo Molina's *History of Mexico* within easy reach, the rector found himself thinking again about the professor. His name was Óscar Amalfitano, he was Chilean, he had previously worked in Europe. And then he had the vision. He wasn't drunk or especially tired, so it was a real vision. (Or I'm going crazy, he thought, but immediately rejected the idea.) In his vision, Amalfitano was riding one of the horses of the Apocalypse through the streets of Santa Teresa. He was naked, his white hair was wild and bloody, and he was shouting in terror or joy, it wasn't clear which. The horse neighed as if it were in its death throes. Its neighs stank, literally. As the horseman rode by, the dead piled up in the doorways of the old city. The streets filled with corpses that decomposed rapidly, as if time were dictated by the fiendishly swift passage of horseman and horse. Later, as the vision faded, he saw miniature tanks and patrol cars at the university and torn banners, though this time there were no dead bodies. They've taken them away, he thought.

That night he couldn't find Pedro anywhere and it took him longer than usual to fall asleep. The next day he called the General Sepúlveda police station and tried to reach his brother. He wasn't there. He called him at home and didn't catch him there, either. At night, from his office, he called the police station again. He was asked to hold. From the window he watched the lights of the neighboring buildings go out and the last students scattering across the campus. He heard his brother's voice at the other end of the line.

"I need a report on a foreign national," he said, "a discreet inquiry, just for the sake of curiosity."

It wasn't the first time he'd asked his brother for such a favor.

"Professor or student?" asked Pedro Negrete, who had taken the call in the middle of a poker game.

"Professor," he said.

"Name, first and last," said Pedro, gazing gloomily at his cards.

The rector gave them to him.

"You'll have his life and complete works in a week," promised his brother, and he hung up.

5

Amalfitano was born in 1942, in Temuco, Chile, the day the Nazis launched their offensive in the Caucasus.

He completed his secondary education at a high school lost on the muddy plain and wreathed in the mists of the south. He learned to dance rock and roll and the twist, the bolero and the tango, but not the *cueca*, though more than once he bounded under the leafy bower, handkerchief at the ready and driven by something deep inside of him because he had no friends in his burst of patriotism, only enemies, purist hicks scandalized by his heel-tapping *cueca*, his gratuitous and suicidal heterodoxy. He slept off his first drinking binges under a tree and met the imploring eyes of Carmencita Martínez and swam one stormy afternoon in Las Ventanas. He felt misunderstood and lonely. For a brief time he heard the music of the spheres on the bus and in restaurants, as if he had gone crazy or as if Nature, sharpening his senses, were trying to warn him of some invisible menace. He enrolled in the Communist Party and the Association of Progressive Students and wrote pamphlets and read *Das Kapital*. He fell in love with and married Edith Lieberman, the most beautiful girl of his generation.

At some point in his life he realized that Edith Lieberman deserved the world, which was more than he could give her. He drank with Jorge Teillier and he discussed psychoanalysis with Enrique Lihn. He was expelled from the Communist Party and he continued to believe in the class struggle and the fight for the revolution of the Americas. He taught philosophy at the University of Chile and he published essays on Gramsci, Walter Benjamin, and Marcuse. He signed declarations and letters by leftist groups. He predicted the fall of Allende but he did nothing to prepare for it.

After the coup he was arrested and brought in blindfolded to be interrogated. He was tortured half-heartedly but believed that he had endured the worst and was surprised by his resistance. He spent several months in prison and when he got out he joined Edith Lieberman in Buenos Aires. At first he made a living as a translator. He translated John Donne, Spenser, Ben Jonson, and Henry Howard for a series of English classics. He found work as a teacher of philosophy and literature at a private middle school and then he had to leave Argentina because the political situation had become untenable.

He spent a while in Rio de Janeiro and then they went to live in Mexico City. There his daughter, Rosa, was born and he translated J.M.G. Arcimboldi's *The Endless Rose* from the French for a Buenos Aires publishing house while listening to his beloved Edith speculate that Rosa's name was an homage to the title of the novel and not, as he claimed, a tribute to Rosa Luxemburg. Then they went to live in Canada and then Nicaragua because both of them wanted their daughter to grow up in a revolutionary country.

In Managua, he was paid a pittance to teach Hegel, Feuerbach, Marx, Engels, Lenin, but he also taught classes on Plato and Aristotle, Boetius and Abelard, and he realized something that in his heart he had always known: that the Whole is impossible, that knowledge is the classification of fragments. After that he taught a class on Mario Bunge that was attended by a single student.

A short while later Edith Lieberman got sick and they left for Brazil, where he would make more money and be able to afford the medical care that his wife needed. With his daughter on his shoulders he swam on the most beautiful beaches in the world while Edith Lieberman, who was more beautiful than the beaches, watched from the shore, barefoot in the sand, as if she knew things that he would never know and she would never tell him. He was active in a Trotskyist party in Rio de Janeiro. He translated Osman Lins and Osman Lins was his friend, though his translations never sold. He taught courses on the neo-Kantian philosophy of the Marburg School—Natorp, Cohen, Cassirer, Lieber—and on the thought of Sir William Hamilton (Glasgow, 1788–Edinburgh, 1856). He was with his wife until her death, at 3:45 a.m., while in the next bed a middle-aged Brazilian woman dreamed out loud about a crocodile, a mechanical crocodile chasing a girl over a hill of ashes.

After that he had to be father and mother to his daughter, but he didn't know how and he ended up hiring a servant for the first time in his life: Rosinha, northeasterner, twenty-one, mother of two little girls who stayed behind in the village, and who was like a good fairy to his daughter. One night, though, he went to bed with Rosinha and as he was making love to her he thought that he was going crazy. Then he got himself into the usual hot water and had to leave Brazil with time enough only to pack the little they could take with them. At the airport his daughter and Rosinha cried and his friend Luiz Lima asked what's wrong with these women, why are they crying.

After that he lived in Paris, his savings at a low ebb, and he had to work hanging posters or mopping the floors of office buildings while his daughter slept in a *chambre de bonne* on avenue Marcel Proust. But he didn't give up and he strove and strove until he found a job at a high school and then a German university. Around this time he wrote a long essay on Macedonio Fernández and Felisberto Hernández, focusing on their importance as Latin American thinkers rather than their literary achievements. And on the first vacation he was able to permit himself he took his daughter to Egypt and they went sailing on the Nile.

His situation seemed to improve. Their next trip was to Greece and Turkey. He wrote about Rodolfo Wilcock and the phenomenon of exile in Latin America. He took part in a colloquium in the Netherlands and he bought a laptop computer. Finally he ended up at the University of Barcelona, where he taught a course on idiocy and self-awareness that was so popular that his contract was renewed for a second year. But he never finished the course. Around this time he received a letter from a friend in Mexico, Isabel Aguilar. She had been a student of his in Mexico City and at one time she was in love with him. Now she was a professor in the philosophy department at the University of Santa Teresa and she offered him a job. She said that she was friendly with the head of the department, Professor Horacio Guerra, that for a month now there'd been a position available in the department, and that if he wanted it it was his. Amalfitano discussed it with his daughter, wrote to Professor Aguilar to thank her, and asked her to send him the contract as soon as possible.

6

The four policemen got up from their seats at a table at the back of Las Camelias, the bar across the street from the General Sepúlveda police station, when they saw Pedro Negrete and Gumaro coming toward them. The policemen were in tracksuits and Pedro Negrete and Gumaro were wearing suits and ties, though Gumaro's suit and tie were cheap and wrinkled and Don Pedro's were expensive. It was eleven in the morning and the four policemen had been at the bar since ten, eating ham-and-cheese sandwiches and drinking beer. Don Pedro instructed them not to get up and ordered a whiskey with water and ice. Gumaro sat next to Don Pedro and didn't order anything. When the waitress brought Don Pedro the whiskey he asked what his boys owed. The policemen protested, no, no, Don Pedro, it's on us, but Don Pedro said to the waitress:

"Charge it to me, Clarita, and that's an order."

Ten minutes later Pedro Negrete called for another drink and encouraged the policemen to follow suit. The policemen said that one beer was enough for them, but this time they were paying.

"Out of the question," said Don Pedro, "I've got it."

The waitress brought another round of beers and another whiskey for Don Pedro.

"Aren't you drinking?" asked Don Pedro.

"My stomach is funny today," answered Gumaro in an spectral voice.

The policemen looked at Gumaro and Don Pedro and then they started to eat the peanuts that the waitress had left on the table.

"Young people today can't hold their liquor," said Pedro Negrete. "In my years in uniform I knew a cop who drank a bottle of tequila every morning before he went on his rounds. His name was Emilio López. Alcohol was the death of him in the end, of course. We never let him drive the patrol car, but he was a good guy, the kind of man you could trust."

"He died of a burst liver," said Gumaro.

"Well, those are the risks."

"His liver was the size of a plum."

Don Pedro Negrete ordered another whiskey. The policemen accepted another round of beers.

"Did you know General Sepúlveda, lads?"

"No," said one of the policemen. The others shook their heads.

"You're young, of course. Did you know him, Gumaro?"

"No," said Gumaro with a sigh.

"Right after I joined the force I was assigned to guard his house. He lived on this very street, which was already named after him, General Sepúlveda at Colima. It was a big house, with a pool and tennis court. I was stationed at the door and my two buddies were in the street, so I didn't have anyone to talk to and I just stood there thinking. Then it started to rain, only a drizzle, you could hardly see it, but to be safe I took shelter under a gazebo in the yard. Then the door to the house opened and General Sepúlveda himself appeared. He was wearing a burgundy robe and underneath it he was in pajamas, it was the first time I had seen him in person and I thought he must be at least ninety, though he was probably much younger. At first he didn't notice I was there. He glanced out into the yard and up at the sky. He seemed worried about something. Maybe he was afraid the rain would ruin some of his flowers, but I don't think so. When he saw me, he beckoned me over. At your service, *mi general*, I said. He didn't say a word, just looked at me, and with a wave of his hand he signaled me to follow him into the house. Of course, as you can imagine, my orders were to stay outside, in case some asshole got past my buddies in the street, but *mi general* was a tough old son of a bitch and I obeyed without a murmur. As impressive as that house was from the outside, boys, on the inside it was stunning. It had everything. Paintings over six feet tall. It was more like a museum than a house, which pretty much sums it up. Of course, I couldn't stop to get a good look because *mi general* was walking quickly and I had to follow close behind so I didn't get lost in those endless hallways. At last we came to the kitchen and *mi general* stopped and asked if I wanted coffee. I said I would be delighted, of course, but since I saw that his hands were trembling I offered to make it myself and then the old man sighed, he said all right, go ahead, and he dropped into a chair. I remember that while I was making the coffee I heard him breathing behind me and for a moment I wondered whether something was wrong. Has anything like that ever happened to you, boys?"

The policemen shook their heads.

"Well, there I was, making coffee, and I could hear *mi general* breathing and I said to myself: careful, Pedro, you don't want General Sepúlveda to die on you. And I was about to ask the general whether he was feeling poorly and whether I should call a doctor, when all of a sudden the old man asks what's your name. And I say: Pedro Negrete, at your service, *mi general*. And he asks how old I am. And I say: twenty-three, *mi general*. And by then I have his coffee ready and I set it on the table and I notice that the general is staring at me, his eyes are boring into me, and I think, this man is sizing me up, but why is he sizing me up? And then the general says he doesn't feel well and I say if you want I can call a doctor, *mi general*, or an ambulance, all you have to do is say the word, but the general looks me up and down and laughs. Not just any laugh. The kind of laugh that makes your hair stand on end, especially when you're young, and he says I don't need a doctor. And I got the sense that the word *doctor* struck him as funny, because when he repeated it he laughed again. And then I thought, old age is making *mi general* soft in the head. A naïve, foolish thought, because after all, how old was *mi general* back then? fifty-eight or fifty-nine, in the prime of life, as they say. And a single look at him was enough to tell you that no such thing was possible, the man was saner than you or me, boys, nothing screwy about him. And that's where I was, my mind flitting from one thought to the next, when I heard *mi general* ordering me to pour myself a coffee, too, a gesture I appreciated, since I could really use one. And when my coffee was ready, *mi general* pointed at a cupboard and told me to open it and I opened it and found a stash of whiskey, because *mi general* drank only whiskey, boys, like me. And he said—I remember like it was yesterday—Negrete, get down a bottle of whiskey and warm up my coffee a little. And I poured a nice splash of whiskey into his cup, which was almost empty, and then *mi general* said warm yours up, too, jackass, because you're going to need it. Which was an offer that sounded more like a warning or a threat, don't you think? but I ignored it because frankly I felt like a drink. So I poured whiskey in my coffee and I drank it down. And when I was done *mi general* made a toast—to life, I think—and I raised my glass too. And as we were going on the fifth or sixth shot the old man said that in the servant's room there was a dead body. And I said: you're kidding, *mi general*, and he looked me in the eyes and said that he never kidded anyone. Go take a look, he said, see for yourself. Then I got up and went searching all over the house for that goddamn room. I got lost a few times, but at last I found it. It was under the main stairs, the ones that went up to the second floor. And what do you think was the first thing I saw when I went in? *Mi general* Sepúlveda sitting on one of the beds, waiting for me! I almost shat myself I was so scared, lads! What do you say to that?"

"Incredible," said the policemen.

"Of course, there was nothing uncanny about it. While I was looking all over the house for the room, the old son of a bitch had gone straight there. That was all. But the scare of it almost killed me. The first thing I managed to say was: *mi general*, what are you doing here? The old man didn't answer or if he did I instantly forgot what he said. Next to him on the bed was a shape with the sheet pulled up over its head. The general got up and motioned for me to come and take a look. I crept forward, boys, and lifted the sheet. I saw the face of a man who might have been sixty or eighty, his face covered in wrinkles, some of them deep grooves, though his hair was black, jet-black, cut very short, fierce, if you know what I mean. Then the general spoke. I swung around as if I'd been touched with a live wire. The general was sitting on the other bed. He's dead, isn't he? he asked. I think so, *mi general*, I said. But I uncovered him again, the dead man was wearing only his pajama top, but this time I pulled the sheet down to his knees, Christ, I've never liked the genitals on a stiff, boys, and I examined him carefully to see whether there were any signs of violence. Not a one. Then I checked his pulse. He had rigor mortis up the ass, as our friend Dr. Cepeda says, and I covered him back up with the sheet. This man is dead, *mi general*, I said. I thought as much, he said, and then for the first time he seemed to collapse, though it was just for a second, I thought he was about to fall apart, bit by bit, but as I said, it was just for a second. He pulled himself together instantly, rubbed his unshaven face, and ordered me to sit across from him, on the dead man's bed. The funeral home will have to be called, he said. I thought to myself that who he should really be calling was a doctor to issue a death certificate, and the police, but I didn't say anything, after all, I was the police and there I was, wasn't I? Then *mi general*, seeing that I wasn't asking any questions, said that the dead man was his employee, his only employee, and that he had been with him for longer than he could remember. This man, he said, this motherfucking corpse, saved my life three times, this bastard was by my side all through the Revolution, this dead meat nursed me when I was sick and took my kids to school. He repeated this several times: he nursed me when I was sick and took my kids to school. Those words made an impression on me, boys. They summed up a whole philosophy of dedication and hard work. Then *mi general* looked at me again that way he had of looking at you like he was grabbing your heart and he said: you'll go far, kid. Me, sir? I hope you're right. And he: yes, you, jackass, but if you want to go far and hold on to what's yours you have to keep your head on straight. Then it was as if he had fallen asleep and I thought: poor guy, the shock of finding his man dead must have exhausted him. And I started to think, too, about what he'd said to me and about other things and the truth is that suddenly I felt this great sense of calm or quiet fill me, sitting there on the dead man's bed, across from *mi general*, whose head had fallen to one side and who was snoring a little. But then the general opened one eye and asked me whether I knew where Nicanor was from and I gathered that Nicanor was the dead man and I had to tell him the truth, which was that I didn't know. Then *mi general* said: he was from Villaviciosa, damn it. And I took note of that. And *mi general* said: those jackasses are the only men in all of Mexico who can be trusted. Really, *mi general*? I asked. Really, he said. Then I called the funeral home and I led *mi general* into another room, so he wouldn't feel bad when he saw Nicanor being put into a coffin. We talked until his lawyer and secretary got there. That was the last time I saw *mi general*. The next year he died," said Don Pedro as he ordered his fifth whiskey.

"He must have been quite a man, General Sepúlveda," said one of the policemen.

"More than a man, he was a hero," said Pedro Negrete. The policemen nodded.

"And now get to work," said Don Pedro. "I don't want any bums on the force."

The policemen got up instantly. Two of them were wearing shoulder holsters under their tracksuit jackets and the other two were carrying their guns on their hips.

"You stay here, Pancho, I want to talk to you," said Don Pedro.

Pancho Monje said goodbye to his comrades and sat down again.

"What are you working on?" asked Don Pedro.

"The shooting in Los Álamos," said Pancho.

"Well, you'll have to take a break for a few days to tail a university professor. I want a complete report in a week."

"Who's the individual?" asked Pancho.

Don Pedro pulled a bundle of papers from his suit pocket and began to go through them one by one.

"His name is Óscar Amalfitano," said Gumaro. "He's Chilean. He teaches philosophy at the university."

"I want a careful job," said Don Pedro. "You'll deliver the report to me personally."

"At your service," said Pancho.

7

Homero Sepúlveda (1895–1955) showed an aptitude for military leadership from an early age: at eight he was tall and dauntless and he captained a gang of kids that made itself hated and legendary in the neighborhoods surrounding the old Municipal Slaughterhouse that once stood on the east side of Santa Teresa, where the man soon to be so prominent in the Revolution grew up. His father was a schoolteacher, originally from Hermosillo, and his mother was a self-effacing housewife, born in Santa Teresa. He was the third of a litter of three brothers and four sisters, all tall and strong, though none of them with Homero's eyes. He didn't attend high school.

When the Revolution began, he and his older brother Lucas took up arms with Pancho Villa. Soon his skill at mounting ambushes, planning raids on enemy supply bases, and moving his troops at lightning speed earned him a well-deserved reputation for bravery and intelligence, a reputation he would never lose. But unlike his brother Lucas, who was brave and intelligent, too, and who died in a cavalry charge in 1917, Homero Sepúlveda was also (and chiefly) cautious and prudent and possessed the ability to predict the twists and turns of fate. It wasn't long before he earned his general's stripes, bestowed on him by Pancho Villa himself aboard his private train.

He battled Porfirio Díaz and was a dyed-in-the-wool Maderista (though in his heart—like his father, who read the Latin American classics—he was never too deeply convinced of anything), he fought tirelessly against Huerta and Pascual Orozco, and then he retired, young and newly wed, and returned to Santa Teresa until the Villistas went back to war, this time against Carranza, whom Sepúlveda fought with few resources but great art, winning respect near and far and earning himself the nickname Epaminondas of Sonora or—it depended on the poet and the spot where the ode was composed—Scipio of Chihuahua, not to mention the Spanish baker who called him El Empecinado of the North or the Milans del Bosch of the Border, though General Sepúlveda always preferred the Greek and Roman references.

He was the only Villista chief (except for Ángeles and Lucio Blanco) who fully exploited the marriage of cavalry, mounted artillery, and mobility: he was skilled at exploiting victories and penetrating the enemy's rear guard, creating chaos.

He didn't fight against Obregón. For a while he retreated to his house in Santa Teresa, supposedly writing his memoirs but really letting matters take their course. Then he was admitted with full honors into the Obregonista camp. He was a personal friend of General Plutarco Elías Calles. In 1935, his friendships and clout got him named state governor. He prospered, like all of them, and his house in Santa Teresa grew like an Erector set, without rhyme or reason, with new wings and stables and staff quarters and even a tennis court used only by his children. As a politician he was a disaster and there were those who said he was like some notorious Greek tyrant or deranged Roman general and others who likened him to Napoleon the Small or the bloodthirsty hypocrite Thiers, but General Sepúlveda didn't give a fig about the nicknames and comparisons, classical or modern.

He survived three assassination attempts.

He had three sons, two of whom went to study and live in Texas, married American women, and founded the Austin branch of the Sepúlveda family. The third never married and lived in the big house in Santa Teresa until his death, in 1990. General Sepúlveda hardly undertook or encouraged any public works during the long years in which he served Mexico as governor of his home state or senator of the Republic. Three years before his death the street where he lived was rechristened Calle General Sepúlveda. After he died his name was given to a street in Hermosillo and the Santa Teresa State Hospital.

A life-size bronze statue memorializes him now in the city's main square. Its creator was the sculptor Francisco Clayton and it portrays the general staring nostalgically into the distance. It's a strange sculpture, with much more dignity than the intellectuals of Santa Teresa, with their sarcastic and naïve mockery, give it credit for, and it's also a sad sculpture—so sad, one might say, that it is rendered absent.

8

Pancho Monje began to tail Amalfitano one Monday morning. He watched him leave at nine for the university and then, half an hour later, he watched his daughter leave. The usual thing would have been to follow Amalfitano, but Pancho let himself be guided by his instinct. When Rosa had turned the corner he got out of the car and followed her. Rosa walked along Avenida Escandón for a long time. For a moment Pancho was convinced that she didn't know herself where she was going, then he thought that maybe she was on her way to school, some school, but the lightness of her step and the fact that she wasn't carrying any books convinced him otherwise. At the intersection with Calle Sonora, Avenida Escandón changed name and got more crowded, and suddenly Rosa disappeared. There was no lack of coffee shops nearby, and Pancho went into one of them and ordered a breakfast of coffee, *huevos a la ranchera*, and toast. When he took the first sip of his coffee he realized that his hands were shaking. That night, at the police station, he was told that a girl had turned up dead in Parque México and he learned that Álvarez and Chucho Peguero were on the case. He went to see them and asked who the dead girl was.

"Edelmira Sánchez, sixteen, hot stuff," said Álvarez, and showed him a picture of a girl in a torn dress.

While his buddies were working, he thought, he had spent the whole day at home, watching television and doing nothing.

On Tuesday he began his vigil at Amalfitano's house at seven in the morning. He left the Ford parked a block away and waited. For a long time he thought the house seemed empty, as if life inside had ceased that night while he was away, unable do anything about it. At nine the door opened and Amalfitano appeared. He was wearing a black blazer, and his white hair, perhaps too long for a man of his age, was still wet. Before he closed the door he said something to someone inside the house and then he set off walking. Pancho let him get a head start and then he got out of the car and followed him. Amalfitano's strides were long. In his right hand he was carrying a cheap briefcase and there were two books in the pocket of his blazer. He passed several people but didn't say hello to any of them. When he got to the bus stop he stopped. Pancho walked on past and went into a store, some fifty yards away. He found a can of Nestlé evaporated milk, paid for it, took out his penknife, punctured the top in two places, and drank from it once he was back out in the street. He passed the bus stop again, but didn't pause. Amalfitano was reading one of the books. Pancho walked to where he had left the Ford and started it. Then he headed down the street until he found the bus that Amalfitano was waiting for and followed it. When the bus got to the stop, Amalfitano was still there. He got on with some other people and the bus pulled away. At nine forty Amalfitano entered the university amid a stream of students. Pancho followed him into the philosophy department and spent a while chatting with a secretary. The secretary's name was Estela and she liked to go out dancing on Saturday nights. She was twenty-eight and divorced. She believed in friendship and honesty.

"Clearly you work in the philosophy department," Pancho said.

When he got back to Amalfitano's house Rosa had already gone out. Pancho rang the doorbell for a while. Then he went back to the car and put on some music. He felt his eyes closing and he fell asleep. When he woke up it was past noon. He started the car and drove away. He spent the rest of the day at El Jacinto, a bar on Calle Nuevo León that catered to policemen. At seven he went to wait for Amalfitano at the entrance to the university.

The next day Pancho arrived a little before nine. At nine fifteen a taxi stopped in front of the house and Amalfitano ran out. At nine thirty Rosa emerged and set off on foot toward Avenida

Escandón. This time she was carrying a plastic bag full of video-cassettes. When Rosa turned the corner Pancho got out of the car and headed for the house. Getting in was no problem.

The house consisted of a living room with an open kitchen, two big bedrooms and one small one, which was used as a junk room, and a bathroom. Behind was a yard with no plants or flowers. Pancho spent a while poking around the bedrooms. He didn't find anything of potential interest, except some letters from Barcelona. He sat in a chair by the living room window to read them. He didn't read all of them. Then he spent a while in Rosa's room. He liked the smell. He looked for pictures but all he could find were a few snapshots of a beautiful woman with her arms around a girl. Hanging in the closet were clothes that might have been a girl's or a woman's. Under the bed were a pair of plush Pluto slippers. He smelled them. They smelled good. Like the feet of someone young and healthy. When he put them back under the bed his heart seemed to leap into his throat. He knelt there, still, his face buried in the blankets, which also smelled good, of lavender, warmth. Then he got up and and decided he had seen all he wanted to see.

9

That night Professor Isabel Aguilar was thinking about Amalfitano when he called on the phone. Though it was still early, she had already put on her pajamas and poured herself a whiskey, which she planned to drink while she read a novel that she had been wanting to read for a long time. She lived alone and in recent years she had even found a certain satisfaction in that. She didn't miss being part of a couple. There hadn't been many men in her life and almost every relationship had ended in disaster. Isabel Aguilar had been in love with a philosophy student who ended up turning to the occult sciences, a militant Trotskyite who also ended up turning to the occult sciences (and bodybuilding), a truck driver from Hermosillo who made fun of her love of reading and who only wanted to get her pregnant (and then run off, or so she suspected), and a Santa Teresa mechanic whose intellectual horizon was soccer matches and weekend drinking marathons, marathons to which she herself became addicted. The only real love of her life was Óscar Amalfitano, who had been her philosophy professor at UNAM and with whom she had never gotten anywhere.

Once Isabel Aguilar went to see him at his house, in Mexico City, prepared to confess her feelings for him, but when she knocked at the door it was opened by a woman so beautiful and with such a visible look of happiness and self-confidence that she almost turned and ran down the stairs.

From that day on she became very good friends with Edith Lieberman, whom she admired and loved wholeheartedly, and she banished the love she felt for Amalfitano to the limbo of platonic affections. When Amalfitano and his family left for Canada their ties weren't severed. Once a month, at least, Isabel wrote a letter telling them about her life and her professional advances and each month she got a letter, usually from Edith, updating her on the vicissitudes of the Amalfitano family.

When Edith Lieberman died Isabel was truly sad, but deep down she thought that her day might have come. At the time she was living in Mexico City with the militant macrobiotic Trotsky-ite and for a few weeks she went so far as to dream of getting on a plane and leaving for a new life in Brazil, with Rosa (whom she planned to care for as if she were her own daughter) and Amal-fitano. But her timidity and indecisiveness were insurmountable obstacles and for one reason or another in the end she never trav-eled to Rio.

The letters, nevertheless, continued with even greater inten-sity than before. In them Isabel told Amalfitano things that she didn't tell anyone else. When she separated from the Trotskyite he was her greatest source of support. Later, with the changes, they began to write less. Isabel fell in love with the truck driver and experienced a brief period of sexual fulfillment. It was for his sake that she went north, to Hermosillo, where she taught at the uni-versity. There she met Horacio Guerra, who at the time was put-ting together a new philosophy department at the University of Santa Teresa. When she broke up with the truck driver she didn't think twice before accepting the offer that Horacio Guerra kept extending year after year.

The first months in Santa Teresa were lonely. At some point Isabel Aguilar dreamed of a more active social life, the kind that because of the truck driver (or because of her faculty mates, who despised the truck driver) she hadn't had during her time in Her-mosillo, but she soon discovered that in Santa Teresa the philoso-phy professors didn't associate with anyone and that the professors from the other departments shunned the members of the philoso-phy department as if they had the plague. This loneliness and her sexual proclivities (warped by her daily contact with the truck driver) led her almost without realizing it into the arms of the soccer fiend mechanic. When she was able to break up with him at last, she felt even lonelier than ever and she resumed with new vigor her correspondence with her former professor. At the same time—Isabel Aguilar would have had to be very dense not to notice it—her friendship with Horacio Guerra, after the interregnum of the mechanic, became closer, and at some point she even went so far as to think that after all they didn't make such a bad pair.

But Horacio Guerra, though far from avoiding Isabel's presence, never seemed prepared to take the crucial step, to speak the precise words that would make Isabel, tired of sleeping with her intellectual inferiors, fall into his arms.

Sometimes Isabel Aguilar thought that all her problems could simply be attributed to the fact that she had no luck with men.

When Amalfitano arrived in Santa Teresa it was like a rebirth. For the first few days she was at his side almost constantly. She located a motel where he and Rosa could stay until they found a house. She helped them look for a house that was to Rosa's liking. She drove them everywhere, like an absolutely loyal and selfless taxi driver. She took them to eat at local restaurants and showed them the city. To her surprise, Amalfitano and his daughter seemed not to appreciate any of her efforts. Rosa was in a perpetual bad mood and Amalfitano was lost in his own thoughts. One afternoon she decided that rather than being a help to the Amalfitanos, her presence had become an annoyance, and she stopped seeing them. She wasn't capable, however, of distancing herself entirely, and on weekends they often got together. Isabel would pick up her car and arrive at the Amalfitano residence at the cocktail hour. Then they would go for a drive, never a very long one. Sometimes Isabel would take them to a place on the edge of town for a drink. Other times she saw Amalfitano alone, in the evenings, and they would go for a stroll or to the movies.

When Amalfitano called and said that he wanted to see her, Isabel thought they would make a date for the following Saturday, so her astonishment was great when he said he wanted to see her that very night.

"I'm in my pajamas," said Isabel, accustomed to being the one who always visited Amalfitano.

"I'm coming to your house," said Amalfitano. "I'll be there in twenty minutes. I need to talk to someone and I can't do it over the phone."

Isabel downed the whiskey in a single gulp and then began to tidy up. She picked up some things in the living room, made the bed and straightened the bedroom, opened a few windows and aired out the house, closed the windows and sprayed a bit of Holiday Forever air freshener in the corners, then she splashed water on her face, put on a little makeup, and poured another whiskey.

10

By Thursday Pancho could have delivered a full report on Amalfitano, but he didn't.

That morning he followed Rosa: he followed her along Avenida Sonora, followed her into a covered market where she did
the shopping, and then followed her back to the house. It was
noon before she appeared again. At twelve fifteen, one of the windows in the living room opened and he presumed that she was
cleaning. Then he watched her go out into the yard, walk to the
fence, bend down, and look for something. Then he watched her
get up and head back to the house with surer steps. Muted pop
music drifted on the breeze to the windows of his car. Then Rosa
closed the window and all he could hear was the whisper of the
sun falling on the pavement and the trees.

At four in the afternoon Rosa went out again.

He followed her on foot. Rosa walked at a good clip, in the
same direction as always, toward Calle Sonora and then Avenida
Revolución. She was wearing jeans and a gray sweatshirt. She had
on low boots, with no heel.

11

Padilla's next letter was torrential. He began by saying that one night, drunk and high on pills, he had somehow ended up at a used-book store on Calle Aribau and suddenly, as if the book had leaped into his hands, he found himself with an old copy of J.M.G. Arcimboldi's *The Endless Rose*, translated by Amalfitano. Your name in that tattered and precious volume!

Arcimboldi, he said, had overnight become a fashionable author in Spain, where they were publishing or about to publish everything he'd written. Not a week went by without an article on the great French writer, or a profile of him. Even *The Endless Rose* (his third or fourth novel?)—a difficult and deceptive work despite its apparent simplicity, to the point that sometimes it seemed like a book for morons—was already in a second printing, when it had scarcely been out for a month. The new Spanish translation was by a writer from Navarra, suddenly revealed to be an expert—which he was, though he'd certainly kept it under wraps—on the Arcimboldean oeuvre. I prefer your translation, said Padilla, and every page that I reread makes me imagine you in that storm-tossed Buenos Aires, freighted with omens, where your innocence triumphed. Here Padilla gets it wrong again, thought Amalfitano, because even though the translation was for a Buenos Aires publishing house, he had done it while he was living in Mexico City. If I had translated Arcimboldi in Buenos Aires, he thought, I would be dead now.

Of course, continued Padilla, he, too, had succumbed to the fashion for Arcimboldi and in a week he'd devoured the three novels in Spanish translation, plus another three in the original French that he'd found at the Librería Apollinaire on Calle Córcega, plus the controversial novella or long short story *Riquer*, which he'd read in Juli Montaner's Catalan translation and which seemed to him a kind of long-winded Borges. In Barcelona there are those who say, said Padilla, that Arcimboldi is the perfect blend of Thomas Bernhard and Stevenson (old R.L., you heard me right), but he placed him somewhere nearer the unlikely intersection of Aloysius Bertrand and Perec and (brace yourself) Gide and the Robbe-Grillet of *Project for a Revolution in New York*. In any case, French to the hilt. Finally, he said that he was starting to get sick of the flocks of Arcimboldi exegetes, whom he equated with donkeys, animals he had always pitied though he hadn't seen one in the flesh until he was nineteen, in Gracia, the property of some Gypsies who moved like metropolitan shepherds from the grazing lands of one Barcelona neighborhood to another with the donkey, a monkey, and a barrel organ. Despite Buñuel and Dalí, I always loved Platero, it must be because we faggots get a kick out of all that Andalusian shit, he wrote, and these lines wounded Amalfitano deeply.

As he saw it, Padilla was a poet, an intellectual, a fighter, a gay free spirit who dispensed his favors liberally, an engaging companion, but never a faggot, a term he associated with cowardice and enforced loneliness. But it was true, he thought then, he and Padilla were faggots, and that was all there was to it, period.

With sadness, Amalfitano realized that he in fact wasn't an authority on the work of Arcimboldi, though he had been the first to translate him into Spanish, more than seventeen years ago, when almost no one had heard of him. I should have kept translating him, he said to himself, and not wasted my time on Osman Lins, the concrete poets, and my atrocious Portuguese, but I struck out there too. And yet Padilla, Amalfitano realized, had overlooked something in his long letter (as had probably all the other Arcimboldians of Barcelona), a crucial feature of the French writer's work: even if all his stories, no matter their style (and in this regard Arcimboldi was eclectic and seemed to subscribe to the maxim of De Kooning: *style is a fraud*), were mysteries, they were only solved through flight, or sometimes through bloodshed (real or imaginary) followed by endless flight, as if Arcimboldi's characters, once the book had come to an end, literally leapt from the last page and kept fleeing.

Padilla's letter ended with two pieces of news: his breakup with his SEAT boyfriend, and the imminent—though why it was so imminent he didn't say—end to his job as a proofreader. If I keep proofreading, he said, I won't enjoy reading anymore, and that's the end, isn't it? About *The God of Homosexuals* he had little or a lot to say, depending: it's a waltz.

In his reply, which was as long as Padilla's letter, Amalfitano entangled himself in a series of disquisitions on Arcimboldi that had little to do with what he really wanted to get across: the state of his soul. Don't leave your proofreading job, he said in the postcript, I imagine you with no money in Barcelona and it scares me. Keep proofreading and keep writing.

Padilla's reply was slow in coming and it seemed to have been written in a state of trance. Right off the bat he confessed that he had AIDS. I got the package, he said between jokes. Immediately after that he told Amalfitano to get tested. You might have it, he said, but if you do I promise that you didn't get it from me. For a year now he had known that he was HIV-positive. Now he had developed the disease. That was all. Soon he would be dead. As far as everything else was concerned, he was no longer working and he had moved back in with his father, who had guessed or gotten some inkling of his son's illness. Poor old man, said Padilla, he's had to watch all the people he loves die. Here he rambled on about people like jinxes or dark clouds. The good news was that he had run into the baker from Gracia who used to come to the soirées at the studio near the university. Without asking for anything in return, the baker, having heard that Padilla was sick, had given him a bimonthly allowance, which was what he called it. It wasn't enough for Padilla to rent an apartment and live alone, but it did cover most of his costs: books, drugs, rooms by the night, dinners at neighborhood restaurants. His prescriptions were paid for by social security. Paradise, as you can see, he said.

He had already been hospitalized once, two weeks in the contagious-disease ward where he shared a room with three junkies, down-and-out kids who hated faggots though they were all dying by giant steps. But I changed their minds, he said. He promised details in the next letter.

With *The God of Homosexuals*, he said, he was proceeding at a snail's pace. The baker—"my dear Raguenau," Padilla called him—is my only reader, a dubious privilege that fills him with joy. He had a new lover, a sixteen-year-old rent boy, infected with AIDS and marvelously oblivious, oh, to be him, sighed Padilla as the letter shook in Amalfitano's hands. Not working for the publishing house was a fascinating feeling that he'd thought he'd lost. Living like a loafer again, I who was put on this earth solely to amuse myself. To amuse myself and make a nuisance of myself every once in a while.

The Barcelona days were glorious. The Mediterranean shone. Padilla was writing from the terrace of a bar on the Ramblas. People stroll by, he said, and here I sit drinking a double whiskey and I'm happy.

12

Near an assembly plant on the edge of town belonging to Don
Gabriel Salazar, on a plot designated as a future industrial park,
though it had yet to attract a tenant, another girl was found dead.

She was seventeen, a year older than Edelmira Sánchez. Her
name was Alejandra Rosales and she was the mother of an infant
son. The cause of death was the same. Her throat had been cut with
a large knife, though no trace of blood was found at the scene (as
in Parque México), which meant that there was no question that
the crime had been committed elsewhere.

The body of Edelmira Sánchez had turned up on a Monday
and her parents had reported her disappearance on Sunday morning. The last time she was seen was Saturday at dinnertime. The
body of Alejandra Rosales turned up a week later, but the last
time she was seen alive was on Saturday, just before Edelmira said
goodbye to her parents. The only one who might have reported
her disappearance was her mother-in-law, with whom she lived,
but her mother-in-law thought that Alejandra had run off with a
man and she had enough on her hands already taking care of her
late son's baby without trying to get to the police station to report
the disappearance of a woman she hated and whom she wouldn't
have minded seeing dead.

According to the medical examiner, both were raped multiple
times, presenting slight lacerations to the legs and back, bruising
around the wrists (leading to the conclusion that both women had
at some point been bound), a fatal slash or two to the neck (sever-
ing the carotid artery; in Alejandra's case the cut was so deep that

it almost decapitated her), contusions to the chest and arms, light bruising about the face. No traces of semen were found in either case.

In Chucho Peguero's report it said that Alejandra occasionally worked as a prostitute and that on Saturday nights she often frequented La Hélice, a nightclub on Calle Amado Nervo. The night that she disappeared she was seen there by a witness, her friend Guadalupe Guillén. According to the latter, at about 8:00 p.m. Alejandra was on La Hélice's dance floor, dancing a merengue. Guadalupe Guillén didn't see her again for the rest of the night. No one saw her leave the club. Edelmira Sánchez, meanwhile, spent her Saturday nights at the New York, a club mainly for teenagers on Avenida Escandón, where she arrived at around 7:30 p.m. By midnight she was usually already on her way home with her boyfriend or her friends, because Edelmira didn't have her own car. That Saturday night, Alejandra wasn't seen at the New York, nor was Edelmira seen at La Hélice.

Edelmira was almost certainly killed on Sunday, between noon and midnight. Alejandra, meanwhile, was held for longer: she was probably killed on Thursday or Friday, twenty-four hours before some children found her body near the assembly plant.

13

Gumaro guided Pancho's first steps on the Santa Teresa police force. When they ran into each other at the station in the morning, he would say: come with me, let your buddies pick up the slack, I want to talk to you. And Pancho would drop whatever he was doing and go with him. Gumaro was nondescript in appearance, neither very tall nor very big, and he had a small head, like a lizard. It was hard to guess his age and he might have been older than everyone thought. To some people, he came across as none too impressive, too small and thin to be a policeman, but if they looked him in the eyes they could tell that he was no ordinary man.

Very late one night, at the bar La Estela, Pancho watched him closely for a while and discovered that he hardly ever blinked. He reported this to Gumaro and asked why he did things differently from ordinary mortals. Gumaro answered that when he closed his eyes it gave him a terrible pain in the head.

"So how do you sleep?" asked Pancho.

"I fall asleep with my eyes open and once I'm asleep I close them."

He had no fixed address. He could be found at any of the Santa Teresa police stations and he never seemed to be busy, not even when he was performing his duties as Don Pedro Negrete's driver. Everyone owed him favors, favors of all kinds, but he only took orders from Don Pedro.

He told Pancho that he was going to teach him how to be a policeman. It's the best job in the world, said Gumaro, the only one in which you're truly free or you know for a fact—without the shadow of a doubt—that you aren't. Either way, it's like living in a house of raw flesh, he said. Other times he said that there should be no police force, the army was enough.

He liked to talk. He especially liked to carry on one-sided conversations. He also liked to make jokes that only he laughed at. He didn't have a wife or children. He felt sorry for children and avoided them, and women left him cold. Once a bartender who didn't know him asked why he didn't find himself a wife. Gumaro was surrounded by on-duty and off-duty officers and all of them fell silent, waiting to hear his reply, but he didn't say anything, just kept drinking his Tecate as if nothing had happened, and ten minutes later the bartender came over again and said he was sorry.

"Sorry for what, pal," asked Gumaro.

"For being rude, Sergeant," said the bartender.

"You aren't rude," said Gumaro, "you're a jackass, or just an ass."

And that was it. He didn't hold grudges and he didn't have a temper.

Sometimes he stopped by the place where a crime had been committed. When he arrived everyone stood aside, even the judge or the medical examiner, with whom he was on first-name terms. Without saying a word, absorbed in his own thoughts, his hands buried in his pockets, he cast an eye over the victim, the victim's effects, and what some policemen call the scene of the crime, and then he left as silently as he'd come and never returned.

No one knew where he lived. Some said that it was in Don Pedro Negrete's basement, while others claimed that he didn't have a place to call home and that he did sometimes sleep in the cells, empty or not, at the General Sepúlveda police station. Pancho was one of the few who knew from the start (in an extraordinary show of confidence on Gumaro's part) that in fact he sometimes slept in Don Pedro's basement, in a little room that had been fixed up especially for him, and sometimes in the cells at the station, but most nights, or days, he slept at a guesthouse in Colonia El Milagro, five blocks from Pancho's apartment. The owner was a woman in her early fifties with a lawyer son who worked in Monterrey. She treated Gumaro like one of the family. Her husband was a policeman who had been killed in the line of duty. Her name was Felicidad Pérez and she was always asking Gumaro for little favors that he never granted.

Many times Pancho followed him from bar to bar until dawn.

Gumaro drank a lot, but he almost never showed the effects of alcohol. When he got drunk he would pull his chair over to the window and scrutinize the sky, saying:

"My brain needs air."

This meant that he was elsewhere. Then he would start to talk about vampires.

"How many Dracula movies have you seen?" he asked Pancho.

"None, Gumaro."

"Then you don't know much about vampires," said Gumaro.

Other times he talked about desert towns or villages or hamlets that only communicated among themselves, with no regard for borders or language. Towns that were one or two thousand years old and where scarcely fifty or one hundred people lived.

"What towns are those, Gumaro?" Pancho asked.

"Towns of vampires or white worms," said Gumaro, "which amounts to the same thing. Godforsaken shitholes where the urge to kill runs as strong as the urge to live."

Pancho imagined two or three cantinas, one grocery store, and courtyards paved in concrete, facing west. Like Villaviciosa.

"So where are these towns?" he asked.

"Here and there," said Gumaro, "on either side of the border, like a renegade state inside Mexico and also the United States. An invisible state."

Once, for work, Gumaro had to visit one of these towns. Of course, he didn't know what it was at the time.

"You never know these things," he told Pancho.

The road was dirt, but it wasn't bad, though the last twenty miles were only a track through the rocks and the desert. They arrived at four in the afternoon. The town had thirty inhabitants and half of the houses were empty. With Gumaro were Sebastián

Romero and Marco Antonio Guzmán, two veteran Santa Teresa policemen. They were going to arrest a Mexican who had wiped out his two Yankee partners in San Bernabé, Arizona. It was the San Bernabé police chief who had gotten the tip and he called Don Pedro Negrete and came to an arrangement. The Santa Teresa policemen would arrest the killer and then cross the border with him. The men from San Bernabé would be waiting on the other side, and they would receive the prisoner. Afterward, they would say that they had found the killer wandering in the desert, howling at the moon like a coyote, with everything happening on the American side, everything perfectly legal.

Guzmán got sick as soon as they arrived. He was shivering with fever and vomiting, so they left him in the backseat of the car, covered with a blanket and babbling about masked wrestlers. Then Gumaro and Romero went from house to house through the town, guided by an old woman with a limp, but they didn't find anything. Either the information they had gotten from the San Bernabé police chief was no good or the killer had long since disappeared, because they didn't find a single scrap of evidence that he had ever been there.

One of the strange things that Gumaro saw as they went back and forth, aware already that the search was useless, were the eyes of some of the animals. They were rubbed-out eyes, he said to Pancho. Eyes from the beyond. Fading into nothing. As if the donkeys and dogs were intelligent and their souls were bigger than human souls.

"If it was up to me," said Gumaro, "I would have drawn my gun and shot all those animals."

Before it got dark they left without the man they'd come to find and back in Santa Teresa Don Pedro Negrete was very upset because he owed the police chief of San Bernabé a favor.

Gumaro talked about towns of white worms and towns of buzzards, towns of coyotes and towns of tiny birds. And these were precisely the things, he said, that a true policeman needed to know about. Pancho thought he was crazy. At dawn they went to eat pozole at El Almira, owned by Doña Milagros Reina, who in her day had been one of Santa Teresa's top whores. By this time Gumaro wasn't talking about anything: not policemen, not towns of vampires, not white worms. He ate his pozole like a man near death and then he said that he had things to do and he vanished all of a sudden down some random street.

"Come sleep it off at my place," Pancho offered many times, sorry to see him looking so pale and shaky. "Come and stay for a while until you feel better."

But Gumaro always ignored him, and suddenly, before he had finished talking, he would vanish. Without saying goodbye, as if at that hour everyone was a stranger to him.

14

Padilla's next letter seemed to have been written by a different person, someone who had just been operated on and was still under the effects of the anesthesia. It said that he had gone with Raguenau and a kid called Adrià to Tibidabo, the amusement park, and everything, absolutely everything, had been so beautiful that he was unable—on repeated occasions, on repeated and baffling occasions, on repeated and crystal clear occasions—to contain his tears. I cried, he said, like someone who finds true religion and sees it for what it is and knows that his salvation lies in it, but carries on regardless.

On the roller coaster, he said, as the lights of Barcelona and the endless darkness of the Mediterranean swam in and out of view, I had one of the most glorious erections of my life, my cock was rock hard, it swelled so big that my testicles and the shaft hurt, I was afraid to touch it, the bulge under my jeans throbbed, it beat like a racing heart, its length reached almost to my navel (my God, thought Amalfitano), good thing it happened where it did, in a public place, added Padilla, because it would have been more than any ass in the world could handle.

Then he said that Raguenau and the kid, who was apparently his nephew, had brought him to the pastry shop of another baker, an old friend of Raguenau's, a guy in his seventies who presented them with an assortment of delicious cookies and cakes, nice relaxing conversation, and the music of Mompou. I'd like to live like that always, said Padilla, surrounded by people like that, sharing pleasures like those, though I know that if you scratch the surface you discover that it's all just polite anguish, genteel anguish, or if you're lucky, anguish chased by a good shot in the arm of Nolotil, but the friendship they offer me is real, and that should be enough, whatever the circumstances. About *The God of Homosexuals* he said nothing.

Around this time Amalfitano was too busy preparing his classes (combing American libraries and universities for the scattered and forgotten books of Jean-Marie Guyau) and all he could send was a postcard in which he explained clumsily how busy he was and inquired about the progress of the novel.

Padilla's reply was long and cheerful, but hard to follow. I'm sure you've found a new love, he said, and I'm sure you're enjoying yourself. Carry on! He reminded him of the Byrds song (was it the Byrds?), the one that goes if you can't be with the one you love, love the one you're with, and—strangely, if this was what he really believed—he didn't ask for any information about Amalfitano's new lover, I imagine, he said, that it's probably one of your students. And yet in the next paragraph the tone of the letter changed dramatically and he implored him not to let his guard down. Don't let anyone play you, he begged, anyone at all, even if he's the hottest guy around and he does it better than anyone else, under no circumstances should you let yourself be taken advantage of. Then he rambled on about the loneliness that Amalfitano bore and the risks to which that loneliness exposed him. By the end, the letter recovered its cheerful tone (in fact, the lines about loneliness and the danger of being played were like a small anxiety attack enclosed within parentheses) and talked about the winter and the spring, the flower stands on the Ramblas and the rain, about glossy shades of gray and the black stones hidden in the walls of the Old City. In the postscript he sent his regards to Rosa (for the first time, since Padilla usually acted as if Rosa didn't exist) and said that he had read Arcimboldi's last novel, 105 pages, about a doctor who upon inheriting the ancestral home finds a collection of masks of human flesh. Each flask—in which the masks float in a viscous liquid that seems to swallow light—is numbered and after a brief search the doctor finds, in a thick book of accounts, a collection of explanatory verses, numbered in turn, which, as in *New Impressions of Africa*, cast spadefuls of clarity or spadefuls of coal dust on the origin and destiny of the masks.

Amalfitano's response was feeble, to put it mildly. He talked about his daughter, about the vast skies of Sonora, about philosophers Padilla had never heard of, and about Professor Isabel Aguilar, who lived alone in a small apartment in the center of the city and who had been so good to them.

Padilla's next letter, four pages typewritten on both sides, struck Amalfitano as melancholy in the extreme. He talked about his father and his father's health, about the way he, as a boy, had noticed the fluctuations in his father's health, about his clinical eye for his father's aches and pains, spells of flu, attacks of weariness, bronchial infections, fits of depression. Then, of course, he didn't do anything to help, didn't even care that much. If my father had died when I was twelve I wouldn't have shed a single tear. He talked about his house, about his father's comings and goings, about his father's ear (like a broken-down satellite dish) when it was he who was coming and going, about the dining room table, sturdy, made of solid wood, but soulless, as if its spirit had fled long ago, about the three chairs, one always unoccupied, off to one side, or perhaps stacked with books or clothing, about the sealed packages that his father opened in the kitchen, never the dining room, about the dirty lamp that hung too high, about the corners of the apartment or the ceiling that sometimes, on euphoric or drug-fueled nights, looked like eyes, but closed or dead eyes, as he always realized a second later despite the euphoria or the drugs, and as he realized now despite how much he would have liked to be wrong, eyes that didn't open, eyes that didn't blink, eyes that didn't see. He also talked about the streets of his neighborhood, the little shops where he went to buy things when he was eight, the newsstands, the street that used to be called Avenida José Antonio, a street that was like the river of life and that he now remembered fondly, even the name José Antonio, which was so reviled but which in memory retained a trace of beauty and sadness, like the name of a bullfighter or a composer of boleros who dies young. A homosexual youth killed by the forces of Nature and Progress.

He also talked about his current situation. He had become friends with Adrià, Raguenau's nephew, though no sex figured into the friendship: it was a kind of monastic love, he said, they held hands and talked about any old thing, sports or politics (Adrià's boyfriend was an athlete and an active member of the Gay Coordinating Committee of Catalonia), art or literature. Sometimes, when Adrià begged him to, he read bits from *The God of Homosexuals*, and sometimes they wept together on the balcony, in each other's arms, watching the sun set over Plaza Molina.

Raguenau, meanwhile, he had slept with. He gave a step-by-step account of the proceedings. Raguenau's bedroom, awash in Caribbean blue and ebony, African masks and porcelain dolls (what a combination! thought Amalfitano). The timid nakedness of Raguenau, a touch ashamed, his belly too big, his legs too skinny, his chest hairless and flabby. His own nakedness reflected in a mirror, still acceptable, less muscle mass, maybe, but acceptable, more Greco than Caravaggio. The shyness of Raguenau curled up in his arms, the room dark. Raguenau's voice saying that this was enough, he didn't need to do anything else, this was wonderful, perfect, feeling himself being held and then falling asleep. Raguenau's smile, sensed in the darkness. The phosphorescent red condoms. Raguenau's trembling upon being penetrated with no need for Vaseline, ointment, saliva, or any other kind of lubricant. Raguenau's legs: now tensed, now seeking his legs, toes seeking his toes. His penis in Raguenau's ass and Raguenau's half-erect penis caught in his left hand and Raguenau moaning, begging him to let go of his cock or at least not to squeeze too hard. His laugh of joy, unexpected, pure, like a flare in the dark room, and Raguenau's lips issuing a faint protest. The speed of his hips, their thrust unimpaired, his hands caressing Raguenau's body and at the same time dangling him over the abyss. The baker's fear. His hands grabbing Raguenau's body and rescuing it from the abyss. Raguenau's moans, his panting growing louder and louder, like a man being hacked to pieces. Raguenau's voice, barely a thread, saying slower, slower. His crippled soul. But don't misinterpret me, said Padilla. That was what he said: don't misinterpret me, the way you've always done, don't misinterpret me. Raguenau's innocent sleep and his own insomnia. His steps echoing through the whole house, from the bathroom to the kitchen, from the kitchen to the living room. Rageunau's books. The Aldo Ferri armchair and the vaguely Brancusi lamp. The dawn that finds him naked and reading.

15

The clinic in Tijuana where Amalfitano took the AIDS test had a window that looked out onto a vacant lot. There, amid the rubble and the trash, under a blazing sun, was a stocky little man with a giant mustache who seemed to be the enterprising type and who was carefully assembling a kind of tent from a collection of sheets of cardboard. He looked like the red-bearded pirate from the Donald Duck cartoons, except that his skin and hair were very dark.

After Padilla let him know that he had the antibodies, Amalfitano decided to be tested, but in Tijuana rather than Santa Teresa, so there would be no chance of running into some university acquaintance. He told Isabel Aguilar and she decided to drive him there. They set out very early and made their way across a plain where everything was a deep yellow color, even the clouds and the stunted bushes scattered along the highway.

"At this time of day it's all like that," said Isabel, "the color of chicken broth. Then the earth shakes itself awake and the yellow vanishes."

They had breakfast in Cananea and then they continued on to Santa Ana, Caborca, Sonoyta, and San Luis, where they exited the state of Sonora and entered Baja California North. Along the way Isabel told him about a Texan who had once been in love with her. He was a kind of art dealer, introduced to her by an art professor. This happened after she had ended her relationship with the mechanic. The dealer looked like a boor in his cowboy boots, string tie, and Stetson, but he knew a fair bit about contemporary

American art. The only problem was that she had taken a dislike to him, spooked as she was by her previous relationships.

"Once," said Isabel, "he came to my house and invited me to a Larry Rivers show in San Antonio. I just stood there looking at him and I thought: this guy wants to sleep with me and he can't figure out how to say so. I don't know why I said yes. I had no intention of sleeping with him, or at least I didn't plan to make it easy for him, and the idea of a car trip to San Antonio wasn't tempting, either, but suddenly something made me want to go, I felt like seeing the Larry Rivers and even the hours on the road seemed appealing, the meals along the way, the motel where we planned to stay in San Antonio, the excruciatingly monotonous scenery, the weariness of travel. So I packed some clothes, a volume of Nietzsche, and my toothbrush and off we went. Before we crossed the border I realized that the Texan had no interest in getting me into bed. What he wanted was someone to talk to (strangely enough, he had taken a liking to me). Basically, I realized that he was a pretty lonely guy and sometimes that got to him. The trip was very nice, not much to report, luckily things were clear from the start. When we got to San Antonio we checked into a motel on the edge of town, into separate rooms, ate fairly well at a Chinese restaurant, and then we went to the show. Well, it turns out that this was the opening and the press was there, a couple of TV cameras, lights, drinks, local celebrities, and—in a corner, surrounded by people—Larry Rivers himself. I didn't recognize him, but the Texan said: that's Larry over there, let's go say hi. So we went up to him and shook hands. It's an honor, Mr. Rivers, said the Texan, I do believe you're a genius. And then he introduced me: Miss Isabel Aguilar, professor of philosophy at the University of Santa Teresa. Larry Rivers looked him up and down, from the Stetson to the boots, and at first he didn't say anything but then he asked where Santa Teresa was, Texas or California? and I shook his hand, not saying a word, a little bit shy, and I said Mexico, the state of Sonora. Larry Rivers looked at me and said wonderful, Sonora, wonderful. And that was it, we said goodbye very politely and we moved on to the other end of the gallery, the Texan wanted to talk about the paintings, I was thirsty but I wanted to talk about the paintings, too, we spent a while drinking wine and eating caviar and smoked salmon canapés, and drinking wine, the two of us growing more enthusiastic about the show by the minute, and suddenly, in the blink of an eye, I found myself alone, sitting at a table full of empty glasses and sweating like a mare after a wild gallop. I don't have heart trouble, but suddenly I was afraid I'd have a heart attack, a stroke, whatever. I made my way to the restroom as best I could, and spent a while splashing off my face. It was a strange experience, the cold water never came into contact with my skin, the layer of sweat was so thick—even solid, you might say—that it blocked it. My chest burned as if someone had stuck a red-hot bar between my breasts. For a moment I was sure that someone had put some drug in my drink, but what drug? I don't know. I can't remember how much time I spent in the restroom. When I came out there were hardly any people in the gallery. A very beautiful woman, a Scandinavian blonde, maybe thirty-eight, was standing next to Larry Rivers and talking nonstop. I was amazed that Larry Rivers and a few of his friends were still there. The Scandinavian woman dominated the conversation, talking and gesticulating, but the strangest thing of all was that she seemed to be reciting something, a long poem that she illustrated with her hands, hands that were surely soft and elegant. Larry Rivers watched her carefully, his eyes half-closed, as if he were seeing the blond woman's story, a story about tiny people in constant motion. Jesus, I thought, that's nice. I would have loved to join them, but my shyness—or sense of propriety, I guess—prevented me. The Texan was nowhere to be found. Before I left, the Larry Rivers group smiled at me. On my way out, I bought the catalogue and took a taxi back to the motel. I went to the Texan's room, but he wasn't there. The next day, at the reception desk, I was told that he had left the previous night, and that before he left he had paid for everything, including my room and my breakfast that morning at the motel restaurant. I thought about eating all there was to eat, even eggs and ham, which I hate, but all I could get down was the coffee. What had caused the Texan to leave so rudely? I never found out. Luckily I had my credit cards with me. At two that afternoon I got on a plane to Hermosillo and from there I took a taxi to Santa Teresa.

16

Padilla's next letter talked about a girl he had met at the hospital and it went off on a long and rather sinister tangent. I promised to tell you how, when I was in the hospital, I settled my dispute with my roommates, he said. Those upstanding young men, rudderless sons of the proletariat (also called lumpen proletariat, thought Amalfitano, who deep down was still a Marxist), treated me the way the Arabs treated the Jews in 1948, so I decided to act, make a show of force, sow fear.

One night, he said, I waited until the whole ward was in the arms of Morpheus and then I got up. Moving stealthily (like a ballerina on the moon, said Padilla) and dragging his IV pole, he headed to the nearest bed (where the most threatening—also the most handsome—boy lay), closed the curtains, and began to strangle him. With one hand he covered his mouth, and with the other, which held the catheter, he throttled him until he gasped for air. When the sleeper woke and opened his eyes and tried to get away, it was futile. Padilla had him at his mercy and he tortured him a little more, then made him swear that the fun was over. The other two woke up and through the curtain they could see the shadow of Padilla on top of their friend. They probably thought I was raping him, said Padilla, but they were so scared that nobody said a word. In any case, the next day the mocking, contemptuous glances had been replaced by looks of fear.

The girl he met was the sister of the guy he had tried to strangle. One afternoon she brought him a present. A huge, juicy-looking yellow pear speckled with brown. The girl sat down next

to his bed and asked why he had hurt her brother. The three junkies, remembered Padilla, were smoking in a corner, by the window, while the girl talked to him. Padilla's answer was: to clear
the air. So even the terminally ill aren't allowed to fuck with you?
asked the girl. Actually, I love it when they fuck with me, said
Padilla, and then he asked her where she'd learned a technical
term like that. The girl raised her eyebrows. *Terminally ill*, said
Padilla. The girl laughed and said at the hospital, of course.

They became friends.

Two weeks after he was discharged he ran into her at a bar
near the Urquinaona metro station. Her name was Elisa and she
sold heroin in small quantities. She said that her oldest brother was
dead and her other brother, the one in the next bed, didn't have
long to live. Padilla tried to cheer her up, citing statistics, survival
rates, the introduction of new drugs, but he soon realized it was
useless.

Her name was Elisa and her turf was Nou Barris, where she
lived, though she bought the drugs in El Raval. Padilla went with
her a few times. The dealer's name was Kemal and he was black.
In other circumstances Padilla would have tried to screw him, but
sex wasn't something he cared much about just then. He was more
interested in listening and watching. Listening and watching: new
sensations that might not offer much comfort but that did slow his
despair and make it more deliberate, allowing him to take a more
objective view of something that at the same time he realized
could not be viewed objectively. Elisa was eighteen and lived with
her parents. She had a boyfriend, also an addict, and once a month
she saw a married man who helped her out financially.

The letter ended with a description of the girl. Of average
height; very thin; too-big tits; olive skin; big almond-shaped eyes
fringed with long, dreamy lashes; almost nonexistent lips; a pleasant
voice, though trained or grown accustomed to shouting and curs-
ing; well-proportioned hands with long, elegant fingers; finger-
nails nevertheless chewed and crooked, badly crooked; eyebrows
darker than her hair; smooth, strong, flat belly. On the subject
of her belly: once, he said, he brought her home to sleep. They

shared his bed. Aren't you afraid that in the middle of the night I'll fuck you and infect you? No, said Elisa. Which led Padilla to the conclusion, logical after all, that she was HIV positive too. For a while, before they fell asleep, they made out. Unenthusiastically, or in what you might call a friendly way, explained Padilla. The next morning they had breakfast with his father. My father, said Padilla, tried to not show how surprised and happy he was, but he couldn't help himself.

On the subject of his health he had only vague things to say. His lungs were weak, but why they were so weak he didn't explain. He ate well, his appetite was good.

Amalfitano wrote back instantly. He told him about his day trip to Tijuana to be tested, he urged him to speak frankly about his illness (I want to know exactly what kind of shape you're in, I *need* to know, Joan), he beseeched him to work without pause on his novel, to the extent possible. He didn't tell him that he had already received his test results and that they were negative. He didn't tell him that he had been dreaming of leaving everything and flying to Barcelona to take care of him.

17

Padilla's next letter was written on the back of a reproduction of a Larry Rivers painting: *Portrait of Miss Oregon II*, 1973, acrylic on canvas, 66 x 108 inches, private collection, and for a moment Amalfitano was unable to read, astonished, asking himself whether in a previous letter he had told Padilla about the trip to Tijuana and Isabel's story of her trip to San Antonio to visit the Larry Rivers show. The answer was no, Padilla didn't even know Isabel existed, so the apparition of Larry Rivers had to be pure coincidence. Coincidence or a trick of fate (Amalfitano remembered a time when he believed that nothing happened by chance, everything happened for some reason, but when was that time? he couldn't remember, all he could remember was that at some point this was what he believed), something that must hold some meaning, some larger truth, a sign of the terrible state of grace in which Padilla found himself, an emergency exit overlooked until now, or a message intended specifically for Amalfitano, a message perhaps signaling that he should have faith, that things that seemed to have come to a halt were still in motion, things that seemed like ruined statues were mending themselves and recovering.

He read gratefully. Padilla talked about a Rauschenberg show (but if it was a Rauschenberg show why had he sent a Larry Rivers postcard?) at a gallery in the heart of Barcelona, about the hors d'oeuvres and cocktails, about young poets whom he, Padilla, hadn't seen for ages, about a long walk to Plaza Cataluña and then down the Ramblas to the port, and then the streets became a labyrinth and Padilla and his poet friends (renegades who wrote indiscriminately in Spanish and Catalan and who were all homosexuals and who had no love for critics in either Spanish or Catalan) vanished with open eyes into a secret night, an iron night, said Padilla.

Then, by way of a postcript or curious side note, on a half sheet of paper and in tiny handwriting, Padilla talked about a trip to Girona to visit the parents of one of the poets, and about the nearly empty train that transported them through the "Catalan countryside," and about a North African who was reading a book backwards, prompting the poet from Girona, polite but exceedingly nosy, to ask whether it was the Koran, and the North African's answer was yes, the sura of mercy or compassion or charity (Padilla couldn't remember which), which led the poet from Girona to ask whether the mercy (or compassion or charity) preached there applied to Christians, too, and again the North African's answer was yes, certainly, of course, absolutely, all human beings, and he spoke with such warmth that the poet from Girona was emboldened to ask whether it also applied to atheists and homosexuals, and this time the North African answered frankly that he didn't know, he supposed so, since atheists and faggots were human beings, weren't they? but that in all sincerity he didn't know the answer, maybe yes, maybe no. And then the North African asked the poet from Girona what he believed. And the poet from Girona, preemptively offended, tacitly humiliated, answered haughtily that he believed in what he could see from the windows of the train: woods, gardens, houses, roads, cars, bicycles, tractors— progress, in short. To which the North African replied that progress wasn't really so important. Which made the poet from Girona exclaim that if it weren't for progress neither he nor the North African would be having this comfortable chat in a half-empty train. To which the North African replied that reality was an illusion and that at this very moment they might just as well be talking in a Bedouin tent in the desert. Which, after it made him smile, made the poet from Girona say that they might be talking in the desert or they might be fucking. To which the North African replied that if the poet from Girona were a woman, he would definitely take her to his harem, but since the poet from Girona seemed to be only a faggot dog and he was only a poor immigrant, that possibility or illusion was barred. Which made the poet from Girona say that in that case the sura of mercy meant less than a bicycle, and that he should watch what he said since the tip of a bike seat had been known to give more than a few people a poke in the ass. To which the North African replied that this would be in the poet's world, not his own, where martyrs always walked with their faces held high. Which made the poet from Girona say that all the Moors he had known were either rent boys or thieves. To which the North African replied that he couldn't be responsible for the kinds of friends a faggot pig might have. Which made the poet from Girona say: go ahead, call me a faggot and a pig, but I bet you won't let me blow you right here. To which the North African replied that the flesh was weak and that he might as well get used to torture. Which made the poet from Girona say: unzip your pants and let me suck you off, darling. To which the North African replied that he'd sooner die. Which made the Girona poet ask: will I be saved? will I be saved too? To which the Maghrebi replied that he didn't know, he honestly didn't know.

I would have liked, said Padilla in conclusion, to take him to a hotel, he was a North African open to the poetry of the world, and I'm sure he'd never been buggered.

Amalfitano's reply was written on the back of a Frida Kahlo postcard (*The Two Fridas*, 1939) and he said that on Padilla's advice, though he actually couldn't remember whether Padilla had suggested this explicitly, he had begun to look for Arcimboldi's novels. Naturally, his search was restricted to the Mexico City bookstores that received new releases from Spain, and the International Bookstore of Tijuana, which carried hardly any books in French, but where he had been assured they could be found. He had also written to the French Bookstore in Mexico City, though it had been a while and he hadn't heard back. Maybe, he ventured, the French Bookstore has gone out of business and it will be years yet before word reaches Santa Teresa. About the Larry Rivers postcard he chose to say nothing.

Padilla's next letter arrived two days later, not long enough afterward to be a response to Amalfitano's letter. It was, along general lines, a synopsis of the novel that Padilla was writing, though for a synopsis, thought Amalfitano, it was rather vague. It was as if something—during the two-day trip to Girona or in his previous postcard or in the Girona home cooking he'd eaten—hadn't agreed with him. He seemed drunk or drugged. Even his writing (the letter was handwritten) was agitated, at points almost illegible.

He talked about the novel in general (randomly citing Emilia Pardo Bazán, Clarín, and a Spanish Romantic novelist who had drowned himself in a river in one of the Baltic states) and about *The God of Homosexuals* in particular. He mentioned an Argentinean bishop or archbishop who had proposed moving the entire non-heterosexual population of Argentina to the pampa, where, lacking the power or opportunity to pervert the rest of the citizens, they would set about building their own nation, with its own laws and traditions. The wise archbishop had even given his project a name. It was called Argentina 2, but it might just as well have been called Faggotlandia.

He talked about his ambitions: to be the Aimé Césaire of homosexuals (his handwriting in this paragraph was shaky, as if he were writing with his left hand), he said that some nights he heard the tom-tom beat of his passion, but he didn't know for sure whether it was really the beat of his passion or of his youth slipping through his fingers, maybe, he added, it's just the beat of poetry, the beat that comes to us all without exception at some mysterious hour, easily missed but absolutely free.

The God of Homosexuals, he said, would take shape first in dreams and then along deserted streets, the kind visited only by those who dream waking dreams. Its body, its face: a hybrid of the Hulk and the Terminator, a terrible and repulsive colossus. From this monster they (the homosexuals) expected endless bounty, not the republic on the pampa or in the Patagonia of the Argentinean archbishop, but a republic on another planet, a thousand light-years from earth.

The letter ended abruptly, as if his pen had run out of ink, but he sent kisses to Amalfitano and his daughter.

18

Padilla's next letter talked about Elisa. It said that one night when he got home he found the girl outside his building waiting for him. She was sick, with bruises on her neck, a slight fever, and not much interest in sleeping. We got in bed together, he said, it was very late and we tried to make love, but her general lowness was matched by my own despondency, my fever, my shivers. At first they just masturbated on opposite sides of the bed, gazing into each other's eyes, saying nothing for a long time. The result was that neither of them could come and sleep fled them both for good. Wide-awake, said Padilla, we talked until dawn, and only then were we finally able to fall asleep.

So Padilla began to talk about the first thing that came into his head, and all of a sudden he found himself telling the story of Leopoldo María Panero, his poems, his madness, what he imagined his life must be like at the Mondragón asylum. The next thing he realized, the girl was kneeling over him or curled around his legs or tying him to the bedposts or asking him to tie her up, said Padilla, or the two of them were sitting on the rug, naked, or they were talking for the first time about death in an innocent, idiotic, desperate, brave way, making plans and promising each other that they would carry them out. Of course, we didn't end up making love, said Padilla, at least technically we didn't.

The problem, said Padilla further on, is that the next day I was sober again (if you could say that what had happened the night before took place in a state of drunkenness), but not Elisa, who all through breakfast couldn't stop going over the things they'd talked about, remembering bits of everything that Padilla had told her, sometimes priding herself on her incredible memory, since their late-night conversation hadn't exactly been a model of coherence, and also, when he got like *that*, admitted Padilla, he talked in bursts, too fast, confusedly, it was a coprolalic kind of thing, so that whoever he was talking to (and Padilla himself) tended to miss more than half of what he was saying, but Elisa, apparently, remembered everything: names, book titles, the petty intrigues and small excesses of a (literary) life long gone.

So the breakfast in question had been very strange.

Suddenly I had a vision of myself. But as a woman. Which (as you know) is something I've never wished for. But there I was, on the other side of the table, a woman with very thin lips, sick, young, poor, unkempt. A woman with the look of someone near death. I'm surprised I didn't kick her out of the house on the spot, said Padilla, clearly not quite persuaded, clearly a little scared. About his novel he said nothing.

Amalfitano's response was brief and epigrammatically ambiguous: he began by saying that Padilla's friendship with Elisa must have some meaning that they had yet to understand, and he ended with an ominous list of the daily problems he faced, both in the philosophy department and at home, in his father-daughter dealings with Rosa, who was distancing herself from him more and more.

As had become habitual, Padilla didn't wait for Amalfitano's response to send him another letter.

He talked again about Elisa.

For three days he had lost sight of her. On the fourth, when he was finally beginning to forget that strange mnemotechnical epiphany, he found her outside his building at a similar time of night and in similar circumstances. Again they slept together. Again they masturbated (this time they both came). Again they talked.

The girl, said Padilla, had come up with a plan to cure herself. The plan was to hitchhike from Barcelona to the Mondragón asylum. When she told him this, Padilla burst out laughing. But she kept talking. This time it was dark and the only light filtered in the window from the skylight in the inner courtyard. She spoke, said Padilla, in a monotone, but it wasn't a monotone, it was full of inflection, but it lacked inflection, it was contaminated by the slang of Barcelona's blue-collar neighborhoods, but at the same time it was the voice of a young lady from Sarriá. You, thought Amalfitano, have read too much Gombrowicz.

The rest of the letter continued at great length on the same subject. The dark room. Elisa's voice describing an impossible trip. Padilla's questions: why did she think she would be cured by traveling? what did she expect from Leopoldo María Panero and the Mondragón asylum? The urge to laugh, and Padilla's laughter and teasing. Sleeping with a faggot is messing with your head. Elisa's laughter, which for a fraction of a second seemed to light up the room and then shoot like backwards lightning through the window joints, upward, toward the courtyard skylight and the stars.

But the letter ended on a less than festive note. Elisa is here with me, said the last paragraph, when I went out this afternoon she stayed here, in bed, my father and I talked about taking her to the hospital but she refused, we made her some chicken broth, she drank it, and then she fell asleep.

19

Padilla's next letter, the first that Amalfitano didn't answer right away, talked about the pilgrimage to San Sebastián and the terms on which it would be conducted, terms dictated by the wavering voice of Elisa, who, he reported, was in the hospital now and with whom it was best not to argue, at least until she recovered. At the hospital, he said, I've gotten to see her family again, the junkie brother I tried to strangle, her mother, who's a saint, assorted aunts and cousins. Once Raguenau had come with him, and another time Adrià, both of them worried about the interest Padilla had taken in the girl. His friends, he said, advised him to stop visiting her, stop taking care of her, start taking care of himself. But Padilla ignored them and spent a night or two at the foot of Elisa's bed. She asked him to talk to her about Panero. When Raguenau and Adrià heard this they didn't know whether to laugh or cry. But Padilla took it seriously and told Elisa everything he knew about Panero, which wasn't much, actually; the rest he made up. And when he couldn't think what else to make up he brought volumes of Panero's poetry to the hospital and read them to Elisa.

At first she didn't understand them.

I think, said Padilla, that she understands even less about these things than I realized at first.

But he was undaunted and he devised a method (or something resembling a method) of reading. It was simple. He decided to read Panero's poems aloud in chronological order. He began with the first book and ended with the last and after each poem he offered a brief commentary that didn't pretend to explain the whole poem, which was impossible, according to Padilla, but rather a single line, an image, a metaphor. This way, Elisa understood and retained at least a fragment of each poem. Soon, wrote Padilla, Elisa was reading Panero's books on her own and her comprehension of them (but the word *comprehension* conveys none of the desperation and communion of her reading) was luminous.

When she was discharged, Padilla—in a rather crepuscular gesture, thought Amalfitano—presented her with all the books he had loaned her and left. He didn't expect to see her again and for a few days he was happy about it. Raguenau and Adrià took him out to the movies and the theater. He went out on his own again. He got back to work, though unenthusiastically, on *The God of Homosexuals*. Very late one night, coming home drunk and high, he found her sitting outside his building, waiting for him.

According to Padilla, Elisa was death.

Amalfitano's response was a five-page letter, hastily written between classes, in which he begged him to listen to the baker and his nephew, and in which, with perhaps exaggerated optimism, he related the giant steps that science was taking in its fight against AIDS. According to some doctors in California, he claimed, the disease was steps away from becoming simply another chronic ailment, something that didn't necessarily mean a death sentence.

About the latest developments in Santa Teresa he chose to remain silent.

Padilla's response arrived shortly afterward, too soon to be a reply to Amalfitano's letter.

It was written on the back of an airmail postcard from Barcelona and it said that his life had taken a radical turn. Elisa is living with me now, he said, and my father is beside himself with joy. Of course, Elisa and I are like brother and sister. Some nights we masturbate side by side. But really, it doesn't happen very often. I do the shopping. Elisa cooks and deals heroin in her old neighborhood. We live in the most delightful holding pattern. At night we sit on the couch and watch TV, my father, Elisa, and me. Something's going to happen soon. I'll keep you posted.

EDITORIAL NOTE

Woes of the True Policeman is a novel whose parts are at different stages of completion, though the general level of revision is high, since all the chapters were first written by hand, then transcribed on an electric typewriter, with many of them—approximately half—subsequently polished on a computer, as Roberto Bolaño's files show.

A number of additional documents deposited in the same files confirm that this is a project that was begun in the 1980s and continued to be a work in progress up until the year 2003: letters; dated notes in which the author describes his projects; an interview from November 1999 in the Chilean newspaper *La Tercera*, in which he states that he is working on *Woes of the True Policemen*, among other books. The title is a constant in all the documentation relating to the work.

At least two manuscript versions of the novel were found on Roberto Bolaño's work table and among his papers, making it possible to state with certainty that the novel was carefully revised and that the computer files were part of the transcription of the novel that the author had been carrying out. The most complete manuscript version was organized in four folders, each labeled with a number, title, and page count: 1. Amalfitano and Padilla, 165 pages; 2. Rosa Amalfitano, 39 pages; 3. Pancho Monje, 26 pages; 4. J.M.G. Arcimboldi, 38 pages. Another folder, bearing the title "Cowboy Graveyard," contained eight additional chapters, as well as material related to another unfinished project.

After careful study and compilation of this material as well as of the chapters found on Bolaño's computer (more recent but only accounting for part of the novel), the final shape of the book was determined. The first and fifth parts of the novel come from the computer files, and the second, third, and fourth parts from the manuscript copies. This edition was undertaken with the unwavering intent to respect Bolaño's work and the firm pledge to offer the reader the novel as it had been found in his files. Any changes and corrections have been kept to a bare minimum.

My thanks to the Andrew Wylie Agency, and to Cora Munro, who with the greatest respect for the legacy of the author has lent her literary counsel and the support of her invaluable knowledge to this edition.

Carolina López

picador.com

blog
videos
interviews
extracts